ALL KINDS OF LOVE

ALL KINDS OF LOVE

MARAKI

DEDICATION

I dedicate my book to all those who love!!!!

ACKNOWLEDGEMENTS

My sincere appreciation to my daughter Vicky who always believes in me even when I don't believe in myself, to my poetry/writers group of friends who listened and encouraged, to my friends from Steubenville, Ohio who remembered, to my cousins George and Nick who lent me their ears and answered questions about the Village of Kardamyla in Chios, Greece, to my Jewish friends who loved my characters and to Denise Cassino for her invaluable support.

CHAPTER 1

STEUBENVILLE

"Frankieeeee...Frankieee," his mother's shrill voice echoed through the house, "Frankieeee get your butt out outta bed." He heard the creaking and stomping on the wood stairs that she scaled two at a time. *Myrna wasn't exactly a light weight. She tipped the scales at 200...all due to the pizza and pasta she cooked and devoured daily in their diner downstairs.* It sounded like a herd of horses coming closer and closer.

Frankie stuck his throbbing head under the pillow wrapping it tightly over his ears to muffle the incessant screaming. "Oh Lord, here it comes," he thought as he heard her panting over him. She ripped the pillow away, slapped the back of his head and grabbed his ear pulling up as hard as she could. The pain was dreadful and he clenched his teeth trying not to scream like a girl.

"Mama mia, stop…stop, please, I'm sick," he yelled trying to hold back the vile taste of vomit that filled his mouth.

"Sick are you or hung over?" She yanked his ear dragging him out of bed. "You miserable low life… you were at Dixie's Cigar Store with your buddy Timmy gambling in the back room again. I work my fingers to the bone trying to take care of this family and what do you do, Frankie? You spend our hard earned cash on women, booze and gambling!"

"You don't think I'm going to let you sleep the day away, Frankie! Get up! Its noon, Frankie, NOON," she hollered pushing him into the hallway towards the bathroom. Go wash up. You stink of liquor and cigarettes. Hurry up, you lazy bum. You need to make the meatballs and sauce!"

"Talk about stink," he gagged and almost threw up.

"What did you say, Frankie?" She screeched and shoved him into the bathroom. "Our food stinks, eh. Maybe we should close the place up and you can go work in the mill." She swung at him again but missed and hit the door he slammed in her face.

"You're not too old for a whipping," she hissed as she rubbed her bruised hand. "Be in the kitchen in 15 minutes. *Capisce*?"

Her round face was beet red and dripping with perspiration. Her huge breasts bounced erratically to the rhythm of her descent in the narrow stairwell. She paused for a moment at the bottom, wiped her brow with the tomato stained apron she wore and flew majestically into the restaurant. "Ciao, my loves," she cooed and opened her arms wide to welcome the steel mill crowd.

"Myrna...Myrna...Myrna," they called out to her affectionately.

Myrna scanned the room for Easy. It was Wednesday, the day the big Greek came in for a heel. She always stuffed the largest end of Italian bread with lots of meatballs, sauce, gooey, mozzarella and added his favorite hot Italian sausage.

She looked directly across the street to Easy's Diner on the opposite corner and didn't see him. This was worrisome because he was never late and she needed his help to close the place again tonight. She packed the sandwich anyway, left it on the counter and made her rounds to the tables joking and laughing with the guys.

Suddenly, Easy was in front of her, his belly pushing hers'. "You think I no come, eh," he laughed uproariously and slapped his sides. "You miss old Easy, eh?"

"Get outta here fatso," she poked his belly. "Your samich is over there. Come tonight to help me close. You hear me?"

"You no good husband outta town again," he shouted. "I be over to bring baklava and maybe little bit sumtheen else, too. Me and you fix old man. I know we too fat but I put you on counter and take care of you."

"You couldn't find that thing under your big pouch, you old goat," she mused and pushed him to the door.

Everyone was laughing. They were genuinely fond of both of them and enjoyed their banter so

they alternated between their two places for lunch. Although there were other restaurants in town, these two were closest to the mill. The food was hearty and the characters were uplifting after damn hard days at work. And, they were comfortable in an atmosphere where spoken words were not perfect. American was not their mother tongue. Most of them were foreigners who had migrated to Steubenville, Ohio to work in the steel mills.

Steubenville, nicknamed Little Chicago, was bursting with gambling, prostitution and nightlife. Jobs were plentiful. There was a whole lot of money to be made and lost if one wasn't careful. Everyone played the numbers. They heard the game was run by Jimmy the Greek who was a hero in the community. He always seemed to come up with a few bills if someone was a consistent loser, "Just to help out the family." The downtown area was home to five theaters, the Capital, the Grand, the Ohio, the Olympia and the Paramount. The latest films brought people from all over the tri-state area. They were dressed to kill in the finest clothes and hats purchased from the Hub Department Store on Market Street. Fourth and Market Streets were always lit up with flashing lights. Music wafted from every other doorway and cigar smoking was an art form. If you wanted to be seen…this was the town.

As the guys filed out swearing under their breath about their fate in the mill, Myrna realized Frankie hadn't come down yet. She was tired and wanted him to finish cooking for the dinner crowd. Her worthless husband Angelo was nowhere to be found. *He thinks I don't know he's staying with those dames who strip at The Cellar at the end of town. And what do I do… cover for him over and over again.*

She looked into the old square mirror that hung by the kitchen door, pulled up her curly red hair and stuffed it in a net to keep it out of the food. The face that stared back at her was still relatively attractive even though it had rounded out with time. The hint of green in her eyes was what Angelo loved most about her looks.

Oh how he loved me. It has been years, ever since he found out our Angelina would never be normal. Why, God? Why does he blame me? I have prayed and prayed to Jesus, the Holy Mother, the Saints. My prayers are not answered. My baby will never heal and my husband will never be mine again.

She caught a glimpse of Angelina from the mirror and tears spilled down her cheeks. Her beautiful daughter stood by the door to the stairwell waiting for Frankie. The fourteen-year-old had her mother's red hair, fair skin and heart shaped lips. But her eyes were dark crowned with black brows. They were Angelo's brooding eyes that Myrna saw.

Frankie burst through the door. For sure, he wasn't dressed for kitchen duty. His black tee and black pants were painted on his long lean body. His dark hair was slicked back on the sides, a few stray hairs drifted over his forehead. He had a flawless face… black eyes and brows, a perfectly straight nose, and full lips. He tried to look older than his nineteen years by maintaining a serious expression yet, he still had a youthful innocence to his face.

When he saw Angelina, his attitude immediately changed to playfulness. He grabbed her and kissed her on the nose. "You are almost as tall as me ladybug," he teased. She wrapped her arms around his neck and squeezed as hard as she could. The adoration in her eyes was probably the most emotion she ever showed.

Frankie was master of his sister's moods and he sensed a difference in her. It was as though she needed more attention or comforting. She followed him all the time now and became distraught when he was unavailable to her. She would sneak into his room nights, sit in a dark corner and wait for him to come home. No amount of coaxing could get her out. Frankie and Angelina had adjoining rooms. When he came home, he would put her to bed, stay till she fell asleep and always leave the door open. Oftentimes, she would wake up, go into his room quietly and sit on the chair by his bed waiting till he opened his eyes.

Myrna softened up when she saw them together and motioned Frankie to take her for a stroll. He was the only person that could communicate with the severally retarded girl. "I'll finish up the kitchen work. Easy will come over and help me a since he closes early during the week."

Frankie took Angelina's hand and headed for the river stopping for a moment to wave to Easy. "No worry. I no leave Myrna work lone," Easy called out. *Boy nice lookeen but notheen upstairs, he thought and poked his head. He lazy like no good fahder, Angelo. Poor Myrna.* He yelled out to the few people in the diner. "Git out...I close now."

Frankie crossed the tracks singing beautiful melodies to Angelina...just like he had learned in the lounges where Dino Crocetti (Dean Martin) used to sing. When they reached the river he stopped and pointed up. "One day soon I will drive you across, ladybug. You can see the river from up high." The bridge to West Virginia was suspended between mountains and looked absolutely heavenly. It was postcard beautiful even down to the smoke that drifted up from the steel mill chimneys.

He scooped up a handful of stones and began throwing them into the water counting every splash. He opened her hand, dropped in a pebble and helped her toss it by thrusting her arm forward. "One to go," he laughed. He could tell she was tense today.

The wind had picked up and whipped Angelina's pink dress against her body revealing a swollen tummy. Her hair flayed across her eyes blocking the view. In a flash, she took off running towards the river waving her arms and making strange moaning sounds. Frankie was not far behind and caught her before she fell into the water. He had never seen her do this. She was hitting him with her fists until he pushed her hair away from her eyes and held her close. "Now, now, ladybug, I'm here. Everything is fine little one." She continued to make long, frightening, sounds. *Maybe she is in pain, he thought.*

"Where are you hurting, ladybug? Don't be scared. Frankie will make it better." He wondered if she understood anything he said. Oftentimes he thought she couldn't hear him. He decided it was about time he took her for a checkup. The moaning finally subsided but she continued to hold onto Frankie, her cheek pressing hard against his chest. He petted her hair and rocked her gently until he felt her relax. With his arm around her shoulder, he moved slowly towards the diner. By now he was starving and could think of nothing else but his mama's lasagna.

When they arrived, Easy was singing Greek songs and dancing with Myrna. His wife Irini was putting candles on the red and white check tablecloths. She had already put up the frilly curtains, swept and mopped the floor. Easy was kicking up his heels and stomping. Irini was yelling at him to finish up in the kitchen or she would slam him with the mop. He grabbed her, twirled her around with one hand and Myrna with the other.

"You crazy, Easy? We mourning," Irini shouted and pulled away.

"You mourning since I marry you. You no geev any. How we have kids I no member."

Myra was laughing hysterically enjoying every moment.

"She tsortch every day light candle. I no see even underpants many years. Black, black, black she put on for anybody who die…even stranger from village we don' know."

"Shame on you, Easy," Irini pointed her long finger at him. "Neighbor from upper village lose her man."

Just then she saw Angelina and Frankie. She ran over to the girl, cupped her face with her bony hands. "Angeloudi *mou* (my angel)," she said sweetly and kissed her on both cheeks. "You hungry?"

"For lasagna," Frankie answered.

"No lasagna…eggplant parmesan and spaghetti. Lasagna no ready," Easy told him. "Forst we talk in back…very portan."

Easy was comical wearing a hairnet that reached his bushy eyebrows. His eyes were deep set, nose broad and lips were slightly crooked, one end turned up and the other down. He had a perpetual quizzical look about him. The white apron he wore didn't quite fit him and he fastened it on the sides with huge safety pins. When he walked his arms swayed back and forth. "Irini stay wit Angelina."

Frankie followed him to the back office. "What's up, my man?"

"You no have window wash no more. I beat heem and put head in bucket black water. I say you comen again, I take knife from kitchen cut throat. He run like crazy."

"Why Easy? What did he do?"

"Sumbody, he tol me Chester take Angelina to park couple times. He take her from porch wit car.

No tell Myrna. She got nuff worry with you no good fahder."

The color drained from Frankie's face and he clenched his teeth. "I'm going to kill the son of a bitch," his voice was low and menacing.

"No…no…Frankie. If he touch her, I kill him. No worry for this. You take care angeloudi (angel)."

Frankie tried to control his rage. He opened the office door and found Angelina waiting for him. "Hey, ladybug. Let's go eat. Theo Easy will fix our plates." He hoped she hadn't heard the conversation.

"Oooooh, wow, looks delicious," Frankie took the plates from Easy's hands and put them on the table trying to suppress his rage. He opened his mouth wide and Angelina mimicked him. "One for ladybug and one for Frankie." He put a forkful into her mouth then his. There was a tension in his chest that rose to his throat. "Two for lady bug and two for Frankie. Show mama how much you like her cooking." He couldn't shake the feeling that Chester had hurt his sister.

"Mama, I'm taking her to Dr. Horwitz tomorrow."

"Why Frankie. Is there something wrong?" She sounded concerned.

"No. Don't worry. Time for a checkup, that's all." *If there is something wrong, the bastard will pay for it at the end of a knife.*

"Why Pittsburgh? Why Dr. Horwitz? There are good Greek doctors right here."

"She is tops and can handle Angelina better than anyone."

"How much money do you need, Frankie?"

"I won last night, for once. I'll take care of it but I need the Plymouth."

Just as she threw him the car keys, Timmy Paidousis walked in and caught them. "Surprise," he said and pointed to the door. His brother Mike, back from the University of Tennessee, walked in.

Timmy was movie star handsome and had a smile that never quit, as if he knew a secret no one else did. His eyes sparkled like pieces of shiny coal. The girls were mesmerized by his charm. He and Frankie were rivals for the hottest babes in town. Mike, on the other hand, was more grounded. He banked on college and sports for his future. Although they looked alike, Mike was wide and muscular. He was a grand presence in any room he entered.

Everybody ran towards Mike to welcome him. "Mihali you home," cried Irini. She was a short, skinny woman, and Mike had to bend down to give her a bear hug taking care not to crack her fragile ribs. He picked her up and she dangled like a rag doll. "Opaa, Thea Irini." She blushed enjoying the attention. He dropped her gingerly next to Theo Easy who put his arm around her shoulders. "Mrs. Georgia she happy, yes. You famous football play now?" she asked him.

"Sure Thea. I box some, wrestle and play ball. You still wearing black Thea? Did somebody die?" He winked at Theo Easy who was rolling his eyes and making funny gestures behind her back.

"Stamati why you no say Mihali comeen?" Easy shouted at Timmy.

"Sit down boys. Tonight everything is on the house." Myrna threw her arms around Mike. "You're too big for me to hug. How do you find clothes in your size?"

His wide shoulders shook up and down as he laughed, hissing through his teeth. "Everything is tailor made."

"Oh!" She looked around to see who heard him. They were duly impressed wondering though what tailor made meant. *It must be for famous people, she deducted.*

"What a mistake inviting us to eat on the house." They both sat at Frankie's table. "When Mike starts shoveling it in, ain't nothing gonna be left for the other customers." Timmy poked his brother. "Don't be a pig." He turned to Frankie.

"What t' hell's wrong with you buddy? I'm the one who should be upset. My mother nearly broke my nose with her purse when she caught me hiding under the poker table. All them guys are afraid of her. The whole town is buzzing," Timmy shook his head. "They ain't got no broke thing' better to do but yap."

Frankie did not even utter a response. He was afraid if he opened his mouth every curse word he had ever learned would come spewing out. He had to stay cool till the doctor examined Angelina. *One way or another, Chester was gonna get an ass kicking.*

The restaurant was almost full. Every customer was excited to see Iron Mike Paidousis. Timmy saw this distraction as an opportunity to sneak out and head for the bars until he saw his mother peaking in the window. "Oooops, no can do," he realized it was futile to try and outsmart her.

"Hey ma, come in," he waved to her. "Thea Irini and Theo Easy are here, too. Myrna will be glad to see you."

Mrs. Georgia was a five-foot powerhouse. She put the fear of God in anyone who wasn't on the straight and arrow, especially her son Timmy. "Stamati, me glad you and Mihali here. I no wan look for you in bar. You nose okay? Maybe I hit you more hard next time."

Oh shit. Everybody heard her. Timmy didn't embarrass easily except with his mother's antics. "No need, no need, mom. I ain't goin' out tonight with Mike in town."

"I no worry for Mihali. He smart...no drink...no play. He nice boy." She pinched Mike on his cheek.

"He no drink... no play," Timmy mimicked his mother, "but he sure can put it away."

Mike was laughing as he polished off yet another plate of Italian delicacies.

"Angeloudi (angel), I bring you kourambiedes cookies." Mrs. Georgia kissed her on the forehead and put the cookies on the table in front of her. "She love my cookies, Frankie. You feed, okay?"

One thing Frankie was thankful for was his sister was well loved. He knew in his heart she was safe and comfortable with these people. *But how did Chester escape his attention? Was he so caught up with broads and booze that he lost focus?*

"That's enough, ladybug. You ate six cookies. Let's save the rest for breakfast." Frankie wiped the powdered sugar from her lips and took her by the hand. "We'll go upstairs and read bedtime stories. Maybe I'll even sing you Dino songs."

Frankie looked back into the restaurant. He saw Mrs. Georgia hand on hip, hair in a bun on the back of her head and Irini, wearing a black scarf tied under her chin chatting intently in a corner. His mother was waiting on tables, oohing and ahhing with her friends. For such a big guy, Easy was light on his feet running in and out of the kitchen. Timmy and Mike were enjoying all the attention. Timmy was pouring on the charm for the ladies. Mike was scooping up sauce with chunks of crusty bread. For some reason, sadness gripped his heart. He wanted to keep this scene in his memory forever.

CHAPTER 2

The nurses had taken Angelina into the exam room. Frankie was pacing the floor wishing he could be with her. "I'll see you in a few minutes in my office." *Judging by what happened last time he was in Pittsburgh, he could imagine what was about to unfold.*

"Frankie, come in." Dr. Horwitz spoke with authority. He followed her closely smelling her perfumed hair. "Lock it, honey." She slammed the door. Frankie obeyed and when he turned to meet her eyes she had already disrobed. Nothing but a white lace garter belt hooked onto white hose was on her perfect body. Her slender legs and small hips led to a tiny waist but her breasts were oversized and set high, studded with huge dark nipples. She reached back pulled out the clip that held her hair in place and shook her head until her long, burgundy tresses were wild. Her grey eyes were fixed on him with lust. She sat on the edge of the desk, lifted her legs high and opened them exposing a shock of auburn hair against pale skin. "Now," she whispered and wet her sultry, ruby stained lips with her tongue.

Frankie did not remember removing his pants. He lost control quickly but as she dug her nails into his sides he came back with fury. "Slow honey. Take it slow." She kept whispering as she pressed down on his shoulders with her ankles and rocked her body. He was standing up wildly thrusting into her like a cave man, his hands squeezing her creamy thighs. His mouth moved back and forth sucking each nipple that stood at attention.

Suddenly he became angry. No woman had ever taken liberties with him. He was always the one that made the first moves and eased into situations. His goal was to make the girl feel special before gaining precious access to her body. Sandy was not only older, but also in command. *Not this time he thought as he heard her calling his name again and again. He wanted to torment her.*

He pulled back and flipped her over. "No, no. Don't. What do you think you're doing?" she tried to fight him. He picked her up by the waist, threw her face down on her knees into the leather chair. "Don't move." He pushed her legs wide open and her head down. She was shocked and began squirming.

Now who's in control!! Frankie was pleased with himself, especially when he heard her whimpering every time he advanced and slapped her buttocks. He was amazed when he realized she was trying to keep from having several unexpected and embarrassing orgasms. Each time she gasped, it was a boost to his masculinity.

Frankie had lost track of time and count. He finally backed off barely able to stand. "Stay that way till I allow you to get up."

"Please," she begged her exposed body trembling. She was humiliated.

"Don't speak till I say you can." He took pleasure in looking at the pink flesh between her thighs while he dressed. "Back out of the chair slowly."

She did as he said wanting to kill him. Her feet were on the floor and she stood up waiting for another command.

"Now turn around and walk towards me." He sat on the desk feeling powerful.

"Frankie, stop," she sounded vulnerable like a child.

"Did I say you could speak?"

How dare he do this to me, he's just a kid. I'll get even. I'll make him suffer. Her eyes looked down as she came towards him. He reached for the back of her neck, pulled her close kissing her tear stained face and mouth wanting to enter her again. Her tongue darted into his parted lips and she melted into his arms.

Stroking between his legs, she cupped her hand preparing to squeeze with all her strength. He caught her wrist and twisted her hand behind her back. "Don't make me hurt you again, Sandy."

"Dr. Horwitz?" Someone was banging on the door. "Doctor, it's locked. We need to talk to you about Angelina."

"See you in the exam room shortly," she called out scrambling to get dressed. She went into the powder room leaving the door open. Bent over with a small hand held mirror between her legs, she wiped her female parts with wet paper towels tossing them afterward into the waste basket. She washed her hands and splashed water on her face.

"Wait here. I'll be back after I've checked her out."

He grabbed a handful of her disheveled hair. "Don't be long. I need to know."

"I must take my time, Frankie. Although, I have suspicions, I want to be sure." She tried to compose herself but her face was flushed and her heart was still beating erratically when she left the office.

There was a growling noise coming out of the exam room. When she opened the door she found Angelina nude and strapped to the table her feet in stirrups. The sound was coming from deep inside of her.

"What have you done? She shouted at the nurses. "Get out of here. "

They were appalled at her appearance. Her hair was a mess, her face red and her lips were bruised. "You told us to prepare her."

"Shut up and get out now. You're both on suspension."

She threw a sheet over Angelina and removed the straps on her arms and legs. With gentle words, she tried to calm the frightened girl. "I'm the doctor. Do you remember when you came here a long time ago? I made you feel better. I need to check you again to see if you are hurting somewhere." Meanwhile she was examining her neck moving slowly downward. She felt her swollen breasts over the sheet then listened to her protruding belly with the monitor. There was definitely a strong heartbeat.

Oh God, for sure Angelina was at least in her fourth month. Nothing could be done now. Was everyone blind to *her condition? Didn't those fools notice that her shape had rounded out?* "Now, now honey…I need to look down there. I won't hurt you." To her surprise, Angelina did not fight. She parted the child's legs and realized she had been violated numerous times and had a painful infection. *No internal this time. I don't want to cause her more discomfort than necessary.* She gently spread a salve on the wounds then lifted the girl wrapping her in a hospital robe. Angelina stared into space. "Let's get Frankie in here." She rang the front desk and ordered them to send him to the back room.

The door was open and he walked in calmly. Sandy's eyes said it all.

"Can we do anything?"

"It's too late Frankie; she's at least four months along. I have to keep her in the hospital for a couple of days to clear up an infection.

Frankie was completely devastated and blamed himself for not watching out for his sister. But this was not the time to fall apart. He had to make plans to take her away. And then there was the matter of Chester. He knew exactly what he would do to the bastard.

"Well, ladybug. We have to stay here for a few days till you feel better. Don't worry. Dr. Sandy will take care of you and I will be here all the time. Maybe we can go on a long vacation afterward." Angelina put both hands on her belly and massaged it tenderly. He wondered if she understood what was happening.

"I have to call home."

"Will you tell them?"

"Never."

"Use my office phone, Frankie. I'm sorry. I'll do whatever I can to make things easier for her."

"Yeah." He went into the office and sat in the leather chair. There was an odor of sex and perfume in the air. *How fast things had changed. His world had come crashing down.*

He dialed the diner dreading the conversation with his mother.

"Angelo's," she answered.

"It's me, ma. I'll be staying a couple more days. Angelina has a bad cold."

"Oh Lord. Should I come to Pittsburgh?" her voice was panicky,

"Stop over-reacting. Everything is under control. You know I can take care of her."

"Okay son. If you need anything phone me… money…anything at all. I love you. Kiss my baby."

He hung up and put his face in his hands trying desperately to hold back tears. He felt the weight of the world on his shoulders and he had to deal with it alone. *Men don't fall apart. They do whatever is necessary to protect the family.*

He looked up and Sandy was standing there watching him. "I need to go to Steubenville tonight. Can you watch my sister?"

"What time?"

"Midnight, maybe." *He had to take care of business.* "I'll be back early."

"She'll be asleep, Frankie. I'll stay with her if it will make you feel better." She ran her hands through his hair.

"Sorry, Sandy."

"Not necessary. I figured you needed to do it your way," she smiled. "There's no telling what you will be in for next time."

"Next time? I'm thinking it can't get any better."

CHAPTER 3

"You have a long drive ahead. It's already eleven and she's fast asleep. Let's grab a cup of java. Don't worry. I'll stay in her room till you get back."

They went to the end of the hallway into the empty waiting room. She poured. "Black?"

He took the cup from her hand. There was a strange look in his eyes, ice cold and impersonal. "I'll probably return before day break."

"Sit for a minute, drink your coffee and take another with you." Sandy sat in a chair and threw her right leg over the arm. Her uniform slipped up revealing her private place. "Wanted to give you something to think about on your long drive home," she purred.

He sat directly across from her on the sofa, eyes fixed between her legs. There was a slight upwards curl on the corners of his mouth. *After what I'm about to do, maybe I should have one last fling.*

He kicked the door shut and unzipped his pants, exposing his huge organ. "Climb aboard." He locked his hands behind his head and watched her approaching, hips swinging to a secret beat. She lifted her white garb, put a knee on either side of him and began a taunting game, moving up, down and around without having contact. He sucked and bit each breast that she pushed into his mouth all the while keeping his hands nonchalantly behind his head.

Sandy was on fire and couldn't wait any more. She reached below and put it inside of her. Although it was hurting from that angle, she still took it all in by slowly rotating her hips. The pain and pleasure drove her wild. "Oh, God Frankie soooo fine, sooo good."

He tensed up, "Mmmmmmm." They exploded simultaneously; yet, he was still hard. She fell forward and laughed, "The eternal erection. Does it ever deflate?" she teased still breathing heavily. "Nope," He stood up and she fell with a thud on her butt, legs spread open. "Come on," he pulled her up, kissed her and rubbed her behind.

She followed him into the bathroom, helped him rinse and dry it giggling like a school girl.

"Gotta go. See you in the morning." He zipped up and walked out.

The long corridor was practically empty except for an occasional nurse disappearing into a patient's room. Faint buzzing of conversation was floating from the nurse's station until Frankie walked by. They stopped talking and stared at him, some dropping their jaws.

He had thrown his black leather jacket over his right shoulder holding it with one finger. His tiger body moved with a distinct swagger. He had an effect on women where-ever he went.

"Wouldn't you enjoy giving this guy a physical?" The chubby night nurse whispered in a daze.

"And, how may I ask, would you remove his clothes…with a potato peeler?" The head nurse stared at his behind. "Close your mouths ladies and get back to work if you can still concentrate after seeing this gorgeous spectacle of a man." She sighed dreaming of what she would do if she ever got him in a hospital bed.

He went directly to the physicians' lot to find Sandy's black Chevy. He had slipped the car keys out of her purse figuring he would return before she realized it was gone. It would be better not to have his own car in Steubenville if he was going to take care of Chester. He flew out of the lot skidding around the first turn. From then on, he danced that baby up and down the hills and valleys with lightning speed all the while planning his revenge.

He slowed down when he arrived in Steubenville, coasted to High Street and hid the car behind the bushes at the far end. This was a neighborhood of hardworking families who spoke little English. The husbands worked in the mill and the wives took care of the homes and children. They cared for each other and shared everything including their cooking. The young ones romped in the streets all day and chased lightning bugs at night for fun. Their doors were never locked.

Chester lived in the basement of two story owned by a handsome Hungarian couple. It was a windy night and white lace curtains were billowing out of the open windows. Everyone was sound asleep tucked safely in their beds. The only sound that sabotaged the quiet night came from the crickets.

Frankie let himself in through the screen door over the basement steps. He could hear Chester snoring as he descended. The dirt bag had underwear strewn on the floor. Frankie picked one up, sat on the bed and shoved it into his open mouth. Chester started to choke. It took him a few seconds to understand what was happening. His eyes were filled with terror when he saw Frankie. He heard the click of the switchblade, felt the cold knife on his neck and defecated in his shorts.

Frankie couldn't do the deed in the house for fear the children would be traumatized if they found the body. The Ohio River would swallow up the ugly runt.

"Not a word, son of a bitch. Get up."

Chester was crying. His scrawny legs buckled when he climbed the steps. Frankie pushed him out the back door through the yard into the alley. He fell to his knees several times shaking uncontrollably. By then he knew it was over and wanted to make one last plea for his life. He went down and wrapped his arms around Frankie's feet. He heard his ribs crack and felt excruciating pain when Frankie kicked him towards the bridge. Shit and blood ran down his legs. The stench was horrendous.

"On your feet, son of a bitch. Keep walking."

Frankie took aim and kicked or punched him every time he fell until they reached the middle of the bridge. He quickly slashed Chester's throat and pushed him backwards over the railing. His arms and legs were spread out and he watched him floating downwards like a kite. The underwear was still in his mouth. It was surreal.

A car light broke through the fog. Dimitri recognized Frankie, stopped and jumped out.

"What happened, son?" He laid his large hand on the boy's shoulder.

Frankie's voice was barely audible. "He hurt Angelina."

Just then Dimitri saw the bloody knife that was still in Frankie's hand. He removed a large white handkerchief from his breast pocked, wrapped the knife   and pried it away from him. It was obvious Frankie was in shock. He led him to the car and put him in the front seat, then opened the trunk and stuffed the knife into a pile of clothes meant for the laundry. He hurried into the driver's seat of his gold Lincoln.

"He deserved what he got. You, my dear boy, should snap out of it and declare this punishment for your sister's pain. I would have done the same thing."

"Stop, stop," Frankie mumbled before they reached town. Frankie got out and threw up in the grass. *The nightmare was just beginning.*

Dimitri stood next to him speaking words of encouragement.

"Angelina is in the hospital in Pittsburgh. I have to leave right away."

"I will take you." Dimitri didn't want him to be alone.

"No. No. My car is close by. I have to get back before she wakes up."

"Let me look at you, son. Okay. There isn't any blood on your clothes but your shoes need to be cleaned." Stand behind that tree. He took a flask of whiskey from his jacket and poured it over Frankie's shoes and a shot in his mouth. Frankie coughed but was grateful for the drink. "That takes care of it. Now let's find your car."

Dimitri was tall and handsome. He was wealthy and powerful but had the demeanor of an average guy. He came to Steubenville a few times a year to visit friends and relatives who migrated there from the island of the winds, Chios, Greece. He resided in upper Kardamyla Village in a mansion overlooking the sea. People referred to it as the palace.

One thing he never forgot, he came from poor stock. The abundance he was blessed with was meant to be shared. He secretly helped those less fortunate. Although they suspected Dimitri was subsidizing them, he feigned ignorance when confronted.

Dimitri embraced Frankie. "I'll be at Easy's place every morning at nine if you need me."

"Thanks. I will never forget what you've done for me. Angelina and I may need to get out of the country."

"Done. Keep your eyes on the road."

Frankie sped off afraid to think of what transpired. He believed killing Chester would bring him
some relief. Instead he was filled with anguish. There
was no other way. He abused my poor retarded sister,
took away her innocence. He needed to pay.

"God forgive me," he cried out loud

CHAPTER 4

THE PLAN

E asy stayed away from the back booth where Dimitri, Frankie and Angelina were sitting. They were whispering and passing around papers. Angelina was clinging to Frankie more than usual and he had his arm around her in a gentle, reassuring way.

"We will take the Lincoln to New York and embark on the Olympia. Eleven twelve days…we're in Greece. All the arrangements are made from here to the Island. Everything is first class, Frankie. You and Angelina will be royalty the entire time."

"Dimitri you have saved our lives. I am indebted to you forever."

"Frankie, my boy, I am aware of your feelings. The fact that I will keep the child is an extraordinary blessing for me and my wife. Have you decided what to tell Myrna?"

"I'll tell her we're going England to see a specialist for a consultation on Angelina's condition. If I say you referred me that will be the end of any suspicions. How in the world did you manage to get the passports so quickly?"

"I have my ways. We should be leaving no later than tomorrow. I can arrange for Sandy Horwitz to come with us if it will help Angelina. Say the word."

"Dimitri...the police have Easy cornered. He looks damn uncomfortable."

"Take Angelina and leave, now."

Easy was up front waving his arms and shrugging his shoulders. Frankie heard his comments as he walked by slowly, holding onto his sister.

"Who you find in river? Poor thin...was it woman? Chester? No! Crazy Chester fall in river? Come sit in back, we talkin!" Easy avoided Frankie. He immediately realized what had happened and had to protect him.

"Dimitri, this police findem window wash Chester in River. Sit down. Terrible, terrible."

The police officer sat in the booth. "Easy, we heard tell that you dunked this guy in a bucket of dirty water."

"Oh yea...I do. He cuckoo." Easy looked serious as he made circles with his fingers around his head. "Maybe he jump in river cause no more job, eh? What you say, Dimitri?"

"Easy...listen to me. I know you didn't have anything to do with this but I have to ask since you had a history with him. Somebody slit his throat."

Dimitri stared at the officer. "What a way to die. Slit his throat and threw him in the river. Surely, you know Easy is incapable. Let's be serious. His size forbids it."

"Oh, my God. Cut throat...I throw up, Easy wailed. "Who do this more crazy than Chester?" Easy grabbed his head dramatically. *Frankie have lotta guts, he thought.*

"Calm down Easy. We're just checking to see if you know anything. Chester was a regular here and at Angelo's. Did one of you notice someone with him or anything unusual?"

"You no go to Myrna. She poor woman with sick girl. You scare. I go ask she see sumthin. Stay wit Dimitri."

For a huge guy, he flew out of the diner in a flash and ran across the street. Frankie was sitting with Angelina. The minute he saw Easy he froze.

"Frankie, they find Chester. No worry. I take care everythin'." He stayed for a while pacing the floor then ran back to his place.

"Okay...nobody see nothin'. Tonight I ask people here and Angelo's. I call you. I help best way. Poor... Chester."

"Thanks for your help, Easy. I'll talk to you in the next few days."

The officer walked out thinking there was no way these people were involved. A mob hit? Absolutely not...he was a window washer for Christ's sake... unless he stole doe from the numbers boys who would never take him out for that. This was brutal. He was beaten raw and underwear was stuffed in his trap. There was a look of terror on his face, poor s o b.

Whoever cut his throat must have had a vendetta. There's no other explanation unless the guy was not from Steubenville and Chester caught him robbing the house. Go figure. Maybe Chester was foolin' with a married broad and got nailed by the husband…one of those mill guys. The Serbs are tough so are the Dago's. No…no…he wasn't exactly the type to mess around. Who would want him anyway? He was puzzled and decided to go to the place Chester lived and scrounge around for evidence…a long shot for sure.

Easy forced his massive body into the booth next to Dimitri. "Take Frankie from here fast, you hear me. Maybe today…"

"Don't worry Easy. Everything will be all right. You are in the clear."

"I no worry for me, Dimitri. I think for poor family…Myrna, Angelina, Frankie. Frankie should cut balls from crazy bastard Chester. I want to beet Angelo for no take care family."

"I'd better go across. I'll see you later." Dimitri went to help Frankie talk to Myrna. She was in the kitchen preparing for the lunch crowd. Frankie was biting his nails. The angelic Angelina had her hands on her tummy and had a tender smile on her face.

Myrna blushed when she saw him. "Mr. Dimitri, how nice to see you in our establishment. The food isn't ready but we can get you coffee and biscotti. Frankie, will you please get a cup?"

"Mom, we have good news for you. Please sit for a minute. Dimitri will explain. Let me take Angelina upstairs to pack."

"Pack? What are you talking about?"

Dimitri embraced Myrna. "My sweet, lady... don't be alarmed. I have found the top specialist for Angelina in England and we are taking her for evaluation." He hated lying to her. "The arrangements have been made and we will be leaving shortly."

"Mr. Dimitri, will the doctor be able to help my baby? Maybe my prayers have been answered. We must tell Angelo if we can find him." She looked elated and tears were running down her cheeks. "He blames me for her condition, you know."

"Now, now my Myrna... nothing is written in stone but we will do our best to put her in capable hands. Frankie and I will be there. Perhaps I can bring Dr. Sandy to assist us."

"Oh Mr. Dimitri...you were sent by God."

"Myrna, do not allow your worthless husband to blame you for anything. He should be ashamed to leave you here with all the responsibilities working a man's job. This is when you need him the most. I spit on him. Easy is right. Angelo should get the beating of his life." He slipped an envelope filled with money in her hands. "Open it when we're gone."

Dimitri realized they had to leave promptly now that the police had discovered the body. He would take care of everything in a matter of a couple of hours.

"Mr. Dimitri...Mr. Dimitri..." Annie Paidousis was knocking on the window. It's an emergency. I have to talk to you."

Annie was a baby-doll and was always dressed in the latest fashions. Her dimples were deep as rivers and her face was set off by huge, dark eyes. She was petite like her mother Georgia and needed a taller stool to sit on when she worked at the Capital Theater ticket booth. Even though she was small, you wouldn't know it when she bellowed out the latest Greek and American hits. People stopped outside of her house to hear her singing. Her voice had an operatic tone and there was nothing she loved more than singing. Annie's mom was not pleased thinking a girl who sang most of the time would never find a suitable husband. Although she wasn't permitted to date, she was popular due to her upbeat personality. Mrs. Georgia wouldn't consider anyone who didn't come from Chios Island for her daughter or her son Timmy. As a matter of fact, unbeknownst to Timmy, she was planning to take him there soon to introduce him to a sweet young woman she had heard about.

"Come in my flower. What is the matter?"

"They're in Pittsburgh." She was breathless. "They were arrested by immigration after jumping off one of your freighters. They were making their way to Steubenville. We have to get them out." She was overexcited and her expressive eyes were as big as saucers. "I went to the jail where they are keeping three people from one family. No one would listen to me."

"All right Annie. Calm down and explain slowly."

"They are from Kardamyla, your village. Jimmy Houmis is one of them. He is the handsomest man I ever saw. He wants me! When I went through the jail house, he shouted out that I was the woman he would marry."

"Annie, listen to me. Do you have particulars? Where are they being held? I'll have them out by tomorrow. Jimmy is indisputably handsome and a great man. I know the family. We'll make sure they come here. Let me be the first to congratulate you on your engagement."

"He's awfully tall, Mr. Dimitri. I probably won't reach his shoulder but I fell for him the minute our eyes met."

"Annie, please focus. I want phone numbers of the officials, the jail house and names of our people. Can you provide these or do we need to go back to Pittsburgh?"

"Got 'em, here you go." She was proudly prepared.

"Now go home and wait for your man to ask for your hand."

Annie bounced out clicking her high heels, singing a pretty tune. She hadn't been this thrilled in a long while and was anticipating her mother's reaction to the news about her impending engagement. He was from Chios, good looking and had a stellar reputation. What else could she want? Even though he was from another village than her folks, she did not think they would object.

"Myrna, tell Frankie to call me at the hotel. If he wants to pick up Sandy Horwitz, we'll have to leave soon."

Dimitri was exhausted by the drama but felt that his contributions would avoid a lot of heartache. He

went to Easy's to let him know about the trip without
revealing the details of the pregnancy. He figured Easy
suspected but did not want him in a compromising
position since he was close to everyone involved.
Knowing they would be leaving Steubenville would
alleviate the old man's anxiety. "You are a caring
friend Easy. This family is lucky to have you around.
By the way, there will be new Chians in Steubenville.
They will be here tomorrow. It seems Annie may be
getting married soon."

CHAPTER 5

As he walked towards the Ft. Steuben hotel on South Fourth Street his mind wandered to the day he saved the life of one of the wealthiest men in the world. He took a bullet in the back by jumping in front of shipping tycoon Socrates Konstantinides. His entire existence changed from that moment on.

He was laid up, under 24-hour care in Argentina where the tanker he was working on had docked. When his wounds finally healed, Konstantinides personally picked him up from the hospital and laid out his plan to mentor him, teaching him everything about shipping. "You are the captain of this ship now," he said seriously. "Someday it will be yours." The one stipulation - he would marry Konstatinides' only daughter Penelope. She was a hot looking blond with fluid limbs, a long neck and cat eyes like her late mother Ariadne. But, she had an edge to her demeanor that Dimitri found harsh.

Nevertheless, this agreement solidified his position. Konstantinides taught him every secret in the business... the tax codes, the where and how of *import/export...shipping under the Panama flag to avoid paying millions in excessive fees and where to grab fast deals such as tobacco for ultimate profits. Dimitri was sharp, quick and was running the business before the old man retired. He inherited everything.*

By then everyone knew Dimitri was a force to be reckoned with. He was quietly powerful and took swift retribution to those who tried to cross him. He was feared and revered. When the time came for the marriage, a private island in Greece owned by Konstantinides was prepared to accommodate the most prestigious people on the continent...Kings, Queens, heads of state, shipping tycoons...by invitation only. Those who were shunned were furious and devastated. Luxurious yachts pulled up to the island. Security was everywhere. Dimitri's mother was not alive but that didn't stop him from including villagers in the wedding. His two best men were Saranti's boys Yiorgo and Strati who were dumbfounded by the pageantry.

All this and Dimitri was still unhappy. The only joy he knew was with his childhood sweetheart Katina, the simplicity of their romance, the purity of their love. Penelope felt the bite. They were both in their own world never admitting the truth, pretending to be content.

He called the front desk from his suite. "Have my driver on standby and send someone up to pack a few things and take them to the car. Get me Pittsburgh General Hospital, person to person, Dr. Horwitz then call the jail in Pittsburgh. I'll be leaving but keep this floor available as always."

Dr. Sandy barely balked when Dimitri told her to get ready to leave for Greece. "You won't need clothes. Only bring a few essentials. You'll get everything on board. We'll pick you up at home tonight. Be on standby. Angelina needs you."

He paid the fines for the boys in Pittsburgh and talked to Jimmy Houmis on the phone. "Come directly here tomorrow. I have rooms available at the hotel. I expect you to make good on your proposal to Annie Paidousis."

"I'm in love with her," Jimmy cried out. "I will be an excellent husband and father."

"Don't get ahead of yourself." Dimitri had a good laugh. "Her folks haven't agreed yet. I understand her mother is a spit-fire and difficult to deal with."

"I'll charm her."

"Yes, yes, you are certainly a charmer."

He hung up and kicked back on the bed for a few minutes to clear his head. When he closed his eyes, he saw his Katina smiling at him. He yearned for her and couldn't wait to go home, to feel her warmth and unconditional love. Then he remembered his wedding night. Penelope was perfect. She was the image of a Goddess making the right moves and sounds. Every time they were together it was the same ritual yet something was off. He couldn't be sure since her satisfaction was always what he would strive for. She laid there like a cold slab of marble staring at the ceiling after sex. How odd.

The phone rang. "I'll send the car for you now. No luggage, please. We don't want to draw attention. We'll pick up what you need on the way. If we are stopped and questioned, we're taking Angelina to the doctor. It won't happen but we should cover our bases. Sandy is waiting at home. She has a passport so that won't be an issue. Our driver is an undercover agent. We will be well protected."

Dimitri made another important call. Angelo was not going to leave Myrna alone when she needed him the most. He was going home to stay. "You know what to do with him. After he begs for his life make sure he begs Myrna's forgiveness. Also, the s o b should be presentable. You got a couple of hours to get it done. You know where to find him."

The last call was to Easy. "My friend, take Irini and go to Myrna's place. Frankie and Angelina just left. Angelo will be going home soon. We have to help this woman cope."

Dimitri thought he heard Easy cry. "We be there in few minutes. No worry. Angelo try something I beat heem."

Dimitri put on his beige, suit-jacket, adjusted his brown tie and left the room. Two big men in dark suits were waiting at the bottom of the steps. Each one touched the rim of his hat and nodded. "Make sure that bastard is sober. Don't put any marks on him or his bitch."

He walked out with a smile of satisfaction on his face and got into the Lincoln that had pulled up at that precise moment. He spoke to his driver, Myron who looked suspiciously like a wrestler. There was very little hair on his head and his neck was huge and didn't quite fit in his shirt. "First, we're heading for Pittsburgh. Don't be in a hurry till we get to the highway."

"Yes, boss." His voice was gruff and deep. His biceps were pushing out of his jacket. Dimitri figured it was a good thing the car was big...Myron's bulky thighs covered half the front seat.

"Myrna packed food for us." Frankie spoke calmly. "Angelina loves mama's cooking."

"Wonderful," Dimitri laughed. "I love her cooking, too."

Everyone relaxed into the luxury of the car once they were on the road and out of Steubenville. They were quiet each reflecting on his own circumstances. Frankie had his arm around Angelina who was sleeping soundly on his shoulder. He couldn't shake the feeling that Chester's death would haunt him for the rest of his life. He had nightmares of Chester falling into the river, eyes bulging, blood spewing from his neck and his mouth stuffed with dirty underwear. In some dreams he jumped from the bridge trying to grab a hold of Chester before he fell into the river. He woke up screaming every time.

Dimitri's mind was cluttered with business. He was expecting his men to meet him at the ship bringing reports about his latest acquisitions, cargo his ships were moving and to what countries. At this point in time he had wiped out most of the competition allowing only a few families who were respectful of his power to keep their freighters. They spoke directly with him or the company before attempting to take advantage of the market. He gave the nod of approval and oftentimes sent business their way. They in turn kept him in the loop with information of anyone who was attempting to undermine his ventures. His thoughts floated to Papou Georgios Cohen who mentored him since he was a child. He owed his business savvy to him.

He leaned back trying to doze off wondering how Penelope would react to Angelina's baby. After all, she had lost two children in the first trimester of her pregnancies. A child she could love and raise may change her miserable attitude. Dimitri was sure her unhappiness stemmed directly from the fact that she didn't have children of her own. She lived in a palace, had every luxury money could buy but it was never enough. Katina, on the other hand, was happy to spend a few stolen hours with him. He dozed off wrapped in tender thoughts of her.

CHAPTER 6

ANGELO GOES HOME

*T*he brothers were on Dimitri's payroll for years. They were well taken care of financially. Basically, they kept an eye on Dimitri's friends from the island keeping them safe and reported if they had problems. Their activities were minimal except, on occasion they needed to respond forcefully. This is when they felt they earned their keep. There were skillful at avoiding physical brutality. Hints of violence alone would scare the perpetrators half to death.

Tony and Vito walked down the long, dark stairway to The Cellar, a popular strip joint. "Which way to Candy's room? We want to get in quietly through the back…it will be a surprise." Vito spoke slowly dragging each word for maximum effect.

The bartender was setting up for the evening crowd…regulars that came to pant over Candy and the other dames of the night who stripped for a living. When he saw the two men dressed in expensive double breasted black suits, he understood this wasn't the time to play games. He pointed to the hallway and continued his work hoping whatever they did would be quick and painless.

Neither Angelo nor Candy noticed them. Angelo was tied spread eagle on the bed his head was buried between her thighs. Candy's pert behind was over his face moving up and down like a machine and she was bent forward with her ruby lips devouring his enormous erection. She was wearing stilettos, black fish net hose hooked onto green satin garters and no bra. Her breasts were swaying across his thighs.

Vito grabbed a fist full of her bleached blond hair and pulled her up. "I see you are multi-talented." She was about to scream when he covered her mouth with his hand. "Shhh, honey. Nothing will happen to you." He shoved her into the closet. "Now lie down in here till we're finished." He slapped her buttocks and threw her on the floor.

Tony was pointing a gun between Angelo's legs.

"No…No…please." Angelo could barely talk. "Don't do it. What did I do? I'll make it right. Please, I'm begging you. I'll do anything you want."

"What d'ya say Vito? Should we shoot this low life in the balls or the head?" He pointed the gun to Angelo's mouth.

"Let's give him a chance to redeem himself."

"I'll give back the poker money. Please don't shoot me. Everything I got is in the nightstand. Take it all. It's yours. I have more at the diner." He was crying. "You can have it."

"Shut up, you hairy prick! You want us to take the money from your family? The money your wife works for, you bastard." Tony cut the ropes from his legs and arms. "Get your ass into the bathroom...I don't want to get blood on the bed."

"Oh God...no...I'm your guy whatever you say I'll do it. Don't kill me."

"Crawl into the bathroom cockroach." Vito wanted to punch him but Dimitri didn't want marks on the guy.

Angelo was on all fours crawling and begging. "Whatever, you say. You are the bosses. Tell me what to do...anything...I'll do it. I'm your man"

"Take a shower asshole and get dressed in your finest." Vito growled at him.

"Why am I getting dressed? Are you taking me somewhere else to kill me?"

"Don't talk...do as we say or we'll cut you bit by bit starting between your legs." Tony gave him a swift kick in the rear and he fell head first into the shower. He turned on the hot water. "Now clean up."

"Great job so far Vito. Now let's get him the hell outta here."

Angelo stepped out of the shower and looked for an escape. The bathroom window was boarded up and the guys were standing at the door. "Whatever you're gonna do, make it quick."

Tony told him to shave and comb his hair then go pick out his best clothes. "We want you to look great in your coffin, son of a bitch."

"Oh sweet Jesus...I gotta family. I got kids."

"You remember them, bastard?" Vito growled at him and shoved him towards the closet. "Get dressed fast. We're going to get a bouquet."

He pulled open the closet door and there was Candy scrunched up with her arms around her knees and her crotch exposed. She didn't move, utter a word or open her eyes. Angelo wanted to slap her. *No help from this slut.* He was angry.

Angelo dressed slowly and methodically in his best white shirt, burgundy tie, navy pin striped suit and matching leather loafers. *What a waste of beautiful clothes, he thought. He was shaking and wondering if his family would go to the funeral after what he had done to them. My poor Myrna didn't deserve the pain I inflicted on her. If only I had another chance, Lord, I would make her happy.*

"Do I get a last request? I want to tell my wife I love her."

Vito and Tony looked at each other and smiled thinking this was working far better than anticipated. They each latched on to one of his arms and led him out of the room through the bar. Everyone working there ignored them. They dragged him up the steps and outside to the car. Tony was the driver and he put Angelo next to him in the front seat. Vito sat directly behind and aimed a gun at his head.

"What about Myrna? Can I say goodbye?"

"Maybe…you want to bring her flowers, too. What you think Vito? Should we take him to the diner?"

"Watch your step Angelo. You're going home to stay. If we catch you anywhere on the street, we'll cut off your nuts and make you eat them. You got it. We'll be watching you! Make sure Myrna takes you back. If she doesn't...well you know what comes next."

"Oh sweet Jesus...oh Lord......thank you. I'll be the best husband and father that ever was..." He was so relieved he almost fainted.

They stopped the car at the flower shop and told Angelo to pick up Myrna's favorites. He bought two dozen yellow roses. "Please let me walk...my place is up the street. I swear Myrna will be ecstatic."

Angelo ran to the diner and looked in the window. Easy and Irini were there with their arms around Myrna who was crying for her children. He adjusted his tie and opened the door. "Myrna, my love, I'm home to stay if you'll still have me." He gave her the bouquet of golden yellow roses and fell to his knees... forgive me. I've been an ass."

Myrna's heart was thundering. Angelo was handsome as ever and he brought her favorite flowers. She couldn't believe it. She wanted to kiss his face and hold him...instead she gave him a stinging slap that rocked his head. "This will be for how long? Until you get a hard on for one of those strippers."

Angelo was shocked. No woman had ever slapped him before. Even though he deserved it, he was humiliated. But, this wasn't going to stop him from winning her back no matter what he had to do.

Easy knew Angelo was coming home. He took Irini's hand and sat her at one of the tables. He would stay till the bitter end in case he needed to intervene and protect Myrna. What a surprise seeing Angelo

on his knees. He put his arm around Irini's shoulder
and kissed her wrinkled cheek that was wet with
tears. "I am lucky for you my Easy."

"I'll never leave you again, Myrna. You are my
only love. I'm here to make amends. I promise to
take care of you forever. Realizing I love you more
than life has brought me begging at your doorstep.
Give me another chance."

Myrna towered over him with her hands on her
hips. "Head for the kitchen Angelo...we have to be
ready for the dinner crowd." She jerked him up by
his tie. "First kiss me like you mean it." The kiss was
long and very, sexy. "We're alone tonight. The kids
have gone to Europe."

"Europe? What are you talking about? I wanted
to see them."

"I'll explain later."

Angelo took off his jacket and went to the back
to put on an apron and hairnet. He was happy to be
alive and happy to be home. "How do I look?" He
poked his head out of the kitchen door.

"Shut up and go workin' or I seet on you," Easy
warned.

"From this moment on...kitchen duty is mine. You
will be out here doing what you do best...having fun
with your customers. And Myrna, no more tears."

"Well, Easy. You and I won't be working the
kitchen anymore and Irini doesn't have to do all
that cleaning and shining. I'll be doing it. You will
be my guests of honor every single night." Myrna
embraced them.

"You are sister, my Myrna. Easy and me always helpin'." She started wiping down the tables. "You go upstairs fix hair, put pretty dress...look nice for Angelo." She was thrilled for Myrna and started thinking perhaps she should do something to make herself look nicer for her man.

Myrna was walking on clouds as she climbed upstairs to her room. She put clean sheets on her bed and laid out her sheer negligee. As she rummaged through her drawers she came across her wedding picture and realized how much she had changed. Her weight was up and her face showed signs of aging but her eyes were still beautiful.

"I'll work with what I have," she spoke to herself and pulled out black lace undergarments. After her luxurious bubble bath, she slathered perfumed cream on her body and dressed slowly. Her cleavage was perfect spilling out from the top of her silver satin dress. Her makeup was subtle but beautiful and her red curly hair hugged her face. "I'm ready to show him, I can be as sexy as any stripper."

"Ciao, my loves," Myrna flew into the diner swinging her ample hips.

The men howled and whistled when they saw her. She was hot and she knew it.

Angelo poked his head through the kitchen door and felt pangs of jealousy. "She's my woman," he shouted. "You are a movie star, baby." He pulled her close, bent her backwards and gave her a Valentino kiss. "Be careful not to mess with her or I'll come out with a butcher knife next time."

CHAPTER 7

Timmy, Annie and Mrs. Georgia were sitting with Irini. "Wow, I dig it," Timmy shouted. I gotta copy Angelo's moves." He called Myrna to the table. "Where the hell is Frankie? I wanted to say goodbye. Mom and I are leaving for Greece tomorrow. She's afraid to travel alone 'cause her English ain't too good. We're hopping the train to New York and then sailing on the Olympia."

"He's gone away with Angelina. Mr. Dimitri is taking them to England to see a specialist for her. Annie honey, I heard you were getting engaged."

"Shush, nobody knows yet." Mrs. Georgia was busy talking to Irini and didn't pay attention to what her daughter was saying. "Jimmy should be here tomorrow morning before the train leaves. He can speak to my mom then. I love him, Myrna. He is the most beautiful man I've ever seen."

"I hope he deserves you Annie," she touched her hair. "You are an angel. He will be a lucky man."

"Did you hear about Chester?"

"What about him, Timmy? He hasn't been around since Easy dunked him."

"Didn't you guys read the Herald Star?" Timmy ran his fingers across his throat. "Chester was bumped off. They found him in the river."

Myrna was shocked. "What happened? Who could have done such a horrific thing?" She pulled the newspaper from Timmy's hands. "Oh Holy Mother of God...his throat. "He has no family that we know of in Steubenville." She motioned to Easy who was talking with one of her patrons about the article.

"No say nothing to Myrna bout Chester take Angelina to park. No say to nobody. You understand me," Easy scared the old man.

"I ain't talking, Easy. Don't worry 'bout me. Did you do it?"

"You cuckoo ol' man. I no want Myrna know what he do to Angelina. Keep mouth closed, okay?"

Everyone was buzzing about the murder. They were going table to table discussing who may have done it. The consensus was that it must have been an outsider. Chester wasn't the sharpest knife in the drawer but he didn't have enemies. They knew him as a window washer who did a little hop and skip dancing for pocket change...nothing more. Who in Steubenville would want to kill him?

Angelo was putting his famous "chicken caccia-tore" on the counter. He was singing Mario Lanza's Be My Love then Annie caught the fever and added her voice. They were fabulous together.

Mrs. Georgia was ready to pull her daughters hair out. "She never find husband...no brains."

Tony and Vito were sitting in the far corner with smug faces. They insisted Angelo serve them dinner. He came out with a huge smile and enough food for an army. "On the house for my friends," he shouted then dropped his voice. "Thank you for not shooting off my dick. It's my best asset and I'm gonna need it tonight. I'm planning a sizzling reunion with my baby."

"What do the women see in you, arrogant bastard?"

"I'm handsome and hung," he touched himself below.

They polished off the food wishing for more. Suddenly, they were queasy. "Oh shit, Vito. I'm not feeling well. The room is spinning and you look green." Tony was up and running to the bathroom with Vito on his heels. The pains were excruciating and they were doubled over praying they would make it to the toilet before having an accident in their pants. "We should have killed him, Tony."

Myrna saw them flash by and yelled for Angelo who was laughing hysterically. Once he realized they had played him, he couldn't resist a bit of revenge. He laced their food with an abundance of fast working laxatives. After all, they scared the daylights out of him and they needed to pay. Truth be told, the guys did him a favor returning him to the fold.

"Angelo, what's so funny? Your friends look sick."

"They ate too damn much, baby." He had taken off the hairnet and was working the room with Myrna, slapping his friends on the back and making wise cracks. He felt wonderful being home and seeing his old cronies. "I don't understand why I left you Myrna. I must have been insane. This is where I belong."

"Hey Angelo...sing us a Dino song before we leave," someone shouted out.

Angelo took Myrna in his arms and danced with her as he crooned Pretty Baby. She was moved to tears as they glided around the tables. He kissed her eyes and face and sang his heart out. When he was finished, he placed his hands on her cheeks and softly kissed her lips.

"Welcome back Angelo," the guys whistled and the ladies dabbed their teary eyes.

Angelo sat with Myrna at the "Greek" table. For once, Easy had nothing nasty to say to him. Even Mrs. Georgia was dazzled by the performance. "Irini, maybe ask Angelo teach our men sing, eh?" "My Easy, he sing good." Irini gazed into her husband's eyes.

Nobody noticed that Timmy was gone. While everyone was enamored with the romantic performances, he took the opportunity to sneak away to have one last fling before leaving for Greece in the morning. He thought perhaps he could finally jump Candy's bones now that Angelo had left her.

The diner had emptied out and the ladies were picking up the dishes. Annie kicked off her high heels and was bopping around singing and dancing while she cleaned off the tables. Mrs. Georgia was yelling at her in Greek to stop the nonsense.

Angelo had forgotten Tony and Vito until he saw them coming out of the bathroom. "I have a question for you my good buddies. Who put you up to it? I want to thank him from the bottom of my heart."

"It was Dimitri, you ass. He didn't want Myrna alone any more. She needed you."

"Come back soon. I owe you a real meal and I promise to deliver. Capisce?" He pushed them out.

"Tomorrow we will be closed. I have plans for me and my baby. First we will help Mrs. Georgia take her luggage to the train. Then we'll have a stroll by the river. I will buy my Myrna earrings from the Hub. We'll eat at the Green Mill and have ice cream at Islay's. In the evening, we'll visit Annie at the Capital Theater to see the new Errol Flynn flick. From now on, I will spend one day a week enjoying the company of my perfect wife. I have a lot to make up for... What do you say Myrna, my love?"

"I thought I had lost you forever. Now that you're home, I will pretend what you did never happened. The only other thing I will ask from the Lord is to make my Angelina well."

"Go on up baby. I will close tonight." He hugged the ladies and punched Easy in the arm. "Thank you for taking care of my family brother."

He locked up, turned off the lights and went upstairs wondering what was in store. Myrna was a wildcat and there was no telling what would happen. Hopefully, she wouldn't fight him. It had been a long time since they had sex and she was always a hot number. He wasn't in the mood for drama but was ready in case she started something.

"Where's my baby?"

"Here sweetheart...the bathroom. I put bubbles in the tub for you," she said sweetly. "Let me undress you and scrub your heavenly body."

He was getting nervous as she removed his clothing and pulled off his underwear.

"Wow, Myrna, you look luscious." She was wearing her sheer yellow negligee. Her breasts were big as cannons.

"Get in the water, honey." She knelt beside the tub and bathed him slowly rubbing the hair on his chest. "You know how much I love this. My goodness, it has been so long. You have some gray hair. I hope you're not getting too old to play," she cooed.

He had a warm dark tan, muscular shoulders and thighs that met on top. Myrna was always crazy about that part of his body. She reached down, parted his thighs and put her hand under his testicles.

"What the hell, Myrna...who taught you these things? You been foolin' around? I'll kill him and you."

She continued to make little circles with her finger and he went totally mad. He was hard as a hammer and ready to pop. She got up. "Isn't it sexy Angelo? Now come and get me." She ran into the bedroom with Angelo on her heels. He was still wet and was slipping and sliding when he caught her and threw her on the bed.

"Oh no you don't, Angelo...you are not putting that question mark inside of me. You are hung like an elephant with a crooked trunk." She had her legs closed tightly. "I won't let you hurt me."

"Come on baby. You know you want it. I'll be careful...slow and easy. Come on...open up." He tried to pry her thighs open while she screamed and squirmed.

"Damn it Myrna...stop playing games." He held her arms over her head with one hand and tried to put his hand between her thighs. "It only hurts for a little while and then you enjoy it, honey. Let me in... Ahhhh, you bitch." He went flying over the edge of the bed when she pushed him with her knees. He hit the floor and was dazed as he watched her race into an adjoining room.

He went after her. "You are itching for it, Myrna. You'll be sorry when I catch you." He landed on her threw her on the bed and held her down. Making loud grunting sounds he ripped her negligee with his teeth.

"Oh God...you are an animal." She faked tears. "My negligee is ruined, you beast! I'll never ever let you in...Angelo...never...never...never."

"Shut up and stop crying, Myrna. I'll buy you a better one. Now open up before I go nuts."

"No...No...No...not while I'm still breathing. You are not putting that in me."

"Okay, baby...I won't do it. It isn't your first time Myrna...you know you want it."

"No I don't...it's too big. You need to see a doctor and have it straightened and shortened."

"Are you crazy? This is one of a kind...unique. Stop fussing and saying stupid things. Let me look, that's all. I swear I won't even attempt to put it in. I love you too much to be the cause of your pain. Let me take a peek, sweetie."

"Do you really, really want to?"

"You know I do. Please, please let me look."

"Well...maybe. How much do you want me Angelo...more than any other woman in the world?"

"Yes...yes...yes...stop talking and open up." He was frustrated and shouting.

"All right," she sniffled. "A tiny look, that's all. Don't try anything or I'll scream."

"Nothing has changed down here. It is still the cutest pussy I've ever seen." He mounted her and decided to go full force. "No more playing around, Myrna. You're getting the whole damn thing."

She screamed and tried desperately to push him off by moving her behind upward but it didn't work this time. He was in and pumping. "Tell me...Tell me I'm the best...say it."

"Angelo, it hurts...oh God...you're the best." Orgasm after orgasm...scream after scream...she moved her hips in waves and didn't stop climaxing till Angelo was exhausted and fell over.

"Is that it...you can't go anymore? I thought you were a great lover man and you're already tired?"

"Do you want to be a widow, Myrna? I'm having a heart attack. Give me a chance to recover and we'll go again."

Myrna rolled onto him and put her breasts in his face.

"I can't breathe with those monstrosities in my face. I'm being buried alive." He began chewing her nipples.

"Remember when you played telephone with them…one in your mouth and the other in your ear."

"Operator, get me an ambulance. I'm suffocating." He spoke into her breast.

"You were begging before and now you don't want me." She reached below his testicles and started playing with him.

"Stop that." He pushed her away. "What the hell you think you're doin'?"

"It's workin' isn't it bad boy? Show me what you can do with it!"

He flipped her on her back and got on top. "You're a volcano. I'm gonna screw you till you're dry." He shoved it in hard and fast hoping she'd give up but it didn't happen. She moaned and yelled out his name again and again.

"How many times can you go, Myrna? I can't hold it any more. Oh, Myrna baby, I'm coming. This is the greatest yet."

"Stop for a bit then push again." she was breathless. "I was having quick ones, now they are longer lasting." She was adept at the vaginal squeeze.

"Oh…oh…oh honey…can't do it." He fell on her burying his face between in her breasts. "Stop squeezing…stop it. I'm finished." Her legs were wrapped around his back and she continued crushing his penis with all her might. "Damn it Myrna. Don't you ever listen? You're killing me."

"Rest Angelo. I'm taking a shower and I'll return with renewed vigor."

"Lie down baby…forget taking a shower. We both need to recuperate." He laid back and closed his eyes.

She smiled knowing what he was in for during the next round. After bathing, she dipped her fingers in a jar of honey that she always used on her face. She plastered it over her nipples and between her legs.

"Angelo, my love, I brought you something sweet." She used her girly voice.

"Is it a cannoli? Mmm my favorite. Put a piece in my mouth."

"It's a surprise. You'll love it…honey for my honey!" She pushed her nipple into his mouth and he automatically began sucking driving Myrna completely wild. She had an earthshaking orgasm before she gave him her other breast.

"You came again? I had forgotten you need more than one man to keep you satisfied. It's delicious. Now can we take a breather?"

"Oh no you don't, Angelo. I'm even sweeter down below."

"What? You have honey on your pussy? This I've got to see!" He took a dive between her thighs and began examining her. "Wink at me sweetie. Let me see how you do it. Go ahead."

Myrna was laughing as she squeezed her muscles. "How's that for a wink!"

"I bet you could light a cigar with it, Myrna. Of course, with all that hair it could be dangerous. I'll have to shave it for you before we try."

"Are distracted from your goal, Angelo?"

"I forgot to mention, it's a lot plumper than it used to be. I love you this way."

"There's more bounce to the ounce. Now get busy and taste the desert!"

He buried his face there making animal noises as he licked and nibbled waiting for her to fly. Her body was shaking and she pushed his head into her.

"I ate all of the honey," he stopped and got on top of her taking it slow and easy.

"Harder, faster," she yelled.

Angelo wasn't having it this time. Whenever he thought she would climax, he pulled out and waited.

"No...no...no..." she wrapped her legs around him trying to get it back in.

After several attempts at delaying, he was ready to explode with her. He thrust it inside of her with angry force and they had what he hoped would be the last hoorah for the night.

"Stop screaming. Someone will call the police!" He placed his hand on her mouth. "Give up...there is no way I can do it again. I can't keep up with you."

"Ohhhh...my sexy Angelo...I give up. You are the greatest lover I've ever had."

"What? Who are you comparing me with... one of those brawny mill workers? Tell me, Myrna. Who is it?" He shook her. "What did you do while I was away?"

"Jealous? I'll tell you the sordid details. I was taking care of our two children and the diner seven days a week while you were humping strippers, gambling and partying. Do you actually think I had time for sex?"

"Myrna, I don't deserve you. Where have our children gone?"

"Frankie and Angelina have gone to England with Mr. Dimitri. He is taking Angelina to a specialist."

"Dimitri is quite a man. I've been a terrible father. I don't understand where my brain has been allowing other people to support my family. I hope I haven't lost them. Myrna, I swear to God, I will make up for my selfishness."

"It's daylight. Let's rest for a while then go to help Mrs. Georgia. Do you have the strength, Angelo or are you worn out from that tiny bit of sex that we had?"

He was already asleep. She curled up next to him remembering how it used to be. They were in love and the world belonged to them. It was magic. "I love you," she whispered

CHAPTER 8

PAIDOUSIS TRIP

It was a breezy summer day, comfortable for traveling. High Street was brimming with activity. People were coming and going to the Paidousis home bringing gifts for their loved ones in the old country. The front and back screen doors were slamming. Food was everywhere brought from the neighbors for Mr. George and Annie since they would be staying behind. Even in all the confusion, there was organization. Mrs. Georgia had the trunks open adding more and more things as they became available. Two coffee pots were perking continuously in the kitchen. Everyone was dunking Greek cookies in their cups then Thea Irini and Thea Anthipe, Mrs. Georgia's sister, washed them out for the next visitors. It was friendly chaos.

Annie slipped into her brother's room and threw his clothes into a suitcase. He finally arrived and tried to climb in the back window falling down several times before crawling in. "I ain't doin' too good…a little woozy, is all."

"Shut up before mom catches on to your dirty tricks. Your clothes are packed now get washed and dressed."

Mrs. Georgia was calling for Timmy to wake up when she heard a ruckus on the porch. Knowing her husband's temper, she dashed to the front of the house catching him with his hands around Angelo's throat. He was threatening to kill him for humiliating his family. Myrna was trying to pry open his fingers explaining Angelo was no longer a cad. He was home for good and sorry for his actions. Mr. George's English was so poor he didn't quite understand her.

Angelo was gasping for air when Mrs. Georgia grabbed her husband and shook him. He finally let go and looked at his wife for guidance. She was the only person that had complete control over him. He turned into a lamb when she spoke and followed her every command. She told him to wake up his son since they would be leaving for the train station shortly.

"Say sorry Angelo, now. He come help us." Mr. Georgia hung his head and mumbled an apology then went looking for Timmy.

"He gorilla," she told Angelo and Myrna. It was her nickname for him due to his huge hairy chest and temperament.

Myrna tended to Angelo who was still coughing and choking. "That man is dangerous! I could have been killed!"

"You're okay." She suppressed a laugh. "Now drink Mrs. Georgia's eight o'clock coffee and have her homemade cookies. You're lucky she was around when he went berserk. Gotta hand it to him, he was protecting our family."

"Psst, psst, Myrna," Annie was motioning to her to come to the window. "Look across the street. There he is…my Jimmy. Isn't he the most!"

"Wow." Myrna was impressed. "He adds new meaning to tall, dark and handsome."

"Please tell him not to come in here. My mother will lose it. He should meet us at the train station. Hurry before anyone notices."

"Does he speak English or should I tell him go to the choo-choo?"

Myrna ran across the street waving no, no, no to Jimmy. "Wait at the train for Annie."

He got it, blew Annie a kiss and took off.

Mrs. Georgia stood on the porch watching everyone haul the luggage and trunks to the van. She was dressed to kill in a form fitting brown tweed suit over an ivory silk blouse with a cascading bow and matching ivory gloves. On her head was a small brown hat tiled to the right with a rim that turned down over one eye, a gold hat pin with a blue evil eye stone on the end and a whisper of a veil that fell on her face. Two large brown spit curls were glued on each cheek. She resembled a grand dame.

"Big man," she questioned Myrna. "What he want?"

"He was lost." She ran inside to avoid her scrutiny.

Mrs. Georgia suspected the tall man was blowing kisses towards her house. Maybe I should worry for daughter, she thought.

Timmy stepped out of his room looking perfectly polished in his charcoal suit. Mr. George knew his son had been out all night and was proud of him for it. He kept quiet and put money in his son's pocket. "For trip Stamati, no tell mom."

"Thanks, pops. You're always takin' care of me. I'm gonna miss you. Be good to Annie. She will need you more than ever."

Mr. George stood at the doorway looking lost and forlorn. His wife did not want him to come to the train station due to his emotional instability. It would be better for him to stay home and wait for his daughter to return. She told him to be strong and that she would miss him then kissed the air next to both sides of his face taking care not to ruin her lipstick.

Maybe he workin' double shifts at mill till we back from Greece, she thought. When I come home, I have more money.

She always spent every dime he made either for her family in Steubenville or needy families on the island of Chios. The trunks she was taking with her were filled with items to be distributed to the poor in the villages.

Mrs. Georgia, Timmy and Annie got into the Plymouth with Myrna and Angelo. Thea Irini cried and waved goodbye. Many of the neighbors on South High Street were walking towards the station to bid them a safe trip…the Shimkos, Peelas, Olivettis,

Benos, Georgiafendis, Synodinos, Smigonoviches, Hasans, Mastrianis, Evangelinos. It resembled a wedding procession from the old country. This was a reason for the neighbors to declare their unity. Although they spoke different languages, they stood by each other emitting kindness and understanding. Everyone was in the same category…missing their country, unable to communicate fully, trying desperately to fit in American society. The men were all mill workers.

When the car pulled up to the station Annie jumped out first and ran inside looking for Jimmy. There he was hiding behind a post. He popped his head out and winked at her. "Don't worry. I will handle everything," he said.

The whole place filled up. There were tears, well wishes and then the train smoking, grunting and clanging pulled into the station. When the luggage was taken aboard, Timmy waved to Jimmy who ran out, picked up Annie and kissed her on the lips. "I'm a Houmis from Chios and I'm going to marry your daughter," he shouted.

Mrs. Georgia was dumbfounded. Her jaw dropped and she couldn't quite figure out what to say except for, "You are too tall for me to embrace you." She took Annie's hand, placed it in his and told her to go to the Hub and pick out a wedding dress. Everyone cheered.

"Mom, close your mouth and let's go," Timmy pulled her to the train and helped her up the steps.

"You know man?"

"Met him at Easy's."

They found seats and Mrs. Georgia stared out of the window as the train moved out. Jimmy was still carrying her daughter and they were waving and sending her kisses. Although there was a crowd shouting good wishes all she could see was her beautiful daughter and son-in-law to be.

"Don't know first name."

"Jimmy, mom…Jimmy Houmis from Kardamyla."

"You mean not from Kambos? The family don't approve of foreigner."

"Didn't you always say you wanted someone from the island? Who cares about the village? All you need to know that he is a Chian and has a huge heart."

"He know she sing all day?"

Timmy was laughing. "He loves her just the way she is, mom. He's her type of a man. She will be happy."

Her wheels were turning. *Now that daughter is okay, I make sure son gets girl from Chios to take him off streets. I have proposals from many families for eligible daughters but my mind say Angela Atsalis is best. I hear she pretty, good homemaker and come from fine family.*

Timmy had already taken off and was checking out the chicks. There were Greek girls on the train from other towns in Ohio and West Virginia. He didn't want to get involved with them because they would be thinking marriage and he wasn't the marrying kind.

"Hey Erma isn't that Timmy Paidousis? Let's get him to sit with us," Dorothy was excited. "He must be going to Greece. We'll be on the ship together." The girls had freshly coiffed hair and both wore navy blue and white taffeta, dresses. Round rimmed white hats framed the back of their heads. Short white gloves and patent leather shoes polished off their outfits. There were fake beauty marks on their faces; Erma next to her right eye and Dorothy above the left side of her lips. The 16-year-old cousins were pretty, confident in their looks and ability to attract boys. Before leaving home, they both practiced tossing their dark hair in front of the mirror, swinging their hips and dropping their lace hankies suggestively waiting for a handsome guy to pick them up. They had the flirting down pat.

"Hey Timmmmmyyyyyy. Timmmmyyyyyy." Erma rolled his name off her tongue. "Come sit over here with us!" She used her sing song flirty voice.

"Meetin' somebody. See you gals later." He ran to the next car wishing Frankie was with him. Timmy handed him the Greek dames and he took the Italian chicks. It just wasn't the same without his buddy. Besides, he was tired from last night's escapades. Candy was still pining over Angelo so he didn't score there but he landed a couple of other strippers who were always interested in him. They wore him out and he needed rest to be fresh when they hit the ship. He scooted into an empty seat near a window and closed his eyes. He was in lala land in a flash dreaming about last night's conquests.

The girls knew Timmy's reputation with the women but were still disappointed when he refused their company. They were both attractive and weren't use to being ignored. "Forget about him Erma. He thinks he's cool because he's good-looking. We'll meet handsome guys on our trip." Erma grabbed Dorothy's hand, "Let's walk back to see who is traveling with him. Probably his mother, the witch."

"I refuse to talk to Mrs. Georgia. She is rude and insulting," Dorothy wined but she still allowed herself to be led. "Oh my, there's the windbag. All she does is brag about Annie and Timmy."

"Hi Mrs. Georgia." They faked sweetness speaking in unison.

"Where you go dress like this?" She gave them the look of disdain.

"We're going Greece on the Olympia."

"No mother and father?"

"We're old enough to travel alone. They couldn't come along but our uncle will meet us at the train stop in New York." Without giving her a chance to ask more questions, Dorothy inquired about Annie.

"She engage to handsome Chian. Timmy also engage to woman from Kambos," she saw no harm in bending the truth a little. After all, she was positive it would happen once they got to Chios and he met Angela. "Put on serious clothes and maybe you find man, too. No nice you travel without escort." She crossed her arms around her chest disapprovingly.

"Congratulations on both engagements. You must be relieved about Timmy." Erma snipped.

"What you say?" Mrs. Georgia contained her fury at the veiled insult against her son. She opened her mouth to slam them but wasn't fast enough.

"We'll see you on the ship," Dorothy pulled Erma from the line of fire and ran up front to their seats.

"She's hateful...thinks she's the cat's meow. She can't even speak English. Somebody should put her in her place!"

"Dorothy honey, lower your voice and calm down." Erma started running her gloved hands over Dorothy's dress to distract her. "You know how Taffeta wrinkles. Now give me a wide curtsy and sit. There, there. You look great." Then she straightened her own dress, pulled the bottom skirt across the seat trying to imitate a princess before she caught a glimpse of Timmy coming down the aisle.

"Hi, Timmy. Congratulations!" Erma waved at him.

"For what? You mean Annie's engagement?"

"Oh, no. We'll congratulate her when we see her. Your mom told us about your girl in Kambos."

"Which one?" He went along with it figuring it would throw them off.

"Don't you know who you're engaged to?" Erma questioned suspiciously.

"Uh huh, that one. You'll get invitations to the wedding." He realized his mother was weaving tales again. No harm done. It wasn't going to happen anyway. He kept moving till he reached his mother.

"Where you be Stamati? You with girls on train. Stay here or I pull hair from head."

"So I'm engaged, am I? Who is it? It would be nice to know her name."

"No matter. Nobody want you. Gamble…drink… run with woman…Chios people no respect you. I be embarrass if you no find woman."

"Oh for Christ's sake, stop exaggerating. I go out once a week with Frankie to have some fun after working like a dog in the mill. I don't drink or gamble except once in a while." He was almost believable. "I didn't come on this trip to find a wife. You begged me to come so I could help you travel. Now you have me engaged and married off. It ain't gonna happen." Timmy was frustrated.

"Close mouth Stamati." She pinched the inner part of his arm and twisted it knowing exactly how to cause the maximum amount of pain. I you mother. No talk me like this." She was still pulling on his flesh. "I know you say story."

"All right, okay. Let go now before somebody sees us." He was grimacing.

"I come from ol' country with no shoes and starving."

"Let me finish. Pops married you and gave you a life…food…a trunk full of money…a house. And, I don't appreciate how good I have it."

"You spoil, Stamati. Need woman to have kids, take care of you. Family make you real man like you pops."

"I'll keep my eyes open for a woman who has your qualities. If I find her, I will certainly consider it," he lied.

"*Now, I happy. I have list from girls in village want to see you and come to America. I think you like one who pretty and good woman. She clean, cook, nice manner. We see her last.*"

"I thought you were going over there to visit your family. It is clear your intentions were to find me a mate. Why didn't I realize that from the start? You certainly fooled me again. It's all right. I'll check out the babes."

"Stamati, Chios no America. Girls go out with man when they engage. Everybody come with you, mother, father, family. Want go out you bring ring to girl in front family. I got ring for you give who you want."

"How many can I get engaged too…five, ten…I'll take them all out."

"You crazy, Stamati. All family comin. No kiss, no hold hand, no nothing."

"You're shittin' me."

"I put pepper in mouth. Watch how you talkin'. You only engage one time…no more. They shoot if insult woman and family. Give ring, you marry."

"No give ring, no marry. Right?" *How the hell will I get out of this, he was wondering. Maybe I can jump ship in Naples and go back to the states. Pops gave me plenty of cash. It won't be a problem. I'll go along with her and pretend I want a wife. I can play on board for nine or ten days till we hit Italy then I'll leave her a note. Yep…that's how it's done.*

Mrs. Georgia felt she was making progress and didn't want to rock the boat. "Okay Stamati. You no have to do nothing. We visit family. Eat fresh fish. Swim in ocean. Have nice time. No want engage... no do it."

Her attitude surprised him. Maybe he would tour the island after all. If his mother wasn't pushing marriage, he could enjoy the family and the stunning scenery. He heard of a couple of mountain villages the people did not live in the modern age. They still traveled by donkey, had no electricity and did all their work by candlelight. The women covered their heads in beaded scarves and wore long dresses. The men had huge mustaches that curled up and wore yards of pantaloons. The streets were narrow and homes were embedded in stone walls. Everyone lived in close proximity. The men, of course, had outlets. There was one cafe in each village where the men smoked, tossed the stones on their worry beads and played a slow game of backgammon.

Timmy recollected the night that cute Dina left a ladder out for him. When Frankie got wind of it and decided he was more suited for her. Down he went into then bushes when she discovered she had been tricked. Timmy managed to drag him away before her old man came out of the house. He plucked branches out of Frankie's butt that night. Timmy laughed out loud.

"Stamati," his mother poked him.

"Sorry. I was thinking about Pops trying to choke Angelo."

"No funny. Pops maybe kill."

Frankie and me should write a book of our esca-
pades, Timmy was thinking. We got stories that rock.
It will be a best seller.

"I hope we have good cabins. I'd hate to be stuck
in the bowels of the ship."

"Stamati, we no spend for rooms. We need money
for poor people in old country. We together one
room."

His mind was racing. Maybe he could find a chick
with a nicer cabin to bed up with.

CHAPTER 9

Mrs. Georgia and Timmy were in line with hundreds of people by the ship when a couple of gentlemen came and retrieved them. "Mr. Dimitri requested you come with us to first class. Your luggage is already there." They didn't utter a word as they were led away. Mrs. Georgia's heart was thundering when they took her to the suite.

Timmy was ecstatic when he saw the size of his room. Before they had a chance to relax, someone led them out explaining that Angelina needed them. They were excited knowing their friends would be on board.

When they exited the elevator, Mrs. Georgia raced to the Lincoln. Timmy was laughing and slapping his thighs when he saw Frankie. Everything will be okay now that his best bud there.

CHAPTER 10

ALL ABOARD

Spaces were reserved near a private entrance next to the giant ship that was swaying against the pier. Myron pulled the Lincoln up to the Olympia and was followed by a row of cars driving at a safe distance. He knew the drill. He got out quickly, opened the doors to one vehicle at a time and frisked the occupants. Each emissary waited his turn to bring paperwork to Dimitri, whispered a few phrases then returned to his car and drove off.

One presented him with a passenger list and explained the Paidousis family from Steubenville would be on board. "Make sure they are immediately taken to our first class quarters. Familiar faces will be a blessing for Angelina. Timmy can share a suite with Frankie and Mrs. Georgia will share with the girls. This is a perfect. They will be with their friends and sail in luxury." He returned to the Lincoln and told everyone there was a surprise in store.

Myron drove onto the ship and waited for the gates to come down. He whistled for the private elevator and opened the car doors. Angelina was agitated and buried her face in her hands. No amount of coaxing could get her out of the car. She would not budge even for Frankie. Strange noises escaped her throat as if she were trying to make a point.

Frankie remembered when Angelina was four or five years old she used some language. She seemed almost normal at that age. Doctors indicated she could be one of the few children who were late bloomers and that her verbal skills may improve with time. Instead, she worsened and retreated into a shell. Her father was increasingly angry and blamed his wife for Angelina's condition. At one point the doctors claimed she was severely retarded and left no hope for recovery.

"Don't pressure her. She'll be okay in a while." Dimitri promised.

He took Myron aside. "I requested priority boarding for the Paidousis family. They should be in the suites by now. Find them and bring them here. He got back in the car and made small talk with Sandy and Frankie.

"Suddenly someone was knocking on the windows. "Angeloudi come with yiayia. I have kourambiedes cookies. She opened the car door and embraced Angelina who perked up the minute she saw her. She exited the car like a lamb and went to the elevator with everyone.

Hey buddy, I thought you were goin' to England."
Timmy had a wide smile on his face when he saw
Frankie.

"We're bringing England to us." Dimitri answered.
"We think Angelina will feel more at home in the
village and arranged for the doctor to come to
Kardamyla."

For the first time in his lifelong friendship with
Frankie, Timmy felt he was being duped. Why was
Dimitri answering a question not meant for him?
There was something wrong and he expected it was
serious. The fact that Frankie did not take him into
his confidence made him suspicious.

Frankie didn't say much but was obviously glad
to see Timmy. It would make this long voyage more
bearable if he could focus on something else besides
his sister's pregnancy and Chester's death.

Frankie and Timmy shared all their secrets. This
was the first time since they were kids that Timmy
didn't know what was happening. It's not that Frankie
didn't trust him. He was afraid to open the gates to
his hell. How would his friend feel if he knew about
the murder? He would have to explain the excruci-
atingly painful circumstances and didn't know if he
could find the strength to tell him.

They reached first class where an elite group
waited to escort them to their suites. "Make sure
whatever they desire is provided." Dimitri said and
went directly to his quarters which was a cut above
luxurious.

The captain was there to greet him. "It is a pleasure to have you on board, sir. Your suite is ready for you. I understand that you have purchased controlling interests in this vessel."

Dimitri crocked his eyebrow and spoke quietly. "I bought the whole damn thing, Captain Theodore."

He walked ahead to the suite overlooking a private pool that was filled with ocean water. He couldn't wait to take a swim and began disrobing immediately. There was barely a splash when he dove in and glided across. The water caressed his long naked body reminding him of Katina's lovemaking. He turned onto his back and chuckled at his erection. *I must remember to tell Katina, he thought. "She will scold me but I know she'll enjoy hearing it."* He didn't call for a woman. Every bit of his energy would be saved for her.

CHAPTER 11

T he three girls entered their quarters. Mrs. Georgia was not about to reveal that she wasn't accustomed to this elegance. She went on her merry way to her room taking Angelina with her. "Let's go my angeloudi." Angelina saw the box of cookies and began making noises. "They for you but no eat all. Save for later." Angelina smacked her lips after each cookie Mrs. Georgia fed her. "Four cookies ok. I no want you sick. Frankie be mad." There was a sad expression on Angelina's face and Mrs. Georgia could not resist giving her one more.

For some reason she felt Angelina's expression was purposeful. But how was that possible? She didn't remember her doing this before. Perhaps she hadn't noticed that the girl understood more than anyone imagined.

Angelina stood in front of the mirror and caressed her tummy. She had a faraway expression on her face as if deep in thought. "Tummy pain?" Mrs. Georgia asked. Angelina turned towards her and shook her head no. "My goodness...you understand." She threw her arms around Angelina and pulled her close. Just then she realized the child had a swollen belly. "Oh Panagia, a baby," she cried out. *I protect and keep secret. For sure Sandy and Frankie know… Mr. Dimitri too. That's why Sandy comin' to Greece. I no tell nobody.*

"Rest my angeloudi here with yiayia. Long trip make tired." She helped her change, turned down the fancy cotton sheets and covered her. Then she kissed her forehead tenderly. Angelina smiled, closed her eyes and was sleeping soundly in a few seconds.

Mrs. Georgia wept quietly. Her heart broke for the child she always referred to as an angel. She wanted to take away the pain the child would experience.

Georgia was about Angelina's age when she came to America with her brother Stamati and sister Anthipie. Stamati didn't last long. TB claimed his life. She and her sister were married off to strangers who had come from Chios before them and were established.

A gnawing fear gripped her when her parents went back to Greece. "You will never go hungry again," her heartbroken mother told her. At fifteen she bore Annie by the time she was nineteen Mike and Timmy came along. Her husband George gave her every cent he made working at Weirton Steel. Even though life was difficult raising three children at such a young age, she still managed to do better than most. She even sent money and packages back home to help the poor. For the first time in her life, food was plentiful.

Mrs. Georgia wondered how Sandy was getting along. She toyed with knocking on the door but decided to wait till Angelina woke up. The dressing table was calling. She sat on the satin covered stool gazing at herself in the mirror. As she adjusted her makeup and hair she realized her looks were still inviting. Perhaps a handsome stranger would ask her to tango, preferably an Italian. This was her secret yearning. She had never danced but was absolutely sure given the right partner she could sway to the rhythm. She smiled and batted her eyes playfully.

Sandy Horwitz was an only child that came from a well to do family. Her parents were both corporate lawyers whose cases exploded in the newspapers. They were brutal in court, never lost a case and made obscene amounts of money. Although they wanted her to follow in their footsteps, Sandy was more inclined towards the medical field. They explained, if she chose that path it would be at her own expense. "Live at home but pay your way through school," they told her. "If you change your mind, we'll take you into the business." She worked and studied manically graduating with honors. Her parents were proud and gave her a huge loft apartment with carte-blanche to furnish it in her style.

Although Sandy didn't impress easily, she discovered these quarters were beyond stunning. The suite had three bedrooms, each with a lounging area. The common dining room was fit for royalty. A large crystal chandelier illuminated the glass table that sat on marble columns. The suites were dressed in shades of blue and gold; the bedrooms enclosed with mirrors and subtle lighting.

She locked the doors, disrobed down to her undies and threw herself face down on the King size bed thinking what she could do with Frankie in this room. She got on her knees lifting her bottom then twisted her head back to look at her reflection in the mirror. She spread open her knees and pulled apart her buttocks with her hands. The red panties she wore cut into her. She was on fire and wanted to make love. Her hand moved between her legs and she rubbed herself there.

There was a knock at her door. "Frankie?" She ran and opened it. There were three designers ready to roll in clothing racks...a man and two women who were oblivious to her nakedness. "Wait outside for a few minutes. I'll let you know when I'm ready for you."

She took off her panties and returned to the bed falling on her back this time. Her knees went up to her chest and her fingers slipped into her vagina pushing deep inside. She rubbed her swollen clitoris with the wetness while observing herself in the mirror. Her other hand pinched and pulled the nipples on each breast. She had trimmed the hair below leaving only slight tufts of burgundy framing the paleness of her thighs. Nothing was hidden behind long hair that she once had between her legs. She was completely exposed and got a strange enjoyment looking there. This is what Frankie would be seeing soon she hoped. Her body trembled as she manipulated herself into a frenzy. She was kicking up her heels and gasping reaching a strong, long-lasting orgasm.

When she was finally spent, she stayed in her position too weak to move wishing Frankie had witnesses the sexy scene. For sure she would drive him crazy by making him watch her next time. She slowly lifted herself from the bed, pulled her panties over her slender legs and small hips admiring the perfection. Her breasts were ample and high, her nipples extraordinarily large resembling the top of a nursing bottle.

Her heart was still racing when she opened the door. The three moved in quickly bringing an array of outfits.

"Bonjour." The women were haughty in an attractive sort of way. Every strand of their golden hair was folded into French twists. They were probably in their forties and wore tailored designer dresses in muted peaches and soft sunshine. Both had dark eyebrows penciled high over their eyes, red lips and rouge applied to last.

The gentleman was more pretty than handsome. He was also dressed artfully. His tan suit hung over a shirt of the same color that matched his hair and sun glazed face. He was thin and had a feminine sweetness about him.

He extended his hand, "Anre. This is Gina and Fifi." The women had French accents and were discussing accessories that would match the dresses.

Anre turned her around and sized up her behind thinking her hips were rather boyish. He pulled clothing off the racks that he would complement her figure. "Where are the other ladies?"

"I'll bring them in once I'm finished. These are great pieces. Shall I try them on for size?"

"They will fit perfectly." Anre was very friendly. "It is your choice but trust us you will be the finest dressed woman on board and probably the loveliest." He added a grey sequined gown that matched her eyes. "This one will be for the ball the last evening. Here is everything for morning, noon and night as well as clothing for the island per Mr. Dimitri's request. Is anything amiss?"

"Certainly not. Thank you." Sandy was thinking how cute he was and that he could pass for a girl. She kissed his cheek and he turned a full shade of pink obviously enjoying the attention.

Gina and Fifi were matching jewelry and shoes to each outfit. "These must also fit your coloring. Your hair and figure are exceptional. We adore dressing you."

"Now shall we call in the others?" Anre touched his face with his index finger and tilted his head.

Sandy wrapped herself in a robe that popped in lilac and yellow flowers and knocked on the door to the next room.

Mrs. Georgia opened the door slightly and put her finger to her lips. "Shhhh, Angelina sleep." She saw the clothing and was immediately fascinated.

"I'll stay with her and you come in here to get fitted. Mr. Dimitri ordered new wardrobes for all of us." They switched places.

Anre wasn't aware of her size. Until a short while ago, he had only gotten orders for Dr. Sandy and Angelina but he would accommodate her the best way possible. "My, oh my. You are tiny and everyone knows expensive things come in small packages."

Mrs. Georgia was pleased with the comments but kept a serious expression.

"We will fit each piece to your proportions starting with evening wear." the girls focused on her. They measured, cut and tucked. "All these will be ready for you in a couple of hours."

Mrs. Georgia didn't know how to react. She was overjoyed and felt like a princess. "This for Angelina?" she went through a rack of pretty youthful dresses.

"They are extremely versatile, comfortable for all occasions. Angelina will feel happy wearing these." Anre said.

"Hey Mom." The door had been left unlocked. Timmy and Frankie walked in.

"We had the same treatment in our suite. Don't we look great?" Timmy was posing with his hand tucked into his suit collar.

"Good but no brains," Mrs. Georgia said with hands on her hips.

"Where's Angelina?" Frankie looked around.

Sandy poked her head from the other room. "She is still resting. Let's not wake her." Her breasts were pushing out of the robe.

Frankie was immediately turned on. "We're hungry. Dimitri invited us to Captain Theodore's table but if Angelina is asleep we'll wait."

The subtle glances between Frankie and Sandy did not escape Mrs. Georgia. Something is going on, she surmised, but it wasn't any of her business.

"I stay with angeloudi. You go."

"No way are we leaving you here. Angelina should be awake soon. We'll have dinner together tonight and then hit the lounges. If she is restless, we'll decide who will bring her back here." Frankie spoke with authority. "Who knows how she will react to the music. She was attentive when Annie sang to her and I managed to give her a taste of Dino many times. Maybe she will enjoy it."

CHAPTER 12

The evening was perfect. Angelina surprised everyone by picking out a dress with spaghetti straps in powder blue and getting ready with little help. She was pretty as a picture. They went to the private dinner at the Captain's table in attire fit for models.

Captain Theodore stood up waiting for everyone to be seated. He wasn't a very tall man and he wore shoes with heels for height. His hands were locked behind his back, chest pushed up and out. He carried himself proudly extremely aware of his position. His hair was full with a salt and pepper glaze at the temples but his mustache was dark as were his eyebrows that lay straight above his soulful wide set brown eyes. When he saw Mrs. Georgia he was struck by her petite figure and discovered an instant attraction which hadn't happened to him in a long time. He requested she sit at his right and she accommodated bringing Angelina close to her. Frankie sat next to Angelina, Sandy and Timmy on his right. The only one missing from the group was Marvin.

There were two couples from wealthy Chian families who were ship owners occupying seats directly across from them. It was an interesting combination. Mr. Dimitri headed the other end of the table and was deep in conversation regarding freighter business.

The table settings, illuminated by candlelight, were exquisite. Lobsters, shrimp and fish were plentiful. Every food imaginable was served with wines that complimented each course. Fortunately for Mrs. Georgia, the captain insisted on helping her with the lobster. Frankie was very attentive to Angelina who was wide eyed and open mouthed. Flaming cherries jubilee were a spectacular end to the dinner.

Timmy was getting restless and wanted to party. He whispered to Sandy who was itching to head towards the lower decks for music and dancing. "Frankie, shall we?" They extracted themselves slowly saying they were interested in seeing the rest of the ship. The Captain offered to be their escort if there were no objections from Dimitri.

"Go and enjoy. See you later." Dimitri turned his focus to his eager guests. They were waiting for him to give the okay to move cargo from South America. The women hung on his every word. Each locked eyes with him when the opportunity presented itself. They were an attractive product of wealthy families and conducted themselves with an air of sophistication. Their husbands on the other hand were rough around the edges. They over indulged in food, had unsightly pouches and ruddy complexions marred by alcohol consumption. Given Dimitri's reputation, both feared he would bed their wives and were unsure what they would do. No way could they confront him. They expected it could be the end of their shipping careers.

Dimitri sensed their discomfort and decided to avoid any female distractions on this trip. Although he knew every inch of Argi and Yiota's plump, tan anatomies and they savored a threesome with him when he was available, he wanted to save his energy for Katina. Besides, he would be reuniting with her the moment he arrived in Kardamyla.

"Mr. Thanasi…Mr. Ari, take your beautiful wives dancing. Let's not bore them with talk of business. You have my blessing to move the products." He stood up. "I will go to the lounges to look for my friends and hope to see you there enjoying the music." He could feel the women seething and thought that under different circumstances their company would be welcome. He rather favored taming angry females with his brand of lovemaking. He wanted to see them squirm as his hand bounced off their ample derrieres.

Dimitri stood up and waited for them to pass. The two men walked ahead of their wives giving them the freedom to grope Dimitri. *No wonder their women fooled around, he thought. They are pigs.* He graciously opened the door for the girls and they both kissed him on the cheek. "Thank you for an interesting time. You are always a gentleman," the girls told him. He put them on the elevator then decided to stroll the deck and smell the ocean breezes before heading for the lounges.

The moon was a golden lantern that drifted alongside the ship. Couples, dressed in their finest evening-wear, were walking slowly arm in arm, leaning on the railings, embracing and kissing. He recognized a few from Ohio and West Virginia. His name was mentioned and he nodded. He was lonely. Funny how power and money did not take away the emptiness in his heart. He wondered what would have happened if Katina wasn't forced to marry the wretched fisherman after his mother died. Their lives would have been different. She would have traveled the world with him. Now he must be satisfied with only a few stolen hours with her when he went to the village.

He heard the music drifting from the lounge and gazed into the portal. Marvin was sitting at the bar watching Anre who was dancing with woman after woman. The others were huddled around Angelina protectively and Captain Theodore had zeroed in on Mrs. Georgia pulling her to the dance floor for a Tango. Dimitri smiled knowing this was only a dance and would go nowhere. Rather than retiring to his empty room, he decided to join them.

"May I?" He pulled up a chair. The whole place was buzzing when they realized Dimitri had arrived. He ignored them deciding to have a good time without interference. Besides, knowing he had made life happier for his friends made him lighthearted.

"My goodness, Mrs. Georgia. You are a good dancer. May I be your next partner?"

"Oh, yes Mr. Dimitri. This first for me. Now you be two!"

They looked kind of silly together. The top of her head reached the middle of his chest but she certainly held her own as he dipped and lifted her. She was ecstatic and was laughing out loud when he took her back to the table. "I okay Stamati?"

"Good thing pops ain't here. He'd punch them guys in the nose."

The jitterbug was calling and Sandy reached for Frankie. "Let's go baby." They had never danced before and she wondered if he would be a swinger.

He was slow to rise took his time walking to the middle of the floor. She shimmied on behind him. Her burgundy tresses were full and flying as she shook her head back and forth. He turned slowly to face her and ran his fingers into the sides of his hair. Without warning, he reached for her waist and tossed her into the air. She screamed on her way down as he pushed her body between his legs then fell forward on top of her. "Later tonight," he mouthed in her ear and jumped up opening his legs over her. Everyone moved to the side allowing them room for their showmanship.

Frankie lifted and bounced her off of each hip, wrapped her legs around his waist and pushed her face backwards to the floor. Her green lace dress slipped back revealing scanty panties of matching color. The crowd clapped and howled as Frankie reached for her hands to pull her up.

He suddenly realized Angelina had approached him. "Hey lady bug." She threw her arms around his neck and squeezed. Timmy moved into position while Frankie lowered Sandy to the floor and took his sister back to the table. Timmy made a split over her body turned her over to face the floor then grabbed her ankles and stood up dragging her around. He lifted her by the hips, threw her over his shoulder and held onto her legs tightly. She was limp as a rag doll when he brought her back to their table amid bravos, screams and stomping.

Dimitri noticed that Sandy was angry and jumped in to alleviate any problem. "You three were superb. Everyone is raving about the performance. Any time you need a job, the Olympia will hire you."

Sandy flashed him a smile. "This is good to know. The three of us sailing, having fun and getting paid for it." She still wanted to slap the hell out of Frankie for exposing her but would wait for an appropriate moment. Preferably when they were in the throes of passion.

"I tired angeloudi. Come we go bed." Mrs. Georgia took Angelina by the hand and led her out.

Captain Theodore was disappointed. He was hoping for more time with her. "Good night. The Captain's table will have a wonderful brunch tomorrow. Please join me," he called out to Mrs. Georgia. As an afterthought, he invited the rest of the group, too.

The midnight romance music began with "I'm in The Mood for Love." The handsome piano player's voice was Nat King Cole velvet. He was a rich deep chocolate color with eyes bright as stars and a smile that melted butter. Slender, tall with muscular arms and shoulders, he was a winner with the ladies.

Simeon browsed the room for Anre as he crooned his favorite melody. He had vanished. Marvin was the culprit, he deduced. Anre would never admit it, but this happened the last time Mr. Dimitri's body guard was on board. He was hurt and the vulnerability affected his singing making him even more enthralling to his audience. Tears were trembling in his eyes. He would not forgive Anre this time.

Timmy pulled a pretty blond to the dance floor, held her arms behind her back and pressed his cheek to hers. Then he realized she was much too young for anything further but he enjoyed whispering sweet nothings in her ear. She was thrilled with the attention.

Frankie moved to the deck with Sandy. They were slow dancing. "How long do I have to wait, Frankie?"

"Till I say when," he ran his fingers down her neck to her cleavage.

Just then Anre ran towards them. Sandy saw the frightened look on his face and noticed he was crying. She reached out and stopped him. "What's wrong?"

"A mistake in judgment that I have to rectify." He hugged Sandy and took off to Simeon's room. He let himself in, quickly changed into a pair of satin pajamas and slid under the covers. He was still crying at the thought of Marvin's seduction scene. When Anre discovered that handcuffs and whips were involved, he freaked out and ran out when Marvin's back was turned.

Anre had been with the gentle Simeon for years. He couldn't understand what possessed him to jeopardize his wonderful relationship over that demonic Marvin. He prayed Simeon did not suspect anything. He would fake illness and tell him he came straight to bed.

It was only the first evening on board and the ship was a hotbed of interludes and romance. Even Erma and Dorothy had paired up with a couple of young men. They were strolling the deck with their uncle in hot pursuit waiting to jump in if there was any hanky-panky. He was there to protect their virtue and realized there would be plenty of sleepless nights until they arrived in Greece and he found them suitable husbands.

The storm happened fast, without warning. The ship began swaying and rocking. The ocean was flaying angrily and frothy waves washed across the deck. Chairs slid around banging on railings while sailor boys scrambled to contain them. There were sounds of broken glass as drinks flew off the tables. People were frightened and were desperately trying to get to their rooms. Some were regurgitating over the railings and stairwells while trying to keep from falling.

"This is Captain Theodore," his soothing voice sounded over the speakers. "Please don't be alarmed. It seems Poseidon, God of the sea, is having an angry fit. He will be over it soon. It usually doesn't last more than a few hours." He tried to alleviate every-one's anxiety by making light of the problem. "We have soda in your rooms. It will help if you have nausea. Please ring if you need assistance. There are hands on board to accompany you to your quarters if necessary."

Since his group had dispersed, Dimitri went to the bar for an ouzo when the storm hit. The bad weather did not bother him in the least. He was used to being on ships from a young age and had survived many such assaults. It was rather exciting to see the huge waves attacking the ship, he thought. He enjoyed the captain's explanation and would congratulate him at the first opportunity,

Sandy and Frankie went to check on Angelina. Fortunately for them, their rooms were nearby. They were soaked by the time they arrived. Mrs. Georgia was sitting in a chair next to the bed.

"How's my ladybug?" Angelina opened her eyes and looked at Frankie sweetly then went back to sleep. It seemed she was the only one not affected by the storm.

"Here. Take Dramamine for you and Timmy." Sandy also gave one to Mrs. Georgia before taking it herself. "It alleviates the nausea and makes you drowsy."

"Later, Sandy." He kissed Angelina and went across the hall to his room. Timmy's door was open and he was sleeping.

Frankie wanted to talk but took the pill and laid across his bed instead. Nightmares plagued him whenever he closed his eyes. He relived those last moments when he slashed Chester's throat and pushed him over the bridge. "Oh God no…no….. no…," he shouted.

"Hey buddy." Timmy turned Frankie on his back and was wiping the perspiration from his face. "Frankie…you okay? Wake up!"

"God forgive me!" Frankie was shouting.

"Buddy, buddy wake up." He shook him. "You're havin' a bad dream." He thought he heard Chester's name and bells went off in his head. Is it possible that Frankie had something to do with the murder? Oh Lord. Frankie was not a killer. Maybe he witnessed what happened. If that was the case, he would have blown the whistle.

"What's wrong, Frankie? What the hell's goin' on?"

Frankie was shaking when he opened his eyes. "Nothin's goin' on. Bad dream is all." He tried to get up but Timmy pushed him back.

"Talk to me, man. I'm cool."

Frankie realized the ship had stopped rocking. "Hey, no more rock and roll. You were good on the dance floor Timmy but not as fine as me."

"If you're not ready to cough it up, it is okay by me. I ain't goin' nowhere. You know I'm your best bud. Dig?"

"Dig. Let's get some shut eye." He pushed Timmy out of his room and locked the door behind him.

Sleep eluded him. Even though he had taken the pill, his eyes were wide open now. He had discomfort in the pit of his stomach that pushed him to despair. The blame was strictly his. If he wasn't into his damned personal pleasures he could have protected Angelina. Over and over again he told himself he had to be strong for her. It was too late to change the past. Angelina was lucky to be surrounded by people who loved her. The Paidousis family was an unexpected bonus on this trip. Maybe he would take Timmy into his confidence before the trip ended. He was in agony and didn't know how broach the subject.

He went out and sat in a deck chair that was soaked. He wiped some of the ocean water with his hand and splashed his face trying to stay alert. *How will I survive this trip without sleep?* he thought. *Maybe there's a pill I can take to stop the dreaming. Sandy would know but what the hell would I say to her?*

Frankie was exhausted and would give anything for a good night's rest. He splashed more sea water on his face and neck. "God help me!" he cried out.

I went to your room and the door was wide open. Why are you sitting on a wet chair? You're gonna get sick." Sandy was looking down at him. Her red satin robe shimmered in the soft moonlight. Her breasts swayed as she moved her hips back and forth seductively. "You need something to keep you from catching a chill."

"Already sick. Need somethin' to sleep."

"Before or after we take it to the next level." She lifted her robe, sat on him and licked her lips. "No underpants, Frankie…go ahead and do your thing."

The pressure of his fingers in her vagina and his thumb massaging her clitoris drove her insane. "My breasts, Frankie, my breasts." Her head fell backwards and she began moaning. "Deeper."

He bit her breasts hard and heard her cry out. "What the hell are you doing?"

But she didn't stop jumping up and down with her bare feet on the deck till she climaxed.

"Hey. Didn't you hear me, Sandy? I want somethin' to put me out for the night. We can do this any time."

"Is that why you were calling out to God, Frankie? Asking for his help were you?" She gasped. "I have a sneaky suspicion you have a dark secret." Her breathing was erratic consumed by the end of her orgasm. I went to your room and the door was wide open. Why are you sitting on a wet chair? You're gonna get sick." Sandy was looking down at him. Her red satin robe shimmered in the soft moonlight. Her breasts swayed as she moved her hips back and forth seductively. "You need something to keep you from catching a chill."

He got up and pushed her off his lap. "Are you gonna give me a pill or what?"

"Stay here while I get my bag." She tied her robe tightly around her waist. "Hope you aren't afraid of an injection. It will knock you out for the night."

"Get it. Make it a double dose. I'll be in my room."

He left the door open, stripped down to his white underwear and paced the floor.

Sandy came in carrying her medical case. "At least let me take your blood pressure."

"Do it, damn it."

She pulled down his shorts and caressed his behind. "Lie down on your side."

He wanted to slap her. "Tomorrow, baby. We'll mess around tomorrow." He watched her insert the needle in a vile and draw out the liquid.

"This is strong." She pinched him high on his hip and pushed the needle in quickly.

There was a slight burning sensation and he hoped it wouldn't be long before he was out. "Will it happen right away?"

"In a couple of minutes. I'll stay with you till it kicks in."

"No. See you in the morning." By the time he uttered his last words he was asleep.

Sandy left his shorts down but decided to cover him. She sat on his bed for a while wishing the evening had turned out differently. She kissed him and slipped her tongue into his mouth. Even in sleep he turned her on. She touched him between his legs and was surprised to find movement. He was the sexiest man she had laid eyes on but she knew it could never be permanent for the two of them…much too young…not established…not Jewish. *I have to make the best of the time we have left and store it in my memory bank, she thought.* She retired to her room in a sad state.

CHAPTER 13

Everyone stayed close to Angelina who was content being the center of their world. She kept her hands on her tummy most of the time as if to protect the baby. Within the first few days, they all suspected she was with child but did not discuss it. They were supportive and loving. Mrs. Georgia never left her side and the others made it a point to lead personal lives only when she was sleeping.

Frankie's sex life blossomed on the ship. He had sizzling encounters with Sandy at bedtime. After every sex-capade, he insisted Sandy inject him with a drug to knock him out. She worried that he would become addicted and tried without success to discover the secret that tortured him. She didn't want to believe the night he went to Steubenville he bumped off the guy who possibly raped Angelina. She read about the murder in the papers. The man's throat was slit ear to ear. It happened the same night Frankie left Pittsburgh General. He was cold as ice when he took off. Her mind was confused. "Where did you go that night?"

"Leave it alone, Sandy. Don't ask questions that have no answers. Hit me with the needle and get back to your room."

"This is the last time Frankie. I sympathize but there has to be another way for you to sleep. Our sex life is phenomenal. The only thing we haven't done is hang from the chandelier. All that exercise should suffice in making you tired enough to sleep."

"Stop talking baby…tomorrow night we'll play on the railing over the side of the ship. Now give it to me…I'll do it."

"No more Frankie. This is the last time. Turn on your side."

All Sandy wanted was to spend the night in his arms but it never happened. She was the most beautiful woman on the ship and was sought after by many men who would do anything have her. No-one measured up to his perfection. She ignored them to bask in his shadow. Although she wanted more, the realization that he was suffering mentally from something he couldn't reveal gave her license to do whatever was necessary to help him.

Timmy knocked on the door. "You ready?"

She met him every night on the deck for a stroll where he tried to comfort her.

Timmy put his arm around Sandy's shoulders. "He'll be okay once we get to the island in a few days. I'll leave you contact info in case I'm needed. We'll be staying on the other side in Kambos."

"If you knew something would you tell me? Perhaps then I could figure out how to relieve his suffering."

"Wish I did." Timmy had already figured it out but would never jeopardize Frankie's life by telling anyone. "Patience, Sandy. He is going through a trauma that only time will heal. The island is the best place for him to get peace." He wanted to give Sandy a ray of hope.

"Gibraltar was stunning. We'll be cruising into Lisbon next. I think we should take Angelina for a stroll on the cobblestone streets. We can pick up a few souvenirs quickly and get back to the ship before the crowds return. Hope Frankie will be awake in time."

"I'll get him up. Let's crash. See you early." Timmy walked to her room and gave her a warm embrace. "Night Beautiful."

Timmy's love life had tanked on this trip. He was obsessed with Frankie's problems and would have to come up with a cover story for him in case he was caught. Nothing else mattered.

CHAPTER 14

"Captain Theodore. Please make sure my helicopter is ready to go in the morning after the ship leaves Naples. My guests will continue on to Greece with Marvin keeping an eye on them. I've ordered a yacht to take them to Chios. They will have tour guides if they wish to explore Athens for a couple of days. Book a floor at Grand Bretangna Hotel for them in case they decide to see the Acropolis, the old city and perhaps The Temple of Poseidon at Sounion."

"Certainly, I will take excellent care of them Mr. Dimitri."

"No doubt, Captain. Since the Olympia will dock for a thorough inspection, I've invited Simeon and Anre to come to Kardamyla. They will travel with the other guests. Please see to it that the staff has full salary during the layoff."

"Will Mrs. Georgia and Timmy be returning on the Olympia?"

"I believe they are leaving in a couple of weeks on the Queen Frederica. Perhaps you should take that voyage since you will be free for a while." He smiled. "I've booked luxury class for them."

"I wouldn't mind but do you think it would make a difference to Mrs. Georgia?" He hoped for a positive response.

"I doubt it but there's no harm in trying."

"I will have a private business lunch with Mr. Thanasi, Mr. Ari and their wives. I don't want them to feel I've abandoned them. My last dinner aboard will be with my friends in my quarters by the pool. Please see to it that it is special. They will be apprised of my plans and I can explain that I'm leaving early to prepare for their arrival in Kardamyla."

The truth was, he couldn't wait to be with Katina. There was constant pain in his heart thinking of the way their lives were torn apart. *He remembered the first time they kissed. He took her to his secret cave in the village where he hid to smoke. She was only thirteen. Even at that young age Katina knew she was his forever. He touched her breasts and kissed her. "Don't be frightened," he said gently. "When I get my diploma, I will marry you."*

"How can I ever be frightened of you," she said and looked straight into his eyes. "I love you."

As usual, all eyes were on him as he headed for his room. Dimitri was an elegant man of 6'2" who naturally drew attention. His exceptional looks and masculinity attracted the women. He didn't flaunt it but had a hard time keeping the ladies away. Oftentimes, he felt obliged to give them a roll in the sack since they threw themselves at him shamelessly.

He was an expert lover who knew how to provide ultimate pleasures for a woman.

Argi and Yiota were leaning on his door wrapped in towels. "Hello Dimitri. We wanted to see you before lunchtime." Yiota made the first move touching him between his legs. "We miss being with you," Argi spoke breathlessly.

"Come in girls." He pulled their towels off knowing they would be naked. "Now, who goes first." He locked the door.

"Me…me…me…" Argi ran into his arms.

He sat down and pulled her over his knee. "Don't you know it isn't ladylike to go to a gentleman's room uninvited. Count to ten. If you don't I'll double up on the spanking." She screamed and counted while Yiota was desperately trying to find a way out. He hit the bottom part of her backside hard enough to cause the maximum amount of discomfort.

He tossed her into the pool head first and motioned for Yiota to lie over his knees. "If you don't, I'll throw you out naked as the day you were born."

She cried hysterically but obeyed him and began counting per his orders.

When she screamed out ten, he threw her into the pool next to her friend.

They were both frantic over their ruined hair and climbed out rubbing their behinds.

"Nice shade of red." Dimitri laughed and examined their well-rounded rear ends. "Here are your towels." He unlocked the door and pushed them out. "Say hello to your husbands."

Angry and humiliated, they yelled at him as they ran down the hallway.

"Beast...beast...beast!"

Their husbands were pleased that they didn't attend the luncheon since they normally didn't miss an opportunity to see Dimitri.

"Where are your lovely wives?"

"They said something about their hair."

CHAPTER 15

KARDAMYLA, CHIOS GREECE

Dimitri jumped off the sailboat near the shore and with long strong strides pushed through the last few feet of crystal seawater.

"Mr. Dimitri! Mr. Dimitri!" The fisherman scrambled to reach him knowing he would be buying their entire catch for the villagers. He shouted for them to distribute the fish and he would be back later to compensate them. He was in a hurry to be with his Katinaki. He knew she would be all warm and supple waiting for him in the old house.

Wearing only his swimming trunks and a towel draped over his broad shoulders, Dimitri darted around a noisy mule as he hurried barefooted through dirt paths under thick fig trees to upper Kardamyla. He stopped for a moment at the top of the hill to admire the ivory marble steps and columns that led to his mansion.

Mother would have been proud to know what her only son had accomplished, he thought. He was

powerful and rich beyond imagination. He dined
with kings and was sought after by leaders of countries to impart his financial wisdom; yet he derived
his deepest pleasures from the simple things in life,
especially the familiar surroundings of his family
home and the girl he had loved since he was a boy.

The tiny whitewashed house with the creaky blue
shutters sat at the foot of the mansion much to the
distaste of Dimitri's spoiled wife. Except for the addi-
tion of electricity and indoor plumbing, he had left
everything intact down to the tin plates his mother
had always used.

No one had access to the house with the exception of Katina who grew up clinging to his mother's
apron. Katina's own mother had died at childbirth
and she was raised under the strict guidance and love
of Dimitri's mother. She had learned all womanly
duties from Kiria Marika such as sewing, needlepoint
and crochet. More importantly, she became one of
the finest cooks and bakers in the village. She loved
to surprise Dimitri with his favorite foods cooked in
the hearth fourno.

The delicious smell of fresh bread wafted through
the door that was opened wide to welcome him.
Dimitri ducked to enter. His huge frame cut off
the early morning light as he stood in the doorway
watching Katina moving swiftly to prepare breakfast.
Her hair was tied with a black net at the nape of
her neck; her long drab grey dress buttoned up to
the chin. No matter how hard she tried to disguise

her voluptuous breasts and curvy hips by wearing "respectable clothes" it was impossible.

Without looking at him, she pulled out the weather beaten straw chair at the head of the wooden table. "Sit Mr. Dimitri," she commanded. Her arched brows were locked severely. She was always the picture of propriety until they were completely hidden from the outside world.

"I heard the helicopter land on Psalidia and left early to prepare all of your favorites…bread, rusks, homemade cheese, mountain honey, strained yogurt, I stuffed tomatoes from the garden for your afternoon meal," she said seriously. "I picked the figs a few moments ago so you could eat them while they were still cool and moist."

"Katina," he scolded in a deep raspy voice, "haven't I told you not to use the fourno in the heat of the summer? If you must bake, go to the main fourno in the village where everyone else takes their food to be cooked." He leaned back in his chair to get a better look at her as she skirted about. "I think you must be punished for disobeying," he said sternly.

She finally turned to look at him softening her gaze. His hair had dried into a mass of coal black curls. His hazel eyes framed with thick lashes sparkled and his strong square jaw was etched with a deep clef. In her eyes he was the handsomest man alive.

"You are the master Mr. Dimitri," she said breathlessly. She laid a pan of warm water at his feet, then with a slow deliberate sway walked to the windows, closed the shutters and latched the door. The room was dark except for a lantern she had placed on the table.

"Be sure to match the punishment with the crime," she mused dropping to her knees between his legs. She dipped a cloth in the warm water and lathered it with a bar of perfumed American soap that she saved only for him. She washed and dried his hands and bent to bathe his feet.

Her tender strokes brought tears to his eyes. He had never felt more love from anyone with the exception of his mother. "My Katinaki, why do you do these things?" He slapped her behind playfully. " Is it to enslave me?" He kissed the top of her head, removed the net and caressed the shiny black tresses that fell in massive waves to her waist. "You claimed my heart the day you were placed in my mother's arms a few hours after you were born."

She moved the pan of water under the table, laid her hands on his bronze muscular thighs and looked up at him adoringly. "You are my eyes and my breath, my Dimitraki. I live to serve you." Her olive skin was flushed; her full lips were naturally stained the color of purple grapes; her eyes dark liquid pools of emotion. Every fiber of her being ached for him, "I am shameless with the wanting of you."

He took her hands into his and raised them to his lips kissing her palms. "Rise, my sweet Katinaki." He pushed up gently on her chin bringing her to her feet, hook his large fingers into the top of her dress and with one quick jerk, ripped it open revealing the red satin bustier he had brought her from Paris.

CHAPTER 16

DIMITRI'S MOTHER KIRIA MARIKA

Kiria Marika was well respected in Kardamyla. She was a handsome woman who knew how to conduct herself in public. She always dressed properly, did not address a man directly and never engaged in gossip. She was tall with long limbs and had an hour glass figure. Her face was unusually superb. She had high cheek bones and cherry lips. When she cast her almond shaped eyes feathered with black lashes on someone, they froze in their tracks. One look spoke volumes. The church was her life; she and her young son, Dimitri never missed a service.

When Kiria Marika heard the wailing, she was cooking fish soup in the fireplace. She lifted the cast iron pot and placed it on the small cement block outside the kitchen door, made the sign of the cross and walked slowly towards the village square. Her heart was pounding. "Please, God. Not another ship gone down." Her husband Petro had narrowly escaped the last disaster but many women lost their husbands in ship wrecks.

Most of the men took to the high seas to make a living for their families. They knew it could be dangerous but didn't have a choice since there were few jobs on the island. Many hoped to dock in America where they would jump ship and make their way to family and friends who had arrived before them.

She asked him not to go. "Stay home and fish for a living. We will manage nicely. I can take in sewing to help." He refused, saying he needed to finish the house and to save for Dimitri's education in America. "A couple more years and I'll quit. I swear to the Holy Mother."

When she first met Petro she was only fourteen. He was the older, well to do, suitor who came to her home to ask for her hand. Her parents and grandparents were present and allowed her to enter the living room as long as she kept her place. "Make Greek coffee, add a sweet to the small dish and put it on the short table," they told her. "Always keep your eyes lowered." She didn't really get a good look at him.

It was embarrassing when she heard them describe her virtues among which 'wide hips would be good for childbearing.' Her dowry consisted of embroidered sheets, crochet table cloths, a few cooking utensils and a mule. He refused the dowry claiming he could provide nicely for his wife since he had been saving many years for this moment. Everyone was surprised especially when he gave them unique gifts from his travels.

"That's settled," the father made his decision. "The wedding will be when she turns fifteen. In the meantime, if you want to see her, it will be here with the family present. Conversation will be minimal."

Their wedding night was a disaster. Marika was completely oblivious and would not allow him to touch her. "But we must…our mothers will be here in the morning to collect the sheet with the stain. How do we prove you are a virgin?" He was completely covered with hair and had a nasal tone to his voice. She was so frightened that she shut her eyes and would not open them. It was the worse day of her life when she submitted to the man who resembled an animal.

She approached the square, her head held high. The names of those who perished at sea were being read. Women were screaming, beating their breasts and weeping.

"Petros Kontos," he enunciated coldly.

"It is God's will," she turned on her heels and went back from where she came. *There is no time for grief. I must take care of Dimitri and plan for our future. Then there is the matter of a church service.*

Dimitri was fighting with Niko, the neighbor's son. "My mother does not give the evil eye just because her eyebrows meet in the middle." Even though he was only five, he wasn't afraid to punch the nine-year-old in the nose. Niko went crying to his mother blood streaming down his face.

"How many times have I told you to save your toughness for serious things, Dimitri. Apologize to Niko now and come home for a talk."

"But he said you give the evil eye!"

"Do as I say or you will get a whipping." She never laid a hand on her son. He was the sunshine of her life.

"I must break the news about his father in a civilized way so that he knows we are not alone. The Lord will guide and protect us," she spoke to herself.

"You said sorry...I'm proud. You are my brave son. Now is when you will show your true strength. It is the God's will that you become the man of the family."

Dimitri had a strange expression on his face, a mixture of pain and fear. "But the man is father."

"No. You are the man Dimitri. Petro will not be coming home. There was an accident and he has returned where he came from. Be glad he is with his family who went before him."

"Who will take care of us? We need him to provide our bread. Will we be poor like the other families who lost their men?"

"How dare you doubt God. He knows we are capable. We have each other to rely on."

There was a banging on the door. "Kiria Marika, it is me, Mr. Kosta the match-maker and broker. I came in person to deliver my condolences. May I come in?" He was a sleazy looking man who wore a straw hat, a nasty looking brown suit and tie. He held the hat over his breast and bowed, revealing a greasy partially balding head. His face was always red and his arm pits sweaty.

She contained her horror at this invasion but knew it would be necessary to communicate with him in order to sell the house. Petro never left her enough money for emergencies. *"Women," he said, "should have just enough to survive without starving."*

"Allow me the honor of assisting you in your hour of need. Pardon me for saying this but you are, indisputably, the finest woman in Kardamyla and the best cook. With or without my help you will find another husband immediately.

I know them all…

It did not take long for her to extract the broom from behind the door and plummet every angle of his body. "You disrespectful, foul individual…to suggest such blasphemy. You will burn in hell."

He ran fast but was already planning his next move. After all, she would have to sell her house to survive. "What a feisty, beautiful woman," he spoke out loud. "If I was younger and taller, I could ask for her hand."

Dimitri was proud of his mother and threw his arms around her. "Together we will survive, mother."

The very next morning, the broker showed up at her door with money in hand for her house.

"Twice what you are offering," she said and reached for the broom, "and the two rooms in the upper village that are empty."

Much as Mr. Kosta tried, she would not negotiate. She slammed the door in his face stating there was another buyer on his way.

But who could it be? The café or hotel owner? The house was prime property next to the sea. It was well worth the money she was asking. He did not want to lose it. He saw Saranti from the café heading that way and ran back to make the deal.

"Kiria Marika, you are a good businesswoman. I concede to your demands. Here is the money."

"Mr. Kosta, where is the paperwork? I will empty my house within the week and move my things to upper Kardamyla once we firm it up with legal stamps."

"Take it…take the money. I trust you. I will be back with the documents. You know the two rooms up there are not in very good condition. The place needs many repairs."

"My son and I will make it livable. It will be our home."

He ran off mumbling to himself. "I'll be back before nightfall."

"Please help me bring the firewood to the front, Dimitri. I will load the mule and take it up tonight."

As they were bringing out the wood, Saranti showed up with his two sons. He was always respectful and helped widows whenever he could. "I came to warn you about Mr. Kosta. He will try to cheat you out of your home."

Her heart skipped a beat when she saw him. "I made the deal for twice what he offered and the two rooms on the hill. We are loading the firewood to take it up tonight."

"You will not be doing this. My sons will load it on the mule and take it up for you. This will take at least two trips. Yiorgo…Strati… go and bring our mule, we will load both and take them up together saving us time to carry more things tonight."

"No, you must not. I am quite capable of

"Stop now woman. We are the men and we will handle this for you."

She felt faint when she looked at him. His eyes were the color of the sky, his hair bleached blond by the sun and his mouth showed a smile filled with pearls.

Petro had never managed to gain her heart. She respected him and was a good wife but could not give what he wanted most, her love.

Maybe God is punishing me for my unclean thoughts and that is why he took Petro away, she agonized. I must go to confession. But what would I say? I am disrespecting my husband's memory when he is barely cold.

The boys returned quickly and started loading the mules. They had the same muscular built as their father but neither had his blond hair and blue eyes. They did however have his inherent sense of responsibility and politeness.

Dimitri did his best, dragging the wood close to the animals.

Saranti knelt down and ran his hand through the little one's curly black hair, "Would you rather stay here with your mother, son? We'll go up, unload and come back for other things."

"I am now the man in the family. It is my duty to do these things. Mr. Saranti, may I be allowed to ask a question?"

"Of course...ask away."

"Why do you have such a strange color in your eyes? No one else in the village has this. I thought perhaps you don't close them when you swim and they take the color of the sea."

He tried to suppress a chuckle. "Well, I was told my mother drank blue paint by mistake when she was carrying me and I received it through her breast milk. My eyes started turning blue each time she fed me."

"Oh, I understand. It really is very charming. Truth is, my eyes are not dark like everyone's here in Kardamyla. They are hazel. Perhaps my mother drank something with a hazel color."

Saranti picked up Dimitri and sat him on the first mule. "Lead the way."

He turned to Marika who was listening through the doorway. "We can take another couple of loads up tonight."

"Oh you mustn't," she protested.

"Pack your things woman. We'll be back as soon as we unload."

For years, Marika saw Saranti twice monthly when she purchased coffee and tea from his establishment. Once he even touched her hand when he gave her fresh coffee from Hora, the port of Chios, to smell. "Yes, it is far superior to what I've been buying," she told him trying desperately to keep from shaking. "I have brewed some. Please try it." He handed her a cup of Greek coffee which she sipped delicately.

These short rendezvous made her life worth living. Without a shred of doubt, she knew Saranti shared her feelings.

CHAPTER 17

"Our Marika is leaving us," Angeliki and Koula were crying outside her door. "We've done everything together for six years now. Ever since you married Petro and moved close to the sea. Who will we sew and cook with?" They embraced her.

Marika finally broke down, tears were streaming down her face. "My wonderful friends, you will visit me on the hill and I will come down to bathe my feet in the sea with you. I'll be here when you need me. Don't forget, we will meet in church on Sundays and during holy days."

"Yes, yes," Koula sobbed and reached into her huge cleavage where she had hidden a gift for Marika. "This is for you, my Marika. It is my most cherished possession, a book of poetry. Do not open it. Wait till you are in your other home and you need comforting."

Koula was a big woman with an equally big heart. She was always pregnant. Her husband came in from the ships, impregnated her and left. She loved her five boys but was praying for a girl this time. "If I have a girl, you will be the godmother."

Angeliki was a waif of a woman who was pale and looked undernourished. No matter how much she ate, she never gained weight. She was the most gentle of the three of them. "How will I ever exist without you," she said softly.

"You have Koula right next door and I will always be around. We three are sisters."

Angeliki had only one girl child. Christina was petite like her mother and had angelic features. Where ever she went people would call her a baby doll.

"We are going to bring you sacks and papers for packing," Koula pulled Angeliki out of the house.

As Marika sifted through her belongings, she took out a sponge and bar of soap. She pressed the sponge near her heart and closed her eyes thinking of him and the love song he sang. She had never heard anything so lovely.

She remembered the day she caught him washing in a makeshift wooden shower. She had gone to his cafe for the usual purchases and did not see him. "Perhaps he is working in the back," she thought and circled the café to find him. "Mr. Saranti," she called out then stopped in her tracks. He was singing a love song and lathering his body with a large sponge. The wind had blown open the wooden door to the shower. When he turned to see her, a full view of his naked body invaded her senses. His manhood grew before her eyes reaching high on his belly as he continued to wash without shame.

She was stunned. He was the image in the poster of Apollo she had seen hanging in the café. A fire

grew in her body and she could not control the
gushing between her legs; sensations she had never
experienced and didn't know existed. She backed up
tripping several times then ran down the dirt road by
the sea that was playing a melody on the shore. The
wind caressing her hair was perfumed by the ocean.
The sun danced magically on the waves. Beauty was
everywhere. In one glorious moment, the realization
that she was a woman changed her forever.

Later that evening, there was a knock at the door.
"Kiria Marika, you forgot your coffee. I was making
deliveries in the neighborhood and brought it to you."

His voice evoked those same feelings she had when
she saw him in the shower. She held her breath and
opened the door.

His blue eyes were fixed on her and for a while
he didn't say a word. He looked around for Dimitri.

"He is playing at the neighbor's house," she was
brazen.

"For my sweet Marika," Saranti took her hands
and laid several packages in them then took off.

Coffee, tea, sugar lumps which were a rare
commodity, a sponge and bar of soap were in the
wrappings. She hid the luxury items, taking them out
and holding them to her breast when she was alone.

"What is that you're holding?" Koula asked. The
girls had come in through the kitchen door carrying
armloads of sacks. She took the sponge from her
hands. "Is this a sponge? My Lord, where did you
get such a thing?" She gave it to Angeliki.

"Petro brought it for Dimitri," she lied. "When he grows up he'll use it to bathe."

"But why didn't you show us? You always show us everything that is of value," Angeliki was surprised as she examined it. "Why is it hard?"

"It softens up when it is wet, silly girl." Koula answered.

Marika was getting nervous. "Let's get busy packing." She took the sponge and placed it on a shelf with the soap.

The three of them talked about their experiences together, laughing and crying while they packed and placed items in the bags. Marika did not want to discuss Petro so the subject was avoided.

"Now that I am a widow, I must wear black. Where will I find fabric to sew my dresses? There is nothing left in Kardamyla. Must I go to Hora? How in the world will I get there?"

"It is a very long and dangerous trip," Koula said. "The roads are narrow and mountainous."

"Mr. Saranti goes monthly," Angeliki spoke. "I'm sure he will be going soon. You can ask for a ride with him."

"I couldn't do such a thing. What will people say?"

"You could do such a thing. Everyone who knows you will think nothing of it." It was Saranti who spoke. He was already pulling sacks out to load on the mules.

"But Dimitri…

"He'll stay with us for a few days," the girls chimed in.

"Perhaps someone has black dye and I can boil my dresses in it. I heard it has been done." She was frightened but excited at the thought of traveling with Saranti.

"Never mind," Koula said. "Dye washes out. You will need to go to Hora. You can purchase things for us, too. There is nothing to buy here anymore. Let's make a list Angeliki."

Saranti and the boys were finishing up the loading. "Kiria Marika, we are leaving for the hill. After we place these things in the house, we will clean out the well and put a tarp on it. Keep Dimitri home now since we won't be back this way. In the morning, we'll pick up another load, take it up then fix the shutters. I'll have to go back to the café to work for a few hours but I'll leave the boys there with a list of what needs to be accomplished until I return. You need a shed for the wood and the outhouse should be updated.

"Oh, yes. Be ready for the trip. In a couple of days, I'll be leaving for Hora."

Marika was speechless. Everything was being handled and her home would be finished a lot sooner than she anticipated. The girls would come and help her whitewash and hang curtains. Of course there was the matter of the furniture.

"I will bring the mule cart for the dressers and beds day after tomorrow," Saranti must have read her mind. "You will be moved in before the trip. The boys will handle the incidentals."

"What have I done to deserve such caring friends?"

"Haven't you made yourself available to everyone who needed help? Don't pretend you don't deserve this." he said and picked up Dimitri who was fast asleep on the front doorstep. He took him to the back room and laid him in bed. "Good night, son. Watch after your mother."

Mr. Kosta arrived at that moment with papers and stamps in hand. "I am here to make everything legal." he spoke loudly. Sign here and we are finished."

Saranti forcefully extracted the papers from his hands. "I'll take a look. Heaven forbid there are any errors."

"Wait, Mr. Saranti. I have mistakenly given you the wrong ones," he took a deep bow. "Yes, yes. Here are the right papers."

Mr. Kosta was sweating profusely waiting for Saranti to finish reading the documents.

The girls were laughing in the background.

"There is no mention of the two rooms in the upper village." Saranti was angry.

"I apologize. Here is the separate paper with my signature." *These people all have such ugly tempers, he thought. They might even beat me if I don't do my business honestly.*

"So far, so good! We will take it to the town council tomorrow to be registered. Sign the papers and Kiria Marika will sign at the town office."

"Of course, of course," he signed and bowed several times while backing out of the door."

"I will see you tomorrow, Kiria Marika. Good night."

"Thank you Mr. Saranti. Good night." She felt like the weight of the world had been lifted from her shoulders knowing he was there to take charge.

"Get some rest. We'll see you in the morning." Angeliki kissed her cheek and began crying once again. Koula wasn't far behind with an ocean of tears.

CHAPTER 18

The lullaby of the ocean waves would not be putting her to sleep tonight. It was quiet in the upper village. Dimitri was staying with his friends and Marika was alone for the first time in years. Her small two room house was equipped with many conveniences. The fireplace was large enough to hang the cast iron pots for cooking. Everything she owned had its place thanks to Saranti's innovative techniques. "It isn't too bad," she tried to comfort herself.

Unable to doze off, she got up and looked into the dark abyss through the shutters. There were goose bumps on her body either from excitement or fear. Saranti would be picking her up after midnight for the trip to Hora. She lit a lantern and put it in the window then packed and repacked the food she had made for the trip.

She heard the wagon rumbling on the stones and thought it was much too early for him to be there. There were drumbeats in her chest. Saranti knocked on the door. "Are you awake? I couldn't wait any longer. Let's leave now."

Without a word, she gathered the basket of food, a few pieces of clothing, a pillow and blanket.

"You won't need these," he tossed the bed clothes on the cot. "I brought everything for you. These next few days you will be my queen." He blew out the lantern and escorted her out. In one swoop, he lifted and placed her on soft, comfortable cushions in the cart. "Rest my sweet Marika." He plumped a pillow for her head and covered her with a blanket. "The night is cold and I don't want you to catch a chill. I will wake you when we get to the lagoon in the morning."

"Saranti," she whispered his name tenderly.

"I know, my Marika."

The wagon rocked her into a deep sleep. When she finally opened her eyes, he was singing a love song that made her heart burst with joy. He stopped the wagon, jumped into the back and lifted her to see the lagoon hidden in a remote place at the bottom of the jagged mountain. "The only thing more beautiful than this is you," he kissed her and she responded with a passion she didn't know existed inside of her.

"Hold on tight, the road downward is rocky and scary but I won't let anything happen to you. She screamed and covered her eyes peeking through her fingers as he took the narrow curves around the mountain. The wagon wheels flew into the air causing her to hide under the blanket. "Holy Mother, protect us," she cried out.

They crashed at the bottom in no time laughing hysterically. "I think I wet my pants," she giggled.

"I'll wash your pants and you in the lagoon," he teased her. "Look what I brought for you, a swimming dress."

"What on earth is a swimming dress?"

"Go ahead put it on and come to me in the water." His eyes crinkled in amusement realizing she had probably never done this.

"I couldn't…

"I will hold you in my arms the entire time. Don't be nervous. I'm going for a swim and you can change behind the bushes." He stripped down to his swimming trunks and ran into the gorgeous blue lagoon splashing and diving.

"I'm coming," she quickly threw off her clothing behind the bushes and put on the colorful swimming dress. For a moment, she wanted the same type of easy freedom he displayed and almost went out wearing only her bloomers. It was completely natural for him but she wasn't ready take such a dramatic step.

"You could take it off, my sweet," he always seemed to read her mind. "No one else is here but us." He walked out of the water, swim suit in hand and threw it in the air. The water dripping from his body sparkled. He was a Greek God standing there in his naked glory. He pulled her towards him, held her face with both hands, kissed her and guided her into the sea. "I want to make love to you in the ocean, on the shore, in the wagon and anywhere else that I can. Tell me how you feel. Tell me you want me."

"I have never wanted anything more in my entire existence. I adore you. Help me take this off, Saranti."

He was biting and licking the salt water from her breasts as her swimming dress floated away. "I imagined this every night. Your breasts are round melons and your nipples are plump grapes."

She laughed at the descriptions of her body. "I am serving you all of my fruits."

He dove under her, opened her legs, lifting her onto his shoulders he buried his face first into her belly and then between her soft thighs. He licked her there.

"What are you doing to me? I am on fire." She held onto his hair with both hands and screamed.

He lowered her into the water and wrapped her legs around his hips inserting himself into her. Their rhythm was perfection. They danced into the waves climaxing again and again

CHAPTER 19

His muscles bulged as he carried her out of the water. Her arms were wrapped around his neck. Her thick long hair had fallen over her breasts and back. The ocean water dripping from their beautiful bodies glistened. She resembled an alluring water nymph and he her guardian mate. They were gorgeous together.

"I'll bathe you with well water. There are sponges, soap and towels in the wagon." He put her down and gathered everything for their bath.

"Look, Saranti, I brought the sponge you gave me."

"You haven't used it yet?"

"I was waiting for you to wash me with it."

"Let's go." They ran to the well where he pulled up a bucket of water and poured it over her head. She jumped around laughing childishly. He washed her with the sponge, rinsed and dried every inch of her with a large soft towel.

"Bring up more water. It's my turn to wash you, my love."

She sponged him everywhere and realized he enjoyed it far too much. His manhood was not affected by the numerous times they had made love in the lagoon. He was still proudly erect.

"Oh no," she ran from him.

He chased her, threw her down on the towel and pushed open her legs with his. "You are perfect there even though you have a scar. Were you cut during the birth? Was it painful?"

"Of course, but it was worth it to have Dimitraki."

"Let me kiss it for you." He put his hands under her knees, lifted and parted her legs. He hadn't shaved and he rubbed his bristly chin on her thighs and further down as he licked and bit her. It added a heightened dimension to the lovemaking. "I'm drinking the nectar of the Gods." He mumbled without removing his lips from the target.

Her body was shaking and she kept repeating his name. When she arched her back, he mounted her rocking to the sound of the ocean waves. They cried with release and fell into a blissful sleep. When their eyes opened, the golden pink sun was melting into the lagoon. It was mesmerizing.

"You were delicious." He whispered in her ear. "I don't think I'll shave till we get to Hora." He nibbled her breasts and rubbed his face on her nipples making them pop up.

"Stop or we may never make it to Hora."

"I was supposed to fish and cook for us. Instead, I went fishing for sweeter things. I'm starving."

"Me, too." She was laughing. "I made dolmades, fresh bread and brought cheese, olives, tomatoes and boiled eggs for you. Let's get the basket."

"Eggs for me?" Saranti was surprised. "What did it cost you? I can't allow you to incur such expense."

"You need your strength to keep up with me," she smiled shyly.

"I'll build you a coop and fill it with chickens. You will never buy eggs again."

"You are too good to me."

"The dolmades are delicious. I was told you were the best cook in Kardamyla."

"When we go home, I will make all the foods you love."

They ate ravenously ripping the bread apart and feeding each other.

"Saranti, I'm cold."

He pulled her close and rubbed her. "I'll put you under the covers in the wagon."

"Let's sleep in each others' arms tonight."

"Actually, I should be driving the wagon to Hora soon."

"Please, let's stay one more day. It is magical here. You can fish in the morning and I'll cook over an open flame. We can travel tomorrow evening."

"Woman of my heart, I could stay here forever with you. One more day of paradise it shall be."

"Did you bring matches?"

"What kind of a man would I be if I couldn't light fires for my woman?"

He sang a romantic love song as they cuddled under the blanket. It was easy, uncomplicated joy she experienced and didn't want it to end.

CHAPTER 20

"**I** haven't thought of him once." She stretched and rubbed the sleep from her eyes.

"Shhhh," he touched her lips with his fingers. "He was an abusive man who didn't deserve you. Forget him."

"But what about…"

"My wife? I don't feel guilty. She has been institutionalized for years and doesn't recognize me. I have a private nurse for her and make sure she has more than enough of everything. When I travel to the port every month I visit her. My life revolves around our sons now teaching them to be respectful and hardworking."

"May I see her?"

"No Marika. I don't want you to be hurt. There is nothing left of her but an empty shell."

"Stay under the covers. It's cold. I'll start the fire, then fish. Oh, Marika, wear some clothes or I won't be able to do anything but play with you."

"You mean eat my fruits," she teased. "I've been saving the figs for breakfast." She peeled a black fig and fed him then reached for another.

"Don't bother to peel...he popped them in his mouth. "They are almost as sweet as you." He smacked his lips. "Mmmmm."

"I should spank you for hiding these, naughty girl." He turned her over and slapped her backside lightly.

"No, no Saranti, stop or I won't show you what else I have hidden." She feigned tears and kicked her long legs up and down.

"Did I hurt you, my sweet? Let me kiss it and make it better." He caressed and kissed her behind then lifted her to her knees. "Don't be afraid, I won't enter the forbidden gate. Put your head down and raise your hips. I want to see what I'm getting into." He opened her up with his hands. "Ahhh, it is wonderful. I can't hold back." He guided himself into her. It was tight this way and he moved around to insert all of himself deep inside. His desire had reached epic proportions especially when he heard her moaning. "Is it painful?"

"It is exquisite pain and pleasure. Don't stop. It's happening again."

They erupted together and fell over beaded with perspiration. Unable to move, they listened to their hearts beating erratically.

After a long pause, Marika tried to speak. "We... must...go.

"to...the...well..." Saranti finished her sentence. "I...can't... yet. Tell me what else is hidden or you'll get another thrashing?"

"Loukoumia," she could barely talk.

"That was much too, easy. Where?"

"Box…under…pillow…made for you."

He crawled over her, grabbed the box and ripped it open. Powdered sugar flew everywhere as he stuffed his mouth with three chewy loukoumia. "They have almonds, too! Oh you are a woman of many talents. Here eat."

"Can't chew now…too tired."

"Sweets for energy," he shoved a chunk into her mouth with his tongue.

"You are an animal." She licked the sugar from his lips. "Go build the fire if you can." She was shivering.

He wrapped her in a blanket and put on his khaki pants. "I'll be back to carry you to the flames. Then, finally, I will fish for our dinner."

"Really?" she smiled thinking about the cheese pie in the basket.

She slipped into a night dress and left the warmth of the wagon. With basket in hand, she crept up behind him.

"What's in the basket?" He hadn't turned around to see her.

"My goodness, you could burn down a whole village with this raging fire."

"You didn't answer me," he grabbed her and tickled her ribs. "I won't quit till you show me."

"No, please…I'll show you." She danced around and fell over twisting and giggling. "Stop it, I will wet myself and I'm not wearing underpants."

"I have to see for myself. Your word is no longer good." He lifted her nightdress. "Uh huh, you are a wanton woman. Is there an ulterior motive for not wearing bloomers?"

"Yes you crazy person. I want to bathe first."

"I'm heating the water to wash you." He lifted her clothes over her waist and took the kettle of water from the fire. "Open up." he yelled and poured between her legs scrubbing with the sponge.

"Don't you dare try anything. We'll starve to death waiting for the fish."

"Okay, but be prepared when I come back. I can't get enough of you. Watch me wave from that protruding rock on the far side of the mountain."

"Wait...wait...she covered herself and reached for the basket."

"I wondered how long it would take you to produce the cheese pie."

"You knew?" she punched his arm. "When? How?"

"While you were curled up like a kitten, my hand traveled to the bottom of the basket. It was difficult for me to wait but I made the choice to eat you instead."

"Shame on you," she cut the pie in wedges and began feeding him.

He swallowed a whole piece and opened his mouth for another.

"Slow down or you'll choke." She loved that he enjoyed her food.

After the fourth piece, he took a deep breath. "You made enough for an entire village. I guess I won't need to fish until tomorrow. We can do more interesting things." he said sheepishly.

She was still eating her first piece. "Oh no...you will fish...I will cook and we'll have food for our trip. We have bread, olives and enough cheese pie for today."

"Okay...I'd better get out there while the fish are still jumping. When I return, it should be warm enough to play in the water." He bit her lips.

"I've been meaning to ask you. Are you not worried...?" She didn't finish her sentence.

"My sweet, Marika. There aren't many secrets in Kardamyla. I know you can't have more children."

The blood drained from her face and her eyes filled with tears. She buried her face in her hands and cried quietly.

Saranti was shocked knowing he was the cause of her distress. "Forgive me my angel, my life, my love. I never meant to hurt you. Please, please don't cry." He embraced her and stroked her hair. "I am a monster."

Marika was in and out of consciousness during three days of labor. The midwife performed a procedure to free the child and save her life. She also elected to ensure Marika would never conceive again. "This is your son," she placed him in her arms.

"No Saranti, I am the monster. I prayed to the Holy Mother to spare my life when Dimitri was born, promising to be a devoted mother and wife. I didn't manage to do the later. When Petro touched me, I was disgusted. He probably left this world knowing he was never really loved."

"Now, you listen to me," he wiped the tears from her cheeks. "There are many women who do not enjoy relations with their husbands. I should know. The men come to the café and complain of these things. Petro was the lucky bastard who married the loveliest woman on the island. He was proud to have you by his side. There was a collective sigh when you passed the square. Every man desired you but your heart belonged to me."

"Do you think God will punish us?"

"For loving each other? Absolutely not! Petro is gone...you cannot cheat on a memory."

"Marika, my sweet love...we were meant for each other and we shouldn't waste one moment of precious time questioning God's intentions. We are happy together. I longed for you and always knew someday you would be mine."

They sat quietly listening to the sounds of the sea, her head on his shoulder.

"Are the fish still biting?" she teased.

"I only know I am," he bit her neck.

"I'm going. Keep your eyes on me." He took off his clothes, ran into the sea and swam across to his fishing point. He climbed easily onto the rock, stretched out his arms and waved. "Wish me luck!"

The day was magical. They cleaned and cooked the fish. As it got warmer, they spent hours swimming and making love in the sea. They ate and napped under the wagon to avoid the sun...teased each other, played and made love again. When the sun came down they packed their belongings and climbed into the wagon.

"I'll put you to sleep, my sweet and head to town. We should arrive by morning, find rooms and do our shopping. Two days should be enough to finish everything."

"I hate the thought of leaving this place. I'll keep it in my dreams."

"Your dreams? We'll be here every month. Since you will be sewing dresses for the women in the village, you'll have to replenish the supplies. What better way for us to be together?"

She threw her arms around his neck and kissed him. "I am sooo happy!"

CHAPTER 21

The deep roar of the boat whistles announcing departures and arrivals woke Marika. She sat up in the wagon and saw giant ferries floating in the port. A plethora of people were disembarking from the planks with their baggage and bikes shouting and pushing each other. Friends and families were embracing their loved ones. People, horses, mules and carts were everywhere. The cafés facing the port were chock full of morning coffee drinkers. She was aghast at the buzzing sounds that emanated from the activity. In her wildest imagination, she did not expect to see…women wearing pants and dresses that shockingly exposed their ankles and parts of their legs. Some were even sitting in the cafes unescorted.

"Good morning, my love. We are going to Omiros at the far end of the port to find rooms. I should have arrived earlier before the boats docked."

He was speaking to her but she couldn't distinguish a word. The noise was deafening.

"Marika, can you hear me?" He saw she was startled and realized, she had never been introduced to such chaos and was probably unnerved. Comforting

her was out of the question. Until they arrived at the
hotel, he could not get off the wagon.

He tried to maneuver around the crowds and
began shouting that he had an emergency. Luckily,
they made a path for him and when he pulled up to
Omiros, he flew to the back. He found her hidden
under the blanket with her hands over her ears and
her eyes closed.

"Marika! Marika! Are you okay?" he shook her
gently. "We're here."

"I'm fine." She scrambled off the wagon. "Did
I scare you? I'm sorry," When she entered the hotel
lobby she tried to compose herself. She had never witnessed anything this elegant. There were white marble
floors, burgundy velvet sofas and chairs. Unusual art
in gold frames donned the walls. People were dressed
in the latest fashions.

"Mr. Saranti, we expected you yesterday," a gentleman with a thin mustache and raised eyebrow,
spoke. He was wearing a double breasted black suit
with gold trim on the shoulders and a crispy white
shirt. There was a superior air about him.

"Mr. Spyro. I need two rooms on the same floor
with bathing facilities, please; one for my cousin
Marika."

Mr. Spyro was salivating when he looked at
Marika. "I apologize, sir. The only thing available is
a two room suite. We will accommodate you for how
long?" His eyebrow went up again and he touched it
with his pinky finger looking squarely at her.

"At least a couple of nights. Kindly, see to it that two coffees, medium sweet and large plates of loukoumades with a healthy helping of honey and extra cinnamon is delivered to our room. Our things are in the wagon."

"But, of course. Here is your key to 101."

He held her elbow and led her down the hallway to their suite. Everything he requested was delivered promptly and placed in proper order.

The rooms were lovely. In the bedroom, the huge wooden headboard had inlaid gold carvings of Goddesses and animals. The bed covers were of ivory satin and gold. She parted the heavy brocade drapes in the window and could see the gleaming harbor. "You told me I would be your queen on this trip. I didn't realize we would be staying in a palace." She ran her hand over the fainting couch adorned with matching ivory brocade fabric.

He laid her on the chaise and knelt beside her. "I would do anything to make you happy." He added more honey and cinnamon to the round loukoumades, popped them into her mouth one at a time kissing her after each one. "You are an angel laying here. Your eyes are dreamy and your lashes remind me of fluttering butterflies ready to soar."

"If they do, they will melt into the sky blue of your eyes. This luxury is wonderful but the most exquisite thing in my life is your love." She touched his face tenderly. "You must be exhausted from driving all those hours. Lie down and rest for a while."

"I'll sleep tonight. There is much to do. First, I'll take you shopping. I'll see my wife while you relax in Vounaki Square. Then we'll go sightseeing in a horse drawn carriage. I want to show you the mansions in Kambos."

"Relax in the square?"

"All the women stop there after shopping. Believe me you won't be admonished for drinking fresh orange juice under the cover of the platano (maple) tree. I won't leave you for long. Now let's wash our dusty bodies."

"We'll take our showers separately," she said emphatically.

"All right…you first, but I can't promise not to look."

"Is there a lock on the door?" She ran into the bathroom and slammed the door shut. "Oh my God. There is a huge mirror in here and lots of fluffy white towels; soap and sponges on the basin. Saranti, come and see!"

"I knew you couldn't keep me out." They showered and played for much longer than anticipated. When they came out, she hung her meager belongings in the closet, chose a long gray dress which she no longer found appropriate. It was quite plain considering what was being worn in Hora.

When they glided into the lobby, all eyes were on them. They were an exotically lovely couple; he with his tall muscular physic, arresting blue eyes and blond hair; she with her warm chocolate face and huge, black eyes. Although they were opposites in appearance, the marriage of feminine and masculine perfection was striking.

"Is everyone looking at us?" she lowered her voice.

"Yes, because your eyes are magnets."

She covered her mouth and giggled. "Where do you come up with these things?"

Spyro held the front door open. "Will you be needing a ride, sir?"

"Thank you, we'll walk." He led her through a maze of cobblestone streets up to Vounaki Square, the beginning of the shopping district. There were dozens of storefronts in the narrow paths each with its unique charm. The owners were outside plying for customers.

"My jewelry is the finest in all of Hora. Actually in all of Chios."

"Allow me to put my shoes on your perfect feet."

"In here dazzling eyes."

"This way please. I have imported hats."

"Saranti, look at these hats…they have black veils. Would the women in Kardamyla wear these? They are very unusual."

"Try one, Marika."

"Should I?" The saleslady was already placing a hat on her head and pulling the veil over her eyes. A mirror was suddenly in front of her.

"If you don't mind me saying, you are an attractive woman. The hat completes you."

She had no time to protest. The hat was being packaged and the money was collected from Saranti. "It is stunning on you."

"What is happening? I only wanted to try it. I would never wear such a thing."

Everywhere they went someone was pawning products. She refused to enter the stores until the moment she saw the fabrics.

"Black only." She chose several bolts, packages of buttons, thread and a few patterns. Even though she was adept in designing dresses, it wouldn't hurt to try different styles.

Saranti dipped into his pockets to pay.

"Please. I have money from the house sale."

"Are you trying to degrade my masculinity?" He said sternly.

"Don't be angry. That isn't what I was doing."

"You will not spend one drachma! Do you understand woman? Save it for you and Dimitri in case of emergencies. Not another word about it!"

They finished their shopping buying things for their boys and from the list that Koula and Angeliki had given her. Saranti took her to the square, sat her at a wobbly table under the large shady maple tree and bought her an orange juice.

"The oranges come from Kambos. They are huge and taste of honey. Relax here. I'll be back before you miss me." He laid the packages at her feet.

CHAPTER 22

An old man with a long white beard approached her table. "Would you mind if I sit? I get juice here every afternoon."

"Please do. I welcome the company. This orange juice is the most delicious thing I've ever tasted."

"You have an accent. Most of the islanders do but yours is more pronounced. Are you from another village?"

"Why yes, Kardamyla." The old man was pleasant and she felt comfortable with him. She was positive they had never met, yet there was something familiar about him. "Do you live here in Hora?"

"I've been staying at the hotel. I'm originally from Thessaloniki."

She remembered Saranti was born there. His mother was told her only hope to carry a baby to term was to be doctored in Thessaloniki. She stayed for months and was relieved at the birth of a healthy blond, blue-eyed boy. The expectation was his hair and eyes would darken which didn't happen. They assured her, a family member in the distant past must have been fair. "You should count your blessings for this handsome child," they told her.

"I heard the finest doctors in Europe are in Thessaloniki. Is it true? We certainly need one in Kardamyla."

"What a coincidence," he smiled warmly. "I have been planning to go to Kardamyla. Perhaps I should consider doctoring there."

"You are a doctor? Oh how we need you! You must meet Saranti. He owns the café in the village. We can talk about bringing you to Kardamyla. My goodness…I don't know your name. I am Marika!"

"Georgios." They shook hands politely. "Dr. Georgios Cohen." He instantly realized, this young lady was in love with Saranti. She lit up when she mentioned his name.

"Do I detect blue eyes behind your glasses? Saranti is the only blue eyed person I've ever seen."

"I have a rendezvous." He stood up. "When will you be leaving, Marika?"

"In the next day or two."

"I want to see you again. Ask for me at the hotel. Spyro will find me."

"We must meet again. I don't know why, but I have the feeling I know you." She had a quizzical expression on her face.

He kissed her hand and walked off clicking his intricately carved wooden cane.

The aroma of grilled souvlakia floating from the kiosks around the square permeated the air. By this time, she was starving. Saranti was suddenly in front of her with a bag of the skewered meat. "You must be hungry. Eat while I load our things into the taxi. I managed to reserve the only one in Chios. Our packages will be delivered to the hotel and we'll take off in the horse-drawn carriage."

"I will not take one bite unless we eat together." It was difficult for her not to be perplexed by the happenings. A taxi cab, horse-drawn carriage…food at the moment she was hungry. "How will I exist without you, Saranti?"

"You'll never know…I'll always take care of you." He sat at the table. "Okay, we'll eat then leave for Kambos."

"Delicious. I've never had anything this tasty."

"Wait till I take you out tonight. There is a restaurant next to the sea with luscious mezedakia. You'll enjoy every morsel."

"Saranti, I apologize in advance for saying this but I feel you are spending too much money."

"Don't say another word. I am in good shape financially. You'll never want for anything. Although, what I do for you can't be obvious. Your reputation should not be compromised."

They finished their food quietly each in their own complex thoughts.

"How is Xenia?"

"There is no change but she is in excellent hands."

"Marika, I need to confide something strange that has been happening to me. We'll talk on the way."

"I want to discuss a serious issue with you, also. And, we mustn't forget to telephone a message to our children that we are well."

"It's been done. As a matter of fact, we'll go to the phone center in the morning to speak with them."

He lifted her onto the carriage. "Marika, I have an unusual story to tell you. Since my parents passed away from that dreaded disease, I have been the recipient of large sums of money. At first, I believed it was an error but as time went on, I realized someone has been looking after me. I don't understand it. My accounts are never depleted. When I come to Hora, my hotel is always paid. I have tried to discover the source but it is skillfully hidden."

The horse was trotting along down quiet dirt streets where branches heavy with oranges swayed over high stone walls. The mansions in Kambos were barely visible through the huge iron gates.

"Obviously, it is an offering of deep affection or love." For no apparent reason her mind floated to the old doctor. "You should not question why you are being blessed. Now I understand how you have managed to help many forsaken souls in Kardamyla. You are passing on your good fortune."

"Marika, I need to know who is helping me and why."

"When the time is right, God will reveal the source of your blessings, my love. Accept your fate, be thankful. You have honored the person who is your benefactor."

He pulled the carriage to the side and kissed her. "You are wise and kind, my sweet. I will try to be patient." He descended from the carriage and lifted her off. "We are going to visit a lonely old woman."

"Kiria Popie," he banged on the gate. "It is me, Saranti. I brought a friend from Kardamyla to meet you."

"My son…my Saranti." The tiny wrinkled old woman yelled to the gardener to open the gate. She embraced him and wept. "You are the only one who comes to visit. My goodness. Who is this lovely creature? Come in my child. You are just in time to eat. We slaughtered a chicken today and cooked it on wood and stones."

Marika took to the old woman instantly. They held hands as Kiria Popie showed her the lush fragrant gardens then cut jasmine flowers for her hair. "Here you are my beauty. This is nature's perfume." The large fountain with a statue of Aphrodite in the middle of the courtyard was her favorite. Her eyes lit up when she told Marika that her husband had it made especially for her.

"Bring a basket of oranges for our girl," she called out to the gardener. "Put it in the carriage. And, Mano, there is no need to disappear. You've been here for forty years, you are family.

Kiria Popie was ostracized by the Chians when she fell in love and married a Turk. The massacre of tens of thousands of Chians during their fight for independence from the Ottomans was a continuing source of pain and anger. Songs and poems were written about the atrocities and passed on to each generation. Though her Fatih was a gentle man, he was shot and killed by neighbors who didn't want a Turk breathing the air of Chios. She sent her two daughters to America to save them from this anguish but Popie refused to leave the home she shared with her beloved husband.

"I bought you a shawl, a robe for the winter, a sweater for Mano and a few garden tools. The delivery will be in the morning," Saranti told her quietly. "We cannot stay for dinner today but on our next trip, surely, you will be feeding us. An orange juice will be welcome."

"You wonderful boy. I adore you." She was squeezing oranges as she spoke and gave them each a glassful. "Thank you for making an old woman happy."

What she didn't know, Saranti provided food, fuel and other staples to keep her in the mansion. Mano suspected but was grateful and said nothing to Kiria Popie. He was like a brother to her and swore he would protect her till she took her last breath.

Marika blew her kisses. "We'll see you next month."

Kiria Popie cried as they disappeared into the night.

"It is very dark, Saranti. How long before we return to Hora?"

"It is always darker in Kambos because of the large trees that shade the road. There is still some

light up ahead. What was it that you wanted to discuss with me?"

"I met a doctor and invited him to come to
Kardamyla."

"A doctor? I left you alone for a short time and
you met another man!"

"Don't be silly. He was an old gentleman with a
white beard from Thessaloniki, Dr. Georgios Cohen.
He wants to visit our village and perhaps remain
there to treat the ill. Would you please meet with
him? He's staying at the hotel."

"If you wish."

"He told me Mr. Spyro will know where to find
him."

"Shall we invite him to dine with us?"

"What an excellent idea. I felt good vibrations
from him. He seems to have a caring, gentle nature.
I believe, in a short period of time, the Kadamylians
will trust him. He will be an asset to our village if
he decides to stay. Oh, I forgot to mention, he has
blue eyes."

"Now, there will be two of us with blue eyes.

CHAPTER 23

"Dr. Cohen, Mr. Spyro told us we would find you here at the Seaside Taverna. I am Sarantis Patrinos and you know Marika."

"I was hoping you would join me. Anticipating your arrival, I ordered mezedakia."

"We had planned to dine here and ask you to join us. It is the best taverna in Chios. Thank you for inviting us."

"Doctor, I told Saranti how we met. It was my good fortune and will be for the people of Kardamyla if we can entice you to stay in our village."

"Marika, if they are as gracious as you, I will be a lucky man." He spoke softly and took her hand.

His eyes filled with tears when he looked at Saranti. "You are a handsome man and your Marika is lovely."

Saranti put his arm around the old man's shoulder. "Marika is a widow...and well...I'll explain some day."

"No need, my boy. It is in both of your eyes."

"Why are you sad? Do you miss your family?" Marika questioned him.

"The Germans, my dear child, took them away. I was spared because I was a doctor. Forgive me if I made you uncomfortable."

"My heart hurts for you. We have lost our loved ones too. Saranti's parents died of TB and mine moved to America. Maybe the Lord led you to us. We can be your family." She kissed his cheek.

The old man was moved to tears. "I'll be back shortly." He left the table and went walking by the sea.

"Saranti, please go with him."

She watched them walk in silence and thought they looked as if they belonged together. Even though the doctor had a cane, he had a proud strut. "How unusual," she thought, "he and Saranti have the same height and walk."

Three waiters were putting plates of delicacies and fresh bread on the table when the men arrived.

"Did you have a nice stroll? Ocean breezes increase the appetite, you know. I don't suppose we can possibly eat all of this amazing food."

"I can." Saranti spoke. "I have the appetite of forty men."

Marika served both of them before adding a few pieces to her plate. "Please be careful to chew before you swallow Saranti. I have seen you drink your food." She teased him.

The evening flowed effortlessly as if they had always known each other. There were no awkward moments between the three of them. They agreed that Dr. Cohen would come to Kardamyla. Saranti would prepare a place for him to live and practice medicine. The old man smiled when Saranti offered to pay his expenses.

"No my son. I can afford it. As a matter of fact, instead of coming by land, perhaps I will charter a yacht and load it with my medical equipment."

"Don't you think it's a novel idea, Marika? Maybe one day we can travel that way too."

For the first time since he lost his family and friends in the holocaust Georgios Cohen was elated. His heart was filled with the promise of a new life close to people he had fallen in love with. Perhaps he will reveal his secret to Saranti. But not for a long while.

Saranti was finally exhausted. His eyes were closing and Marika wanted to return to the hotel to put him to bed. "We must be leaving," she said sweetly. "May we see you tomorrow morning for loukoumades?"

"Nothing would make me happier." Dr. Cohen embraced both of them. "We'll walk back together. You may need my assistance with this sleepy fellow."

They strolled back to the hotel. Saranti was in the middle with his arms wrapped around both of them. He was already in a dream-state by the time he went to his room and fell into the luxurious bed.

Marika thanked Dr. Cohen, made plans to meet him the next day and bid him goodnight.

Finally, Saranti was in a deep restful sleep. She did not want to disturb him by removing his clothing.

His lips were slightly parted. Each breath he took was long and low. Marika watched him, amazed at his perfection. She reveled in the glory that was bestowed upon her. There was no beginning and no end to her feelings. She had forgotten everything before him and knew only her life began the moment she set eyes on him.

She removed her clothing, put on a bed dress and laid next to him quietly. Before too long, he pulled her close to him crying out her name. He was dreaming about her as he had many times before only this time she was real. He felt her in his arms and relaxed.

They slept peacefully until they heard the morning sounds nudging them to open their eyes.

Saranti traced her face and lips with his finger and kissed her softly. "My sweet love," he whispered. "Somehow we will find a way to be together till the end of our time."

"We will always belong to each other. Even if we can't live together our hearts are one, my wonderful man. How do you feel about telling Dr. Cohen our secret?"

"He already knows without words, my love. He sees it in our eyes."

"We are meeting him this morning for loukouma-des and coffee. What time will we phone our boys?"

"Ours is one of the few rooms with telephone lines. We'll request the call come to our room. Dr. Cohen can wait with us and we'll go out afterward or we can have our breakfast here."

CHAPTER 24

Someone was knocking on the door. Saranti realized he had slept in his clothing didn't want to answer the door in case it was that snooty Mr. Spyro."

"You were exhausted and I didn't have the heart to change you. Go for a shower and I'll bring what you need."

"It is Georgios with your breakfast. May I please enter." She opened the door wide and he came in with armloads of food. Marika and Saranti helped him carry everything to the table. "I had them deliver fresh figs, too."

"I'm starving," Saranti started popping loukoumades in his mouth. "Thank you.

I'm sorry Marika. I should have fed you first." He put a plumb black fig in her mouth.

Dr. Cohen and Marika were both laughing. Saranti's clothes were a wrinkled mess and his hair had risen to new heights.

"He hadn't slept in days and passed out when we got here. I didn't want to wake him to change into his night clothes. Drink your coffee Saranti." She smiled at his spontaneity. He wasn't at all uncomfortable with the way he looked.

"You forgot, Marika. We brought him here together. He was fast asleep before we carried him in."

Realizing she was still in her night dress and ran to the closet to get a shawl. "We wanted you to join us here. You must have read our minds. We are glad to be with you." She beamed and sat next to him on the chaise.

Saranti contacted the call center and was waiting for a response from Kardamyla then he sat at Dr. Georgios feet staring up at him.

The doctor was carving a chunk of cheese. "It is home made from the mountains." He put a piece in Sarantis wide open mouth. *He is like a small child who needs attention, the doctor thought as he reached over and tousled his hair.* He carved another piece for Marika and put it in her mouth. *Her smile is fresh, innocent and full of love. I care for her the same way I care for my Saranti, he thought and wanted to embrace them both.*

Saranti was playing with the doctor's beard. "I've never in my life seen a longer beard. When you come to visit Kardamyla, everyone will comment on it."

"Visit? My decision has been made. I phoned Thessaloniki and they are shipping my medical equipment immediately. I will volunteer my services since I don't need money. While we're discussing my beard, you must see what I have under this hat." He pulled it off and his grey hair tumbled down. "I haven't shaved or cut my hair in many years. You see, it was my way of mourning."

Marika couldn't believe his small hat held that much hair. "We don't mind the hair at all, but, if you are ready to let it go, Saranti and I will cut it for you."

The phone rang and while they were speaking with their children, Doctor Cohen ran out. "I'll be back shortly."

"We'll see you soon. Your gifts are only a small part of it, we are bringing wonderful news," Marika told Dimitri. She wanted the boys to know about the doctor who would probably be a grandfather figure to them but decided to do it after they met him. She was positive they would have the same warm feelings that she and Saranti experienced.

Georgios was back holding packages again. He spread out newspapers on the floor near the window and added a chair. Then he opened the drapes, pulled out his hair cutting paraphernalia and sat down. "You will cut the hair and Saranti will cut the beard," he said seriously.

"Are you sure? Because we love you just the way you are." Marika knelt down and held his hand.

"I can no longer mourn. It is time to live!" He handed her a comb and scissors and placed another set in Saranti's hands. "Anyway you want. Don't be intimidated."

"I am saving your beard." Saranti brought a box from the closet. "This is a major undertaking. First we shall wet the hair. Then I will cut it at the chin. Marika, how far up are you willing to take it off."

"He will have a clean neckline. I will shave it afterward. Is that all right, doctor?"

"I'm old enough to be your grandfather. Call me Papou Georgios?"

"Oh, yes, yes…Papou Georgios is ideal. Isn't it Saranti?"

He sat perfectly still as they laid wet towels on him and began cutting.

"Okay, Papou. This is the last of it." He tied the hair with a ribbon and dropped into a box. "You are quite handsome for an old man. We have a lot of widows in Kardamyla who may be interested in you."

Georgios hadn't been this happy in years. He had a wide smile and was admiring Saranti when Marika backed up to look at him. Suddenly, she saw the resemblance. He was an older version of Saranti with a beautiful smile and sparkling blue eyes. Her heart was thundering and she couldn't speak.

Georgios saw the emotion in her eyes and understood that she had discovered his secret. He shook his head indicating it wasn't time yet. Tears filled her eyes and she bent forward and kissed him on the cheek.

"Go take your shower, my love and I will clean up everything here."

"Clothes?"

"I will bring them to you." Marika gathered the newspapers and threw everything away then took Saranti's clothing to the shower. When she came back, she spoke to Georgios.

CHAPTER 25

"The apple doesn't fall far from the tree. He is a good and decent man as you are. For sure you have been taking care of him these past years. I knew it was someone who loved him very much. When will you tell him?"

"My gentle and kind, Marika. We don't want to make his world upside down. Let's wait till the time is right and he is ready to accept the truth. As long as I have his love, nothing else matters."

"Your secret is safe with me. How you must have suffered losing your family and friends. It is now our responsibility to heal your wounded heart. We will take care of you from now on." She put her arms around him and cried on his shoulder.

"Marika, my sweet. Don't cry." Saranti was out of the shower and dressed. "I will miss Papou, too. Kardamyla will soon be his home and we will be spending a lot of time together."

"Stay with him Saranti while I get ready."

Saranti sat down and threw his arm around the old man's shoulder. "Marika is very sensitive. We must protect her from the bad tongues of the village. They know nothing of our relationship."

"My son, do not worry. My lips will not reveal your secret. I want you to remember the words I tell you. You and Marika will be together, I promise you. I know these things."

"Somehow, I believe whatever you tell me. I am happy you are coming to our village. You will enjoy it and Marika's cooking. She is not only beautiful she is an excellent homemaker. She has a five-year-old son, Dimitri and my two are Yiorgo and Strati. They are ten and eleven."

"I'm excited about meeting the boys."

"There is a small hotel in the square next to my café. It doesn't do much business and I think it would be ideal for your practice."

"That it will. We must purchase it and make it into a clinic."

"What a fine idea. The clinic will be by my cafe and the boys can help you fix it up. They are excellent with tools, respectful, good in school and helpful to those in need. I am a proud father."

"You couldn't ask for anything more of your sons. You taught them well. Perhaps we can train one or both to be in the medical field."

"It hadn't occurred to me, but now that we have you, it would most definitely be a possibility."

Marika had gotten dressed and was sitting in the next room listening to them talk. She didn't want to disturb their conversation and was glad Saranti was confiding in Papou. The three of them had bonded completely in such a short time. She could not imagine life without the old doctor. *I should go to church and light a candle, she thought but I'm afraid after what I have done that the Lord may punish me. Everything was in the name of love. I'll ask forgiveness and thank God for bringing Papou into our lives.*

"Marika are you almost ready? Stop fussing. You couldn't possibly make yourself more beautiful," Saranti called out to her. "Come. We will walk by the sea and give Papou details of our complicated village."

"I've decided to attend church this morning and leave you two gentlemen for man talk. We'll meet later in the square. You see, I am quite reasonable about being alone at the cafe. I can handle it without being flustered. In fact, I believe this means I am a modern woman."

"Oh, no! What have I created? Next thing you know she will be wearing pants and lip tint."

"Go...go...See you later." She kissed both of them.

They walked down the long corridor to the main lobby where Mr. Spyro was greeting the guests. He took one look at them and was aghast. "You didn't say your grandfather was coming, Mr. Saranti."

"It must be the blue eyes he whispered to Papou." He was amused at what he perceived to be mistaken identity. He didn't bother to correct him. As a matter of fact, he rather enjoyed that Spyro thought they were related.

"Mr. Spyro, it is I, Doctor Georgios." He and Saranti were laughing and continued out of the building while Spyro stood there scratching his head. He didn't recognize the old doctor without his beard

CHAPTER 26

T hey sat in a quiet café by the sea sipping Greek coffee, then swished the cup around and turned it upside down to let the grounds dry in unique patterns. It was fun to read the future in each others' cup.

"You will be taking a trip by yacht to a faraway village." Saranti smiled at his own fortune telling skills. "There you will meet a pretty widow who will be mesmerized by your charm and good looks."

Georgios was laughing heartily and slapping his thighs. "Is this what you tell your customers? No wonder they flock to your place."

After a while, they focused on the serious issues that plagued Saranti. He began the soul wrenching journey into his life. For some reason, he felt the need to express his feelings to the old man. He bared his soul explaining that he was a stranger in his family. His parents were simple people without much of an education but they were loving and kind. Yet, they looked at him with an unusual expression as if searching for a familiarity they couldn't find. He always felt he didn't quite belong. When they realized that had

contracted TB and it was life threatening, a marriage
was arranged for him and Xenia through her parents.
At seventeen, he had a pregnant wife who was desperately unhappy. He suspected she loved someone
else. After their second son, she lost her mind. "My
heart broke for her but there was nothing I could do
but concentrate on raising my boys. I needed to put
her in an institution. There was no other way to care
for her." Saranti also revealed he was receiving large
sums of money anonymously. "You and Marika are
the only ones who know."

Papou laid his hand on Saranti's shoulder. "My
dear boy. There are reasons behind everything. As
you become older, you will also be wiser. A deep
understanding will wipe away your doubts and fears.
Now tell me, how did you and Marika find each
other? She is the most beautiful thing that has ever
happened to you with the exception of your sons."

"I have been in love with Marika as far back as I
can remember. Her parents took her out of school
when she was a tike. I suspect she cannot read or write
much but I haven't broached the subject with her. I
still remember the look of dismay on her face when
her father removed her from the class. He claimed
women did not need an education. I was older but
all the students shared the same classroom. I hadn't
seen her except in church until she started coming to
the café to buy coffee and tea twice a month. I knew
her feelings were as intense as mine by the way she
looked at me. I'm talking too much. I apologize."

"No my son. I want to know everything about you. Marika melts at the mere mention of your name. The way you look at each other is the most amazing love I've ever witnessed."

"She is my world. Her husband was an abusive man, yet she honored him by not acknowledging her life was hell. She was always serious and respectful to everyone. I've never admitted this horrible thing, but when he drowned, I knew we had a chance to be together."

"Life has many curves, Saranti. This one opened the path for you and Marika to bring each other comfort, understanding and love. Cherish every single moment you have together. Things can change at the blink of an eye."

"Oh Papou, I'm ashamed of myself for thinking my pain could have possibly been as deep as yours. You lost everyone to the Germans. You had no family until now. Please tell me about your daughter and wife."

"Never be ashamed to express your feelings. If we are family, the freedom to share our secrets, our pain, our joy is a given. My wife passed on when she delivered the greatest gift I ever had. Sarah." *Georgios had a faraway look remembering the day Sarah sacrificed her child when he was born to save him from the Germans.* "She was a strong woman who had no fear. When they took her away she was smiling. I cannot speak of this now. Someday, I will tell you her story, my son." *He wanted to tell him that Sarah was his birth mother but knew it was too*

*soon. The preparation for such talk had to be gentle
and slow, if ever. He endured a stabbing pain in his
heart whenever he remembered her.* "You would have
liked her. She was studying to be a doctor."

"Did she mirror your good looks, Papou?"

"Let's take off our shoes and walk in the sea."
He laid his cane on the table. "We should then find
our Marika who will sooth us. She is exactly what
we need."

They rolled up their pant legs and played tag
with the waves zigzagging and kicking the water. It
alleviated the anxiety felt during the conversation
about Sarah. Georgios was breathing normally again
thinking now he was existing for his grandson. His
mission was to make Saranti's life easier and happier.

"Let's go to Vounaki. I'm sure she will be scanning
the area for us."

"Papou, you are a gem."

They found Marika sitting on the edge of her
chair. "Did the two of you have a nice visit? Saranti
needs a man to talk to that is not from the village.
He can get a new perspective from a voice of experience." She was trembling.

Saranti was alarmed when he saw her but didn't
dare touch her for fear someone would see them.
"Papou, help her. She is shaking."

Dr. Georgios felt her forehead to check for a fever.
"What's wrong my child?" He held her arm leading
her back to Omiros.

"I'm frightened. When we go back home, will I ever see Saranti? I don't know if I can live without him."

"Is that what you are worried about? I'll make sure you see him every day."

"But how?"

"Do you trust me? Leave details to my discretion. I have a plan."

Saranti was about to cry. But he calmed down when he heard Papou telling Marika he would handle everything.

When they entered their hotel room, Saranti embraced Marika kissing her face and eyes. "You heard Papou. We'll see each other every day, my love."

"You two pack and leave while it is still daylight. Spend the balance of the day traveling together. Rest on the way. I'll inform you before I arrive. It shouldn't be more than a few days. There is plenty of food here for the road." Papou pushed them along. "I'm going to my room to wait for communication from Thessaloniki. Don't be surprised if you see me sooner." He hurried them along and ran out of the door.

CHAPTER 27

By the time Papou reached his room he had decided to depart for the village immediately. He phoned Thessaloniki to request a sewing machine be added to the medical equipment and shipped directly to Kardamyla then contacted Spyro to book a small boat and have it loaded with toys, candy and oranges. He would be arriving in advance of Marika and Saranti.

The blue and white vessel was fast even though the water was choppy. He was pleased with himself. The purchase of the hotel had been completed and would be remodeled into a clinic. One end would be Marika's boutique and the other would continue to be Taki's fourno. Although he had never been in the village, he had a feeling he would fit in.

The captain jumped off and pulled the vessel into the harbor. Children were running around screaming. They didn't have many visitors and were excited to see the little boat. "Would you children be kind enough to take these to the hotel?"

The two boys that helped him ashore were the image of their father. "You must be Saranti's sons. He told me all about you when we met in Hora.

"Wow, you have blue eyes."

A youngster was pulling on his shirt. "Excuse me sir. Did your mother drink blue paint, too? Saranti's eyes turned a strange color from his mom's breast milk."

"What a coincidence. Saranti and I both had the same experience." he was laughing. "And who might you be?"

"I'm Dimitri, Marika's son." He held Dr. Georgios hand tightly.

"Marika and Saranti talked about you kids all the time." As he walked to the hotel he saw what he thought was a black sack on the steps. It moved ever so slightly as if caressed by a soft wind. When he came closer he saw a spoon dip into a wooden bowl.

"That's the widow Paraskevoula," the boys told him. "She eats here once a day. We love her because she is good to us."

Taki came out from the bakery and gave a basket to the widow who took it and ran off.

"You must be the doctor. Welcome! Everything is prepared for you." They shook hands.

"Tell me about the widow."

"It has been fifteen years since her husband drowned in a freighter that went down during a storm. He left her with nothing. Poor woman lives in a shack. We try to take care of her but she is too proud to accept our help and prefers to work for the one meal a day that she eats."

He went into the room and began emptying the packages. Oranges, toys and candies were everywhere. "Help yourselves. These are for you. Please don't eat too much candy at once. You'll be sick. I'm a doctor and I know these things."

Except for his great grandsons, the children ignored him and stuffed their mouths with sweets.

He told Strati and Yiorgo he would be staying at Marika's and asked them to carry his suit cases and medical bag. "I also want one of these cots and a chair to be placed outside of the kitchen. I hope you don't mind."

"Right away sir."

"I am the man of the house," Dimitri pulled on the doctor's sleeve. "You need my permission to stay there."

"Of course, Dimitraki. Your mother said you would show me the way. Shall we walk up together?"

"Well, okay. What shall I call you?"

"Papou seems appropriate since I am an old man."

"Is that's what my mother calls you?"

"Certainly."

Doctor Georgios glanced at the fig tree as they climbed the hill. "Voulitsa, is that you up there?"

No-one had called her by that name since she was a child. She was startled and fell as she reached for the basket of figs that had slipped from her hand. Dr. Georgios was able to stop her from rolling down the hill. No man had touched her in years and she was frightened and fighting. "Stop that. I'm a doctor and I need to see if you are hurt." She closed her eyes while he examined her. "Nothing serious, only a few scrapes. I'm taking you to Marika's for a further checkup." She was light as a rag doll as he carried her up.

Dimitri was in awe of the way he took command. No one was able to communicate that way with the widow.

He laid her on the cot and covered her with a sheet. "Find my medical bag and fill a large container with water."

He untied her black scarf, pushed it off of her head revealing black silk hair with a few streaks of gray. He threw it to the ground. "You will never wear this again." He unbuttoned her dress, pushed it off of her boney shoulders and threw it on the ground. "You will never wear this again." He rolled down her black wool stockings from her skinny legs and threw them on the pile. "Never again," he mouthed. She didn't utter a word.

"Thank you for bringing these, Dimitraki. You are truly indispensable. What would I do without you? Now, please go to Taki and order food and ask the boys to join us for dinner. Ask him to send us milk, honey and fresh bread tomorrow morning."

"Whatever you say Papou." He was beaming as he ran down the hill.

Georgios gently washed Paraskevoula's bruises and dressed them. "You will be fine." She looked into his crystal blue eyes and began to cry. "Are you hurting somewhere else?" She took his hand and laid it on her heart. He was sad to see her fingers were covered in callouses.

He wiped her tears with his hands. "From today, I promise to take care of you. You will stay here with us until you gain your strength. This cot is where you'll spend your days and nights rising only to bathe and use the facilities. When Marika comes home, she will make you beautiful dresses." She began sobbing again. "We won't have any of that," he kissed her forehead.

The three boys arrived with food. "Take it to the kitchen and bring me a plate for Voulitsa."

"But she only eats once a day, Papou." Dimitri told him.

"Do as I say then go back inside and wait for me."

Georgios pinched small pieces of chicken, potatoes and bread with three fingers and put it in her mouth. "Eat as much as you can."

"Chicken?" she questioned.

"So you do have a voice." He continued to feed her slowly.

After a while she shook her head no.

"I guess a half plate for your first meal is pretty good." He popped a caramel in her mouth and she smiled. "You like sweets, eh? I'll make sure you will get at least one every day. Now, I am going to give you sleeping powder and when you wake up I'll be here next to you, Voulitsa. Drink the entire glass."

When she dozed off he rubbed her callouses with oil and wrapped her fingers in white gauze then went into the kitchen to visit with the boys. Dimitraki climbed onto his lap. They ate and conversed together as if it was a daily ritual. His great grandsons questioned him about his choice in careers. He marveled at their intelligence and planned to delve more into this subject when Saranti came back. Perhaps he could entice them to the medical field since they already behaved in a manner befitting those who find satisfaction in helping others.

"Boys, Voula will be awake soon and I must take care of her wounds. Please go enjoy yourselves and if you have any time make sure everything at the hotel has been removed and set out in case anyone needs the furniture."

"We've already done that Papou. In fact, the place is being scraped and painted by the villagers."

"Make sure Taki feeds everyone and I will compensate them for the work. If he has rice pudding, please bring it for Voula." He went out to sit with her, unwrapped her hands and began scraping her fingers with a stone. He wanted to do this while she was still asleep in case it was painful. When he finished her eyes fluttered open and she smiled at him.

"My goodness. You've been asleep for more than four hours. I must give you a little more food and then a sweet surprise." He did the same as before, pinching small portions of food and placing it her mouth. "Chew well then swallow." She obeyed him. When she finished the plate, he brought out the pudding. After the first spoonful, she was ecstatic and began eating it quickly and opening her mouth for more. Georgios laughed out loud as she polished off the entire bowl. "I didn't quite expect that but I'm certainly glad. The sleeping powder must have given you an enormous appetite."

"No. You did." Her voice was low and sweet.

"It looks as if you'll be stronger faster than I anticipated." He mixed more sleeping powder and lifted her head. "Down it goes." She floated off within seconds.

Georgios sat in the chair next to her and closed his eyes. He heard a voice calling his name and thought it was a dream.

CHAPTER 28

"Papou. Papou Georgios. Papou," she called out.

He looked around and saw Marika coming up the hill. She ran to him, fell on her knees and put her head in his lap. "I heard about the widow. I will help you with her. You have already changed her life when no one else could. Your heart is large as the ocean." He kissed her cheek and patted her head. "I saw the boutique," she whispered. "I know what you meant about seeing him every day."

"I hope you realize, I love you as much as my Saranti. You are in my heart as he is. I've even bonded with the children. In fact, I think Dimitraki has really taken to me."

"Oh yes. The minute I saw him all he talked about was Papou did this and Papou did that. He gave me details about the widow."

"Where is Saranti?"

"He's picking up my girlfriends with the wagon. They want to meet you. I think we'll have more people here tonight from the cafe also."

"I've missed both of you. Meeting the boys was the highlight of my arrival. I don't feel like a stranger."

"Oh, my Papou. You are family and when Saranti realizes he belongs to you, he'll be overjoyed."

A slew of screaming youngsters stormed up the hill followed by the mule cart carrying Marika's girlfriends. The kids ran around the widow's cot. "Look…she has hair. We've never seen it before. Is she sleeping? Can she hear us?"

"She is in a deep sleep and can't hear a thing." Papou told them. "Go play and if she wakes up, I'll call you."

Saranti lifted the ladies from the cart and they came over to see him. "Dr. Georgios, how nice to meet you! The entire village is talking about you." They went into the kitchen carrying food and cookies for Marika.

"Did you bring coffee, son?"

"Enough for the Greek Navy. We're gonna need it, Papou. All the old goats from the cafe are on their way. Fortunately, they are bringing chairs."

"Where are the boys?"

"They were putting finishing touches on the clinic and will be on their way momentarily. I will be the one to complete the boutique. It needs special touches," he winked at Papou.

Marika, Koula and Angeliki came out with trays of cookies and coffee. They both sat by Papou. He saw a wisp of a blond girl child sucking her thumb and hiding behind Angelika's skirt. "Come here koukla." She shook her head no and smiled.

The boys had just arrived, "She won't go to anyone but Strati, Papou." Dimitraki told him. "Watch this. Come play with me, Christinaki." She shook her head no and stared at Strati. He pretended to be annoyed but when he opened his arms she ran to him and laid her face on his shoulder. Papou was thinking, this tiny beauty would be his great granddaughter one day.

"Koula, your color is a bit off. If you're expecting, I'd like to take your blood pressure and perhaps give you an exam."

"You see those boys…five of them are mine. I had easy deliveries with all of them. I'm hoping for a girl this time. Marika will be the godmother."

"At the very least, please let me take your pressure."

"Koula, listen to the doctor." Angeliki rarely spoke up but she was concerned about her friend. "She's been having dizziness. Let him check you out."

"All right. I'll see him this week."

"Don't wait one more day. I can measure your blood pressure now."

"No, no, no. Perhaps tomorrow."

The doctor was very uncomfortable. In his observation, she was ill and he was rarely wrong.

Everyone was talking at once. The men had arrived and were engaged in macho conversations. Most had open shirts with chest hair sneaking purposefully from the top. They were making references to their virility trying to impress the doctor. He pretended to believe them but suspected sooner or later many would be approaching him for advice regarding their sexuality.

They tried to bring the conversation to the extermination of the Jews but he refused to discuss it. It was too painful and wanted the evening to be lighthearted.

Slowly, they all descended discussing the doctor amongst themselves. "He is quite a gentleman. We are lucky he chose our village for his practice. We'll have our own doctor and won't have to take that dangerous trip to Hora if we are ill."

The boys wanted to sleep by the sea since it was extremely hot that evening. "Dimitri, I'll have to get your mother's permission." Saranti went into the kitchen. "Kiria Marika, we are taking Dimitraki with us to sleep near the sea."

She was a frightened that he may want to swim at night. "What if…"

"Kiria Marika, my sons will take care of him and if it will make you happy, I will stay the night with them."

"All right, Mr. Saranti. He'll be safe if you keep an eye on him." she felt much better.

He put the ladies on the cart. "Papou, where will you sleep. Certainly not in the chair. I will bring you another cot after I drop off the girls."

"Good. I need to speak to you so plan on staying a while."

When Saranti returned with the cot, Papou shooed him into the kitchen. "Go visit with her. No one is around. I'm tired and need to lie down." He took Voula's hand and worked on the callouses before crawling into the cot next to her.

CHAPTER 29

Georgios was at the clinic organizing his equipment. Dimitraki was always under-foot. He watched and listened to everything continuously asking questions. Suddenly, Georgios realized Voula would be waking up and he had to get home. He wasn't giving her much sleeping powder any more. Her appetite had increased and she was stronger. He left her for a while when Marika was home in order to organize the clinic. "Dimitraki hurry and get me a mule." He did everything Papou told him and flew to the rescue.

Almost at the top of the hill he heard her crying. "Where is my doctor? He promised he wouldn't leave me."

Marika was trying to calm her. "Have some orange juice. He'll be here shortly."

"Voulitsa, I'm here. Don't cry." She sprang from her cot and ran to him.

"Well, well. It seems as though you've gained plenty of strength." He put his arm around her shoulder. "Let's go into the kitchen and eat together for a change." He sat her at the table and Marika began serving her delicious meat balls.

"Marika, doesn't she look beautiful. I sat her in the sun for a few minutes every day and there is a warm color on her face."

They were both laughing. Voula took a meat ball and put it in his mouth. "Don't you think it's time I feed you."

"Did you see that Marika. Voulitsa wants to feed me now. That is the best I've ever tasted because it was from your hand."

Marika thought there was a romance brewing and decided to sneak off and leave them alone.

"I don't want to call you doctor or Papou. What do you think?"

"Georgios is fine with me or do you have something else in mind."

"How about my Georgios?"

"That's funny. It is exactly how I think of myself."

He was happy watching her being playful with him. "Let's get you ready for the boutique. Your dresses are finished except for the hems. Will you try them on for me?"

"What will I wear to go there my Georgios?"

He wrapped her in a sheet and lifted her onto the mule. "There, there. You are a lovely princess."

CHAPTER 30

"It looks like our family is expanding. I have a feeling a romance is brewing, my sweet." Saranti was talking to Marika.

"Quiet. Someone may hear us." She put her finger to her lips.

"Someone already has." Papou said. "I'm taking Voulitsa to the clinic for a physical and we'll be back for the dresses. Saranti wait for me here."

He lifted and carried her into the exam room. "Put this on and lie down here while I give you the once over."

She squirmed and giggled during the process. "Sit still. Haven't you ever been to a doctor before?"

"No." She kept bouncing around. "This is just plain silly. I am perfectly fine."

"That you are. Fit as a 20-year-old. Now let's go try your new clothes. We're going through the back. The gentlemen at the cafe are burning holes through us. They must be jealous that I am escorting a beautiful woman who isn't quite dressed."

"We're here." Papou called out.

Marika took her to the room that was lined with pretty dresses.

Papou and Saranti sat and waited for the show. "You know the guys are curious about your relationship."

"Let them be curious. They need an outlet for their frustrations."

Paraskevoula came out modeling the first dress. When she looked in the mirror she couldn't believe her eyes. She threw her arms around Marika then kissed Georgios.

"Isn't she lovely, Saranti."

His mouth dropped open when he saw her. "She's amazing!!"

Marika sent her in for more dresses and hemmed the one she wore.

"All of these are mine?" She modeled them and Georgios was pleased to see the joy in her face.

"I told you, Voulitsa. You will be the best dressed woman in Kardamyla. Wear your favorite, then order food from Taki for the whole family. We'll eat dinner together at Marika's. Come get me. I'll be at the cafe. Let's go Saranti."

"Are you joking? You want me at the cafe?"

"Of course. Everyone should see how beautiful you are." He ran across shouting, "A medium sweet with extra foam." As usual, when Dimitraki saw him, he tagged along and climbed on his lap. He spent as much time as possible in his company and gazed at him adoringly. In his eyes, Papou was the smartest man in the world and he learned something interesting from him every time they were together.

Dr. Georgios had coffee with the men at the cafe whenever he came to the clinic. Their two subjects of interests were sex, of course, and politics. They were quite uninformed about both. Still, he enjoyed their company.

A woman appeared suddenly. She was weeping. "Simo, hurry. Our son is injured. He is in pain and holding his arm."

Simo was a huge man and when he rose up he towered over the others. "How dare you come to the cafe! I should slap you."

"Your son is suffering. Please come home." She ran off dragging her long, ugly dress.

Saranti and Dr. Georgios were both infuriated with Simo. "I'll take care of this. Simo, why do you speak to your wife in that manner. She works hard cleaning, cooking, washing your dirty clothes and I hear she goes to the fields too. What is it that you do all day but gamble? Your son probably has a broken arm. Bring him to the clinic and go next door to buy your wife a new dress. She looks like a poor gipsy woman in rags."

He ran across and asked Voula for her help. "Dimitraki, find one of the boys and tell them to come immediately." He changed into his white jacket and pants. "Voulitsa please wear the long white nurses uniform."

Strati came in quickly. "What do you need Papou?"

"Are you strong enough to hold someone down who is in pain while I work on him?"

"I can if necessary."

Simo and his wife came in carrying Niko who was moaning and biting his lips.

"Put him on the exam table and leave."

"But we want to help."

"Go." He turned his back on them and focused on Niko. "Talk to him, Strati, while I examine his arm."

"What happened, Niko?" He explained how he fell from a tree, heard a crunch and nearly passed out from pain.

"Nikaki, the doctor will take good care of you."

"I'm quite sure it isn't a bad break. Bite this and I'll fix it.

Niko suddenly felt excruciating pain and bit on the rubber stick hard to keep from yelling.

"That wasn't too bad Nikaki. You handled it well." Papou told him. "Bravo."

"Voulitsa, mix two cups of powder from each jar on the top shelf with a cup of water. I will show Strati how to spread the paste on Niko's arm."

"Dimitri is outside. Ask him to bring in Niko's parents."

His mother was crying when she came. "Nikaki are you all right?"

"He was incredibly brave," the doctor said. "When Strati finishes with the cast, you may take him home. I will give him a small amount of sleeping powder to alleviate any discomfort. If you need me, which I doubt, you know where to find me."

"Thank you Strati, for helping me through this. You too doctor. I'm grateful."

Simo was relieved. He picked up his son and left without a word. His wife was still sniffling.

CHAPTER 31

THE MONK

The entire family was sitting around the kitchen table. Marika and Paraskevoula laid out the spread from Taki and lit lanterns. They felt guilty because they didn't do the cooking. "I'm an excellent cook," Marika said. "I can make any number of these."

"How about you Voulitsa? Can you cook too?" Papou asked.

"If I have someone special to cook for, it will all come back to me."

"Well, here is how I feel about it. Marika, you don't need two jobs. You have enough to do at the boutique and now that you've asked Voulitsa to assist you, I don't see the necessity for either one of you to be working in the kitchen. Taki buys fresh fish from the fishermen and does a bang up job of cooking. If you girls want to show us your talents once in a while, like during the holidays, well ok."

"But Papou, you are spending a lot of money and we want to contribute. Right Paraskevoula?"

"Believe me girls. I wouldn't if I couldn't. Now that is settled and we can eat and talk about more important issues."

Marika told Papou that she believed she found his friend the monk and sent him a message to come to the house. "I'm not sure he received it. The monastery has been in lock-down for quite a while."

"Thank you for your efforts Marika. When he discovers I am here, surely he will try to visit me." Papou got all the news about his grandson from the monk who wrote to him every couple of months about Saranti's life.

Papou was content. Dimitraki had climbed onto his lap. The family was all at the kitchen table eating and talking at once. His life had changed dramatically in a blink of an eye. He didn't know when or how he would reveal his true identity to his grandson.

"Being together with all of you has made me realize how precious family is and I want to say how much I love you. Voulitsa, you know I am a Jew. Does that make a difference to you if I were to ask you to be a permanent member of this clan?"

"My wonderful Georgios. I have been yours from the day you fetched me when I fell from the fig tree."

"Well those are the sweetest words I've heard in a long time." Papou touched her hand.

Marika shed tears of joy and embraced her and Papou. She glanced at Saranti who was also touched and hoping that that this wonderful happiness would rub off on him and Marika, some day. "Congratulations. This is the best news. Wait till our friends at the cafe hear about it." he was laughing.

"Papou, we will have to build another room for you and Paraskevoula. I wouldn't want you to live elsewhere." Dimitraki said seriously. "And Papou, what is the meaning of a Jew?"

"I will never leave you my boy whether I'm living here or not and I will tell you what it means to be a Jew soon."

Strati and Yiorgo didn't make such a big deal about it. They knew this was coming from the first day they saw Papou feed her tenderly. It was a perfect union.

"Boys, I want to ask you how you feel about pursuing the medical field."

"What is pursuing?" Dimitri questioned.

"Studying or following. I think you would make excellent doctors if you have the inclination to help people who are ill."

"I would not be adverse to this if my sons want it. In fact, it would make me proud."

"Marika?"

"Papou stop," Dimitri told him. "The way I see it, Strati and Yiorgo would be perfect. They even help cats deliver their babies. I heard if it wasn't for Strati helping you with Niko's arm, it would have been difficult for you to do it alone. Anyway, I hate blood and I want to be a sailor so I can travel the world."

Papou was duly impressed with Dimitri's reasoning and deducted that he would be an excellent businessman. "Well, in a few sentences, you put me in my place and made me see the light."

"Boys, what do you think?"

"I agree with Dimitraki," Strati said. "I felt rather proud to help you with Niko. And Yiorgo would make an excellent doctor and partner with me."

"That takes care of our future. We will be the finest doctors this village has ever seen. When do we start?" Yiorgo asked.

"It isn't that simple. You will study for many years and go to medical school in England. You are lucky that I am also a teacher and we can work together. If my patients allow you may observe at the clinic."

"Someone is at the doorway, my Georgios."

The monk was dressed in black. He wore a tall hat, long robe and a large wooden cross hung on a piece of thin leather on his chest. His salt and pepper beard covered his entire face. "Excuse the intrusion. I am seeking Dr. Georgios. My name is Gabriel."

Papou removed Dimitri from his lap and threw his arms around the monk. "Mitso my good friend. I grew up with him in Thessaloniki. He is a Jew. Don't be alarmed. They are family and will keep your secret."

"We always knew he was a Jew. We kept silent to protect his identity." Marika said softly. "Please join our table."

Tears fell from Gabriel's eyes into his beard. "Let us walk for a while Georgios. Do you have news for me?"

They held each other as they walked in the night. "Your grandchildren are more than well. They are happy living with Greek Orthodox families. Here are pictures that I managed to take secretly. Imagine their good luck that the priest made them phony baptismal certificates and found good loving families to take them as their own. He saved them from the Germans."

Mitso cried and kissed the pictures. "May I keep these?" He held the pictures to his heart.

"They are yours, of course. Mitso, the realization that your identity is not a secret gives you the freedom to leave and go to your grandchildren."

"I refuse to disturb their lives. I have made my life as a monk and will remain in the monastery. Perhaps my prayers saved them."

"I truly understand your circumstances. I must express my deepest appreciation for your continued friendship. The information you sent regarding my Saranti saved my life. He doesn't know he is my grandson but when the time is right I will reveal the truth."

They held each other and walked back to the house in silence. It was an emotional evening and when they came into the kitchen everyone saw the sadness in their eyes.

"Please partake with us." They wanted him to stay.

"I am fasting," he bowed his head. "But if the invitation still stands in the near future, I will return to share food with you wonderful people."

"At the very least, please take fresh bread and olives with you." Marika wrapped a package and gave it to him. "You are always welcome here."

He bowed his head and faded back into the darkness.

Saranti got up. "This was quite an evening. It is getting late and we must leave."

Papou cupped his grandson's face and looked deep into his eyes. Each felt an overwhelming love for the other. "Please let the boys stay here tonight."

"Yes, of course, Papou."

Marika turned her back and began washing dishes. Paraskevoula noticed she was crying and understood there was much going on she did not know yet. "Go and rest. This is the least I can do." Marika went into the other room to lie down.

"I will see you in the morning son. Bring up the milk with honey and bread from Taki if you have time.

CHAPTER 32

T he drama had exhausted them and they slept soundly. When the daylight crept onto Papou's cot he slowly opened his eyes remembering the happenings of previous night. Many positive things transpired yet he still felt sadness in his heart because of Mitso. He didn't want to get up yet and stayed on the cot trying to fall back asleep.

Saranti had already arrived and was in the kitchen preparing the table. When Marika walked in and found him there she was joyfully startled. They came in one at a time rubbing the sleep from their eyes. "Go wash up and sit at the table." Saranti told them as he poured the warm milk into the cups. "Marika, don't do a thing. I will slice the bread and cheese that I bought this morning."

"Where's Papou?"

"I believe he and Paraskevoula are still sleeping."

Dimitri went out to wake him. "Papou we're having our milk. Aren't you coming?"

He kept his eyes closed while Dimitri stood over him. "Is it daylight already?"

"Aren't you coming in the kitchen? Saranti brought breakfast."

"Shush. I don't want us to wake Voula. Let me wash up."

Papou was in rare form when he entered the kitchen. "I think you need to go back to Hora to pick up more products for the boutique and ouzo for the cafe."

"It is too soon to travel again, Papou. What will everyone say?"

"This is business Marika. Besides, I want you to purchase jewelry for Voulitsa. If we are going to get engaged I need rings and chains. Wait a couple of days and go. The children will be well taken care of and Voulitsa can help at the boutique."

Saranti was all for it. He couldn't wait to be alone with Marika. "I say we shouldn't worry about gossip. The people in this village would not dare utter a bad word about you."

"Well, all right, but I must be crazy taking a chance on ruining my name."

"Don't fret. I will lay the ground work by discussing it at the cafe. Of course, I won't mention the engagement till you return. I'll plan a big surprise?"

CHAPTER 33

"Papou…Papou," Dimitri was knocking on the clinic door. "Aren't you finished yet? I'm hungry!"

"I'll be out shortly, son. I have to take a shower first."

"Why? You'll be taking one again tonight. Don't you know too much soap and water is bad for your skin."

"I have to wash off the germs Dimitraki. I shouldn't be more than 20 minutes." Papou laughed. The boy always came up with a funny comment.

"What are germs?"

"I'll tell you later. Order food for all of us and have it sent to the cafe and make sure the boys are there too."

He didn't miss a beat. Whatever Papou said, he did.

Papou scrubbed himself down and was wondering if his parts were still alive. I suppose waiting for intimacy was the best choice, he thought. Besides, he didn't have a moment alone with his girl. Dimitri was always underfoot.

When he came out, Dimitraki was waiting. They went to the boutique and pressed their noses on the window and knocked.

Voula looked up from her sewing. "Is it lunch time, my Georgios?" She tossed her hair back and smiled flirtatiously.

"We'll be eating across the street." His heart skipped a beat. Had she gotten more beautiful since this morning, he thought.

"Only men go to the cafe." She stood at the door and tilted her head. There was a piece of thread stuck on her full rosy lips. Georgios reached over and picked it off. That small gesture inflamed her. She licked her lips and stared into his bright blue eyes wanting to kiss him. The look she gave him did not escape his attention. He was surprised to feel a warmth in his chest that traveled to his loins.

"Papou says, women are equal to men and they can go anywhere they please. Isn't that right Papou?"

"I'm proud that you remember what I say, Dimitraki."

He led her across the street. "Don't be nervous. You are not doing anything wrong. My girl can go anywhere she pleases."

She enjoyed being referred to as his girl and lifted her head high walking regally to the cafe. He pulled out the chair for her and pushed it gently towards the table as she spread out her dress and sat. The stunned expressions on the men were comical.

The food was on the table and his grandsons were waiting to dig in. "We'd better eat soon because the

little one will be falling asleep and I'm not capable
of carrying him up to the house."

"They are staring at us with fire in their eyes."
Voula whispered.

"And so. This is the start of a new era in Kardamyla
and you will lead the way."

"But Papou, you don't understand. This has never
happened before. The men are shocked," Strati told
him.

"I believe we should open the door for women to
come here boys. They have every right to congregate
and share stories about their daily lives with each
other. It is possible communicating with their spouses
in a relaxed environment may lead to better understanding of each other. The men will actually listen
to their women instead of just ordering them around.

"What do you suggest?" Yiorgo asked. "Shall we
raise a sign saying women are welcome?'

"How about Saranti's Ouzeri and Cafe welcomes
women." Voula was excited and dedicated to the
cause. "It should be blue and white like the Greek
flag."

"My God," one of the men whispered. "Next
thing you know the women will be running the whole
town."

"Why not? They do everything now and don't get
respect or credit." Simo spoke up.

"But where will we go for man talk and to swear?"

"We'll have to curb our tongues when they're
here." Simo was their leader and he usually had the
last word. "Besides, the atmosphere will be uplifting

with the women around to admire." He got up and left.

Papou was delighted hearing different opinions. Changing their mind set was a process and he was feeling positive since he heard Simo, the biggest, most hard headed man support women.

"The sign should go above the door. I trust you boys can handle it. We can have it up by tomorrow."

Dimitraki was excited. "What about the widows who have no escorts?"

"Widows are women too. Do you think women are incapable of walking to the cafe and placing an order without a man?"

"I have to remember that one…widows are women, too. My mom can even come over for coffee in the afternoon. Right, Papou? Maybe with Paraskevoula."

"Of course. Any time they have the urge for conversation with their friends or husbands."

"Besides when women are content during the day, they tend to be nicer at night?"

"Why at night?" Dimitri popped up. "What about during the day?"

"It is just a matter of speech." He winked at Voula and she blushed.

Simo returned with his wife on his arm and holding Niko's hand. She was wearing a new dress and he had a fresh, clean Sunday shirt on. He lit a cigarette and placed it at her lips then nodded to Papou as if to say, I'm taking on the cause. Niko showed them his arm. "See doctor…see Strati….it works as well as before." He moved it around enthusiastically,

"It is nice your beautiful wife is sitting here in her new dress." Papou waved at them. "Please allow me the honor of treating you today." Simo puffed up his chest proudly. "She will come here as often as she pleases."

The men were looking at them with disbelief but made no comment. They were defeated and had to accept the circumstances. They decided Saranti's place was already more pleasant and there were only two women there.

"Don't you think we should ask our father before making drastic changes?" Yiorgo asked.

"I guarantee he'll be fine with it. Put up the sign before he returns from Hora and there will be no further discussion. May I please say a few words about you two handsome boys. You are far too serious for your age. Have you noticed girls in the village who are secretly flirting with you? Talk to them, for heaven's sake." The boys were always polite and diplomatic. Papou wanted them to enjoy their youth, be more spontaneous.

"Their fathers would kill us. We're not permitted to even look their way." Strati was horrified at the thought. "Any communication will be with girls Christinaki's age."

Dimitri had dozed off. "Get a mule cart, boys. No way are we going to carry him up. We'll take our afternoon nap and then you can come back down for a swim."

He put Voula and Dimitri on the cart before climbing in. "I have a splendid idea. There will be a huge engagement party in the square. The entire upper and lower village will celebrate. This is where you can venture out and ask a girl to dance."

Both boys expressed their discomfort!

"How long did it take us to change the mindset of the gentlemen at the cafe? Only one day. That is what will happen at the party. As long as you remain respectful, there should not be an issue."

"Whose engagement my Georgios?"

"Ours, my love. The finest bouzouki and clarinet players on the island will entertain us." He lifted her off the cart then picked up Dimitri and laid him in his bed.

"Many things have transpired today, Papou. Strati and I don't think we can sleep."

"Lie down close to the little one and if sleep eludes you, go to the seaside." He embraced them and was filled with adoration for his great grandchildren including Dimitraki.

When he came out, Voula was dancing around in circles, laughing and crying at the same time.

He took her hand and led her to the back of the house, held her face and kissed her moist lips for the first time. She moaned and her breasts pressed softly against his chest. At that moment he knew, lovemaking would not be a problem for him.

CHAPTER 34

Marika and Saranti arrived at the lagoon. They were deliriously happy since they didn't anticipate taking another trip this soon.

"Why aren't you descending? Are we going to admire the gorgeous view first? I was wondering, there won't be a place to stay along the way during the cold months?"

"Have faith, my sweet. You don't think our private world will be disrupted by a few winter months? I simply will not allow it. Now, look directly across the mountain at an opening between two peaks. We are going there before we go down to the sea."

He drove the cart around a dirt path that led to the cave entrance. "Stay here until I give you a signal." He dragged packages that were tied with a rope beneath the cart into the slit in the mountain.

Marika was getting restless. "May I please come with you?"

"Wait until I finish. Then, I will welcome you into my palace." There was a platform that he often used when he traveled in the cold weather. He covered it with blankets and cushions. This is where he went to quietly fantasize about Marika. He cleaned out the fireplace and added a few touches that he brought with him. There was a candelabra that held nine candles he always had on a stone next to where he slept. "Okay, my love. Here is our palace." He helped her inside.

"How cozy. There is even a fireplace with a chimney for the smoke. The candle holder is an unusual touch. Where did it come from?"

"I received it many years ago but there was no name attached. I keep it here for comfort. Do you like it?"

"Very much." For some reason Papou came to mind.

Saranti pulled her legs from under her. She screamed and fell backwards onto the platform. He held her wrists above her head with one hand and peeled off her clothes with the other. They were both on fire. "When my time comes, I want to die here looking into your eyes." He kissed her passionately and undressed himself quickly. His tongue darted into her mouth and he swallowed her sweet sighs in gulps. After their lovemaking, they fell into a deep restful sleep.

Marika woke up first and was startled. "Saranti, get up. We have to get to Hora before nightfall to purchase the jewelry."

"Let's take a dive first and we'll leave after we have a bite."

"It is so comfortable here our nap took up half a day. There won't be time to shop but we can visit Kiria Popie."

"Let's go down and splash around. We'll have to check in at the hotel, visit Kambos and shop in the morning."

They came out of the cave naked, got into the mule cart and flew down the mountainside. Marika screamed for the Holy Mother to protect them. Saranti was laughing as they crashed at the bottom, jumped from the cart and ran into the sea. She was still afraid to swim and held onto him.

"I thought you were over that."

"I've only been swimming once in my life. This makes twice."

"Forgive me, Marika." He began licking the salt water from her body.

"Stop. We'll never get out of here."

"But it tastes good, my sweet

"Never mind…Don't quit unless there's an earthquake." She was breathless. Her breasts were barely above the water. Her head was tossed back and her long hair floated behind her. When her ankles went over his shoulders, it gave him license to play between her legs. He used his mouth and hands, parting and nibbling. When he bit her clitoris, she trembled and pushed herself into his face calling out his name. There was no holding back for either of them. Even though he hadn't entered her, they both had orgasms.

"I always knew you would be fiery." They weren't finished yet. He slowly inserted himself into her and moved at a slow pace as if the waves were controlling his movements. With each push the fire grew into slow long climaxes.

"I can't get enough of you, Marika. My dreams were full of lovemaking and now you are mine, all of you. There aren't enough hours or days for us."

She heard drumbeats in her chest as he carried her out of the water and placed her on a towel. The sunlight flickered in their eyes as they held each other and rolled back and forth playfully.

"This is our paradise, my sweet." They listened to the music of the waves lapping on the shore.

CHAPTER 35

During the trip, they talked about Papou. "People say we have similar features. Of course, it is well-known each of us has a clone in this world. He is a nice looking man who doesn't look his age."

"He is intelligent and kind. Dimitraki is completely under his spell. Best of all, he has changed the widow's life as well as his own. He was lonely, Saranti. Now he has us and Paraskevoula. As far as the resemblance...it is remarkable."

"Isn't that amazing! I'm proud to be his double. Funny thing, he was in Thessaloniki where I was born. Did he ever mention the hospital he worked in?"

"No. He only talked about his daughter being taken by the Germans." Marika wasn't sure if she should hint that they were related. Papou wanted to be the one to tell him. It would be disruptive if she mentioned anything.

"Let's visit Kiria Popie." She changed the subject. "We can do our shopping in the morning and then head back."

"We'll rest at the lagoon on the way home."

"Not for more than a couple of hours. It should keep us satisfied till our next trip."

"Marika, my sweet. I can't get enough of you. Show me your breasts," he smiled at her and his blue eyes had a playful twinkle.

"Wouldn't it be embarrassing if another traveler saw me exposing my breasts? How fast would they run us out of the village?" She looked around and there wasn't a soul to be seen. She threw her shawl over her shoulders, unbuttoned her dress to her cleavage and gave him a quick peak before covering up.

Saranti went crazy and almost drove over the mountainside.

She screamed and grabbed hold of him. "Be careful, my love."

"I'll fix you tonight in our room. Where did you learn such naughty things?"

"I always try to do what you want. Sometimes it isn't easy but I'm learning."

He stopped the mule cart. "You had better climb into the back. We don't want anyone to see you sitting with me."

"No one would be on the road in this heat. They're taking their afternoon siesta."

"You know, my Marika, we are not the only ones who are in love. Maybe others are in the same predicament and are looking for privacy." He helped her to the back, didn't see a soul so he kissed and bit her lips. "You are my life.

CHAPTER 36

The sun was disappearing as they arrived in town. "I am hot, dusty and in great need of a shower, Saranti."

"We'll be at the hotel in a heartbeat. Since the shops are closed, we'll bathe and head for Kambos."

Spyro was not surprised when they arrived at the hotel. Papou had phoned ahead to make sure room 101 was available and their things were taken there immediately.

"There is no time for you know what, Saranti. Let's shower and go. We have the entire night to play."

"What did you call it? You know what! Ha, ha, ha. That is funny. You have it all planned out, don't you? It didn't take long for you to boss me around."

"I would never do such a thing." She was embarrassed by his remarks. "I'm merely making suggestions. You are the man and will always have the last word."

"I was teasing you, my sweet. We'll do as you say. Kiria Popie will be glad to see us. I'll ask Spyro to send someone to pick up food and have a carriage ready for us.

CHAPTER 37

K ambos was aromatic and lush but instead of enjoying the ride Marika was uneasy. "Saranti, I have a feeling something is wrong. A tightness in my chest usually means a tragedy. Stop for a moment and hold me."

Saranti remembered hearing about Marika's premonitions. He held her close and spoke soothing words.

When they arrived, the gates were open and Mano was moving his personal property out. "Mr. Saranti, we lost her a few days ago. It happened fast. I didn't have the heart to call you. She's been buried already."

"What about the girls. Did they come?"

"They refuse to come to Chios after what happened to their father. They were devastated. when I told them. They wanted her to stay with them in Ohio. Regarding the property, they refuse to have anything to do with it. She left me this place but there is no way I can support it. I'll have to put it up for sale and send the proceeds to the girls."

"You will do no such thing. She wanted you to stay here. The expenses will be handled. Besides, I have been coming here for years and will continue to visit. Where is she buried?"

"Near the fountain next to her husband."

"Let's take your things back into the house, Mano."

"I have a letter for you, Mr. Saranti. I found it beneath her pillow."

"You were her loyal friend. She wouldn't have survived this long if it weren't for you."

"Being with her was an honor. Your support is what kept us going."

Marika walked through the garden remembering Kiria Popie's grace and kindness. She picked jasmines and made a bouquet for her grave. Although they only met that one time, she was deeply saddened by her death.

"I think you should find a person without ties or property to share this place with you. A poor widow or family. There is plenty of space and you shouldn't be alone."

"I'll consider it. Kiria Popie would approve, I'm sure."

Saranti and Mano walked through the house. They went into the bedroom where she took her last breath. There was an indentation in her pillow that had ivory lace crochet around the edges. Mano picked it up and smelled it. Suddenly he began sobbing. "She made this herself. This home was always in order and everything you see was designed by her hands. The dresser scarves, the chair covers, the towelettes... look at the colors. She was always busy working on beautiful things. The gardens were her creations. Of course, I helped but could never compete with her exquisite taste."

Saranti placed his hand on Mano's shoulder. "We're only travelers on this earth. It is inevitable that we'll meet on the other side. Don't shed more tears. Let this be an opportunity to spread joy for others. It is what she would have wanted."

"Yes, yes. There was a poor family that she assisted. She gave them vegetables from the garden and blankets in the winter among other necessities. I will invite them to stay here with me. At least they will have warmth in the winter and food in their bellies."

Marika was sitting on the steps and listening to the fountain when they came out of the house. "Kiria Popie is with Fatih and very happy." She laid the flowers on her grave and said a prayer.

They didn't speak on the way back. Marika knew that Saranti wanted to remember his surrogate mother. It was quiet and dark as though Kambos was in mourning. An occasional horse trotting by briefly broke the silence.

An ache in his heart brought him to the brink of tears. He controlled himself for Marika's sake. She held his hand hoping to comfort him. *How sad Papou didn't meet her, she thought.*

"Are you hungry, my sweet. I left the food for Mano."

"Maybe we should have a meze by the sea. I'd like to listen to the waves break against the rocks."

He didn't answer but drove the carriage directly to the Seaside Taverna where they had met Papou. They walked slowly and deliberately to a small lonely table that was waiting near the water. A waiter ran over and dropped plates of sea-fare for them. The waves crashed at their feet.

"The last time we were here, it was special."

"Being together is special, Saranti. Don't allow yourself to be hurt. She wouldn't want that. You will miss her for sure but the memories are everlasting." She always knew what to say to make things better. "When will you read her letter?"

"I'll wait till I am emotionally stronger."

They managed to eat a few morsels and then left for the hotel.

CHAPTER 38

The morning brought another round of sadness. Neither wanted to talk or eat. They had slept but had unusual dreams. Marika was walking in gardens searching for someone beyond her reach. Saranti was speaking with Popie asking when she would return. "Return from where? I am here beside you," she said gaily.

"The stores won't open till ten. Let's have a coffee at Vounaki."

They were surprised to find Mano in the square. His eyes were red and swollen. "I've been here most of the night. I was unable to stay at the house alone. Maybe I'll see the Poulos family. Despina is a widow. Her son and daughter spend a lot of time doing odd jobs in Hora. Kosta is eleven and Eleni is nine."

"I'm surprised you can see anything. Your eyes are slits."

"I know, Saranti. I spent the whole night grieving."

Marika took his hands into hers. "You must allow her to rest. She can't move on if you're weeping. Fond memories will keep her with you."

He buried his face in his hands and sobbed. Suddenly he heard familiar voices calling his name. He recognized the Poulos children. They came up to him and explained they heard about Kiria Popie. "She was a wonderful lady," Eleni told him. She had helped them through many traumas. It was painful to think they were now on their own.

Mrs. Poulos was thin and fragile looking. Her dark eyes were hollow and she always looked frightened. Both her children had the face of desperation. It was pitiful.

Mano reached out to them. "I am thinking I would prefer not to live at the house alone. Perhaps you would consider staying with me. There is plenty of room and the food would not be an issue. The garden is filled with everything."

"But we have no money," Mrs. Poulos cried out.

"Funny thing, I don't expect anything but your friendship. Kosta and Eleni will thrive in the environment. Now that Popie is gone, I could use the company."

"We have a few things in the shack. The children can stay with you while I pack." She was excited thinking they would be living in such a beautiful environment.

Saranti got up and hailed a horse and buggy. "Marika and I will help you pack."

The kids were stunned and weren't sure how to react until Mano embraced them. They relaxed and began chattering at once wanting to know which room would be theirs and where they could play. "Can I go to the school in Kambos?" Kosta asked.

"We'll work everything out once you settle in." Mano was a larger than life, a man with a big heart and sense of humor. The children always cared for him and Kiria Popie. They enjoyed visiting them and left with full stomachs and nice gifts. Now, they would be a permanent part of the mansion, which was a dream come true.

Kiria Despina was back in a flash with two small bags. It seemed they didn't have much.

"Take the children and go home Mano. Kiria Despina has shopping to do and she'll come when we're through." Saranti gave Mano the horse and buggy. He, Marika and Despina went to the stores.

Despina was embarrassed to purchase anything until Saranti scolded her. "This is a personal favor in honor of Kiria Popie. It will be an insult if you don't accept. You and the children are making a fresh start."

They watched her depart with the packages in the only taxi in Chios and laughed as she continuously made the sign of the cross.

"I have never loved you more than I do at this moment." Marika's eyes were brimming with tears.

CHAPTER 39

Saranti and Marika refreshed themselves at the lagoon. It was a short break but a welcome one. After all, it would be a while before they could travel again. Saranti broke down and read Kiria Popie's letter. She expressed her love, thanked him for taking care of her and wrote she knew without a doubt he would keep an eye on Mano. "My place is yours whenever you need solace. Mano should bring someone to stay with him. He needs the company. The Poulos family comes to mind. I'm sure you will handle it, my precious son. Keep Marika happy. Life is short."

Saranti tossed his head back and laughed. "It is as if she's here with us. She even expressed an interest in having the Poulos family stay with Mano." The pain he felt was somehow alleviated. "She wants me to keep you happy, my sweet. Are you?"

Marika kissed him and traced his face with her fingers. "You are my greatest joy, my love."

CHAPTER 40

They pulled into the village at nightfall and found the square lit up. The musicians' stage was at the foot of the cafe. Hundreds of colored lights hung from above. A mass of tables dressed in blue and white covered the plaza.

Saranti scratched his head when he saw cafe sign welcoming women. "This was definitely orchestrated by Papou."

"He is a clever man, Saranti. Your business will probably triple."

"I'll save a table for you next to the spot where I work."

"Oh, no! I would be embarrassed to be seen at the cafe."

"It wouldn't be bad if you were with Papou, Paraskevoula and the boys. You are coming to the engagement, right?"

"Oh yes. I wouldn't miss it."

"There's Papou, Marika. What in the world is he doing here at this hour?"

He ran towards them. "Isn't it beautiful? The festivities will commence in the morning...music, dancing and food all day long. We'll exchange rings in the early evening. Did you bring the jewelry?"

"Let me show you. It is stunning. My goodness Papou, the square has never been this lovely."

They went into the clinic and laid out each piece. "I purchased 24-carat gold. You said nothing but the best for Paraskevoula."

"You have exquisite taste. One day we will be buying these for you, my Marika." Papou said. "It is almost finished and the men will remain until every last thing is done. Paraskevoula knows about the engagement party but she doesn't know details. Saranti, please take us up. I don't think she realizes I'm gone. I slipped away when she fell asleep. The boys are at the house with Dimitraki. I'm surprised he didn't follow me down here," he chuckled

Paraskevoula was awake, sitting in a chair with Dimitri on her lap. "It was hard to keep him home when he discovered you had left. Where, may I ask, did you go at this hour?"

Dimitri went to Papou and took his hand. "Why did you leave me Papou?"

"I want to welcome Marika and Saranti back from their trip. You were sleeping." He picked up Dimitri. "Let me put you to bed."

His mother gave him a big hug and kiss. "Growing boys need their sleep."

"You know what they say about people who walk at night…they step in mud and…"

"Don't say it Voulitsa. Let's go to sleep. Tomorrow is a big day, my sweetheart." He sighed. *I can't get away with a thing in this family, he thought.*

CHAPTER 41

"Papou…Papou…Dimitri shook him. Wake up. I smell loukoumades."

"I know son. The smell is coming from the square. We'll wash up and go down to eat."

Strati and Yiorgo came out. "Dimitri, you don't leave Papou alone for one minute. He needs his rest. Come with us. We laid out your clothes."

"Papou should pick out my shirt and pants," he whined.

"Paraskevoula, wear your beautiful blue dress and we'll go down for coffee."

"This early, my Georgios?"

"Get ready, my love. I have a surprise for you."

CHAPTER 42

T he square was already packed with people
from upper and lower Kardamyla partaking
in loukoumades and coffee. Lambs and pigs
were roasting on a spit. The musicians were tuning
their instruments. Papou held Paraskevoula's hand
while Dimitri trailed next to him to hear his conversations. He welcomed everyone to the festivities.

She was too shy to say much. One of the ladies
said her dress was the color of Dr. Cohen's eyes.
"That's why I picked this fabric." She was proud to
be the center of attention,

"My wonderful Georgios. Is this what you were
up to last night? I can't wait to be your wife."

"Sooner rather than later. We'll take off after we
exchange rings and go to the synagogue in Hora.
I've booked a suite at the hotel. I hope you're ready
to be mine!"

Suddenly, she had butterflies in her stomach. "I'm
afraid but just a little."

"So am I, my love. But just a little," he laughed
and pinched her sun-kissed cheeks. "You are lovely."

The square looked magical and the people were enjoying themselves. Even the widows came without flinching. A few of the ladies were actually smoking. This was the beginning of the modernization of Kardamyla.

Georgios felt a tap on his shoulder. "I wouldn't miss this if there was an earthquake. I'm spending the entire day here to celebrate with you my good friend. The monastery can wait!"

"Mitso," Georgios shouted and embraced him. "You have made this day complete. I know it is early but I remember you enjoyed your ouzo. Let's get a bottle."

The monk began drinking with Georgios. He was a young man the last time he had a drink. He was dizzy in zero time but continued to sip. "To hell with fasting. Today is for feasting." He ripped off a piece of lamb from the spit, dunked it in his ouzo and ate it ravenously smacking his lips."

"The old Jew is having fun. Gabriel is the best monk we ever had in this village." People were commenting. "The doctor calls him Mitso. It must have been his name before he joined monastic life."

"I didn't know he was friends with the doctor. I heard they knew each other in Thessaloniki during their youth."

"Has anyone noticed Saranti resembles Dr. Cohen."

"They both have blue eyes."

"More than that. When I see them together, I think they're related."

"Ridiculous. We knew his mother and father. Unless she had an affair with the doctor, it isn't possible. He's too old. Anyway, Cohen was never in this village and she didn't leave here until she was at least five months along."

"You're right. He is too old to be his father."

Georgios overheard the comments. *Maybe he should tell Saranti the truth, he thought.* He asked Mitso if he was listening but the old monk was woozy and didn't pay attention. Georgios sat him at the family table. "Stay here till the music starts and then we'll dance if you can remember how."

"I was always a better dancer than you Georgios. You can bet I haven't forgotten! I can kick up my legs higher than your head." He slapped his thighs and downed another drink. "Bring me chunk of lamb and a piece of pig."

"Try to keep the food out of your beard." He dropped two huge plates of food in front of the monk. "After I dance with my bride to be, I'll be back for a zeimbekiko, you old goat. We'll see who can really dance."

Marika and the boys showed up dressed in their finest. The boys were quite handsome. They wore ties and white shirts. Their hair was cropped properly and their eyes were filled with excitement at the prospect of meeting girls. Except for their coloring, Strati and Yiorgo were the image of Saranti. "Papou, papou," Dimitri shouted, "How do I look? Is my shirt the right color?"

"You are perfect son. All of you come and sit with the monk. Remember what I taught you young men. When you want to dance with a girl you will go to her table and address the head of the family asking for permission in a polite way. Once it's granted, then pull out her chair and take her hand. The rest is easy. Don't dance too close."

"But Papou, Christinaki will never let Strati dance with another girl," Dimitraki said.

"He'll have to work it out with her."

Saranti was in the cafe making coffees and whistling every once in a while to get Marika's attention. She pretended not to hear but her heart thundered in response.

"One day, you and Saranti will be together. For now, enjoy the interludes. By the way, this belongs to you." He dropped a gold necklace in her hand.

"I couldn't...."

"Oh but you will. It is but a token for my wonderful new life. You cannot refuse!"

At this moment, she was content and gave Papou a sweet smile. She was happy to see Angeliki and Koula since both their husbands were away on freighters and they didn't go anywhere but to church and her house. They embraced and began chatting about their lives.

"Where's the monk?" Papou asked.

"He is inebriated and can barely walk." Marika told him.

"Papou, he is at the outhouse. Should I find him for you?" Dimitri wanted to be helpful.

"Please son. I'm worried he may take a fall."

Dimitri returned holding the Monk's hand and trying to keep him stable. The old man swayed back and forth singing Greek songs that he recalled from his youth.

"Mitso, sit here by me until it's time to dance."

"Papou, he left his underwear in the outhouse. I tried to put it on him but he wouldn't stop moving."

"Thank you, son. This is one hell of a mess. I don't think he realizes it." He and Dimitri had a good laugh. "Keep an eye on him for me when I dance with my Voula."

The three girls were amused when they overheard Dimitraki talk about the monk. Koula hoped he wouldn't take a fall and expose himself. Marika felt sorry for him.

"Maybe we should find his underpants and return them." Angeliki whispered.

"Only you would do that," Koula shook her head. "How embarrassing for poor Gabriel and for you, foolish girl. How do you suppose you could give a drunk man his underwear?"

"I guess you're right. But I'm worried. He has always been a pillar in the community. Now he is drunk and out of control."

The band started playing Syrto, a bouncy island dance. Papou and Voula had perfect rhythm together which surprised them both. The crowds encircled them and clapped. He waved them on to dance and watched for his grandsons to join in. Per Dimitri's prediction, Christinaki hung on Strati's leg and there was no way he could take another girl for a spin.

Yiorgo, however, was free to roam and he was smart enough to request the mother's hand before asking for permission to take the daughters to the floor.

When the band finally played a perfect *zeimbekiko*, the old monk rose up and tripped to the dance floor. "Cohen," he slurred his words. "Here is where I show you how it's done." He snapped his fingers and dragged his legs. The people gathered 'round to clap him on. Although Papou was worried, he decided to accommodate his friend and took a few dips. When he heard the screaming and laughing, he turned to see his friend kicking up his heels exposing his unmentionables.

"The Monk Gabriel has perfect parts," they yelled. The women were not fazed. They rather enjoyed the demonstration. The men, however, were upset to see their women relishing the show.

"Papou tried unsuccessfully to cover him up but he kept jumping up and kicking his heels until he fell back onto the dirt dance floor and passed out. Papou pulled down his robe and asked for help to take him into the clinic. "Bring a lot of raw unions," he yelled as they carried him in and laid him on the exam table. They plastered his private parts with onions, covered him up and strapped him down.

"Dimitri, please stay with him." Papou knew Mitso wasn't going anywhere for a while but he wanted to keep Dimitri occupied since he was planning an exit with the small yacht in the harbor.

"Anything you say, Papou."

When he walked out, he heard the women discussing his friend's exhibition. "Dr. Georgios," a widow called out to him. "If the old monk decides to take off his robes permanently, I would be interested." She giggled.

"I'll let him know. Now that it is over, perhaps we can concentrate on the engagement." He stopped the music and motioned to his family to come up with Paraskevoula. Marika, Saranti and the two boys came to the middle of the dirt dance floor and brought him the jewelry.

"My beautiful Voula. You have made my life complete." He kissed her forehead and reached for the first piece of gold which he hung on her neck. With every kiss he added more gold ropes, pins, bracelets and rings. Paraskevoula and Marika were both crying.

There were whispers coming from everywhere. "She deserves this."

"Who would have known someone would come along and rescue her. And, he's handsome too."

"The jewelry is exquisite." A few women sighed hoping they would be next. Everyone gathered around the couple offering best wishes.

The men felt they couldn't compete with the doctor. They respected him but could never be the man he was. He always gave them good advice about their women and most of it worked fairly well. So what if they couldn't afford fancy things. He said their girls would enjoy flowers and a trip to the cafe with them. An occasional pretty gift from the boutique always warmed them up.

When the music began, Georgios whisked Paraskevoula away to the yacht that was waiting in the small harbor. "Stay here Voulitsa. I can't leave without saying goodbye to Dimitraki. He would be hurt."

A large, blond woman climbed off of the yacht. She had wide masculine shoulders, huge hands and big feet. Her hair was in a bun high on her head. She was attractive in an odd sort of way. Her brown eyes were deep set and topped with feathered brows. Her nose was the only small thing about her. When she smiled her lips almost reached her ears. Her face had a curious cross between determination and humor.

"Dr. Eva, it is nice to see you again."

"You too my friend." She towered over him. "Which way to the clinic?"

He took her arm and led her back. "This is where you will practice till I return. I appreciate your help. I didn't want to leave my friends without a doctor."

Eva knew the villagers would be uncomfortable with her at first, especially since she was a female doctor. The men wouldn't want any sort of exam. Unless there was an emergency, there wouldn't be much work for her in the clinic. Well, she figured, she would be gone in a few days anyway. She would try to have some fun. Dr. Georgios confided that the men in the village refused to have a prostate exam. She could scare them into complying. It wouldn't be the first time.

He walked in to find Dimitri sleeping in a chair next to the monk. "Dimitraki," Papou ran his fingers through his curly hair. "May I introduce you to Dr. Eva. She will fill in for me while I'm away. I want you to take care of her."

The boy rubbed his eyes and gazed up at this giant woman. His expression was comical. He couldn't fathom a woman being that big.

"Papou, where are you going?"

"Paraskevoula and I are going to Hora to be married. You are the man of the family until I return."

"I'll miss you, my Papou." He threw his arms around him. "Don't be afraid. Everything will be accomplished, respectfully. as you taught me."

Georgios had tears in his eyes when he left. He loved his great grandchildren but had a special place in his heart for Dimitraki. He couldn't love him more if he was blood.

"I'm going out to have some fun, Dimitri. Come with me and make introductions. You don't need to be here. The old guy won't move a muscle for a long time."

Dimitri took Eva's hand and led her to the family table. He kind of took to her but was continuously staring. He couldn't believe any woman could be so big. "This is the new doctor until Papou returns." She met Marika and the other ladies. "Do you have husbands here tonight? If not take me around and introduce me to the married women with escorts."

They thought her behavior was strange but complied with her wishes. She launched a campaign of fear regarding what she referred to as the family jewels. The women were on to her but she put fear in the men indicating they could be subject to removal of their parts if they didn't come in for a physical.

"Didn't Dr. Cohen tell you? Something serious is going around and can infect the men. Come in right away for an exam before it's too late. Don't be cowards." The word spread like fire and the men decided to submit to the exam for fear that time was running out. "Is it too late?" someone asked.

"Who knows? We can stop it if you hurry."

"The giant will tear us apart," Simo said. "Let's go together tomorrow morning and get this thing over with before we have serious problems."

She winked at the wives. "Think how bad it would be if these guys had to give birth". The women really enjoyed her. "If you men need support, bring your wives along.

CHAPTER 43

PAPOU COHEN'S HONEYMOON

Georgios and Paraskevoula were married and he took her to the hotel for the night. Spyro was on duty and when he saw the two of them, he couldn't believe his eyes. Dr. Cohen was an older version of Saranti.

"This is my wife Paraskevoula. Did you prepare our suite?"

"Of course, doctor. It is perfect. We have extra help in case you need something." Although I doubt it with this beauty in your arms. Both Saranti and the doctor won the lotto. He felt envious. Maybe I should visit Kardamyla to find a beautiful woman, he thought.

Paraskevoula was taken aback. She had never been out of the village and this hotel was exotic. Her eyes were saucers when they entered the suite. It was decorated with flowers and candles.

"I have something for you to wear tonight. I didn't give you the opportunity to pack. There are a couple of dresses in the closet."

"I actually forgot I would need clothes. I assumed we would be returning tomorrow. Is the bedroom through that door?" She walked into the luxurious room. "Am I dreaming?"

Georgios kissed her and gave her the satin and lace nightgown to wear. "Do you want to shower first or shall I?"

She didn't know how to use anything in the bathroom and called him in to help.

"It really is a lot easier than what we have in the village. As a matter of fact, we'll have a similar one in our home."

"Our home?"

"Didn't I tell you? The big house by the sea is your wedding present. The one you always admired."

Her mouth was open but she didn't say anything.

He slapped her behind. "Hurry up. I need you."

When he got into bed with her and started to play, she kept her eyes closed. "Don't you want to see what I'm doing?

"Why should I? I can feel everything." She was shy about seeing him nude.

"Ok, but can you pretend we're dancing." She opened one eye and closed it immediately. "You are naked."

"Well how else to you think this is done." He stripped her slowly and played with her kissing and caressing her various parts. She jumped a couple of times but that didn't deter him. He was turned on and suspected she was too. When he finally put his lips on her breasts, she screamed. "Good or bad," he asked and continued his mission. She didn't answer him but was ready to explode.

"Which dance do you want me to do?"

"The Syrto is fine. I can't hold back any more. Are you ready?"

He turned on his back and put her on top. She could really swing her hips and had her very first orgasm in years. He came immediately after her. "Wow. This was great. How much longer are you going to keep your eyes closed."

"I'm not sure, my Georgios. Please put on your pajamas and then I'll open them."

Her soft breasts were in his face and he loved looking up at her. "Okay. If that's what you want." He slipped on his bottoms and laid next to her. He didn't expect having sex with her would be so easy considering his age. The timing was perfect and he knew she was satisfied. He was ready for more and began playing with her again.

"May I bathe?"

"Not unless I can come with you."

"Does that mean no pajamas?"

"It sure does. If that's a problem, keep your eyes shut and I'll wash you."

"You mean everywhere?"

"Is there another way?" She was adorable in his eyes and he found the whole experience humorous. Eventually, she would yield, he thought. Till then, they would enjoy it the way she wanted. Still, it was wonderful.

They woke up several times during the night to experiment. She enjoyed everything he did. Finally, she touched him but wouldn't look. "Oh my goodness. It is a large one."

"Do you want to see it? At some point you will. It isn't awful you know."

"Okay a quick look. Oh, you are right, my Georgios. It is smooth and pretty."

"Pretty? Good grief. I'm a man!" He roared over that remark.

"I'm starving Voulitsa. Shall we go out and get orange juice and sweets in the square."

She was ready in a flash and excited to finally see Hora. When they arrived at the square Georgios explained how he met Marika and Saranti.

"My Georgios, now that I am your wife, you can confide in me. You shouldn't keep secrets."

He broke down and explained his relationship to Saranti. "No one must know until I'm ready to tell him about his real family. I don't want him to be hurt."

"How can he possibly be more hurt than he was from the people who raised him. They continuously berated him for not resembling the family. There is a precious bond between you. It is time to tell him the truth. I'm sorry your life has been desperately sad. But that is behind you know."

Georgios was crying quietly. "I love him and my new family more than my life."

"As I love you." She kissed his eyes. "I won't press you, my Georgios by asking too many questions that you may not be ready to answer. One thing though. I have the distinct feeling Marika and Saranti are in love." By the expression on his face, she knew it was true.

He took her hand. "Let's stroll around the town and pick up a couple of things for the boys. We'll eat this afternoon at the Seaside Taverna where I met Saranti.

"I want to go home tonight, my Georgios. Is our home ready?"

"It is in ariston condition. If you want to go back, how about in the morning?"

"I won't mind another night of lovemaking," she said softly. "Maybe I'll open my eyes."

He was having a lot of fun with her school girl antics. It was as though this was her first time.

I'm not far behind, he was thinking. It has been more years than I can count. I guess you never forget because it was incredible.

CHAPTER 44

When Georgios and Paraskevoula returned from their trip, they went directly to their new home. It was ultramodern and she wondered if she would ever get used to it. It looked great but how would she cook? She didn't have the vaguest idea about the appliances. They spent the night there before returning to the square. No one knew they were in the village and were surprised to see them hand in hand walking to the clinic. When the newlyweds showed up, Eva had Strati and Yiorgo with her, explaining different procedures that she performed. The boys were proud to be learning from Eva and were excited to tell Papou what they had learned.

"She's been teaching us interesting things, Papou. We were allowed to stay through several exams. Also, we've been sewing wounds on the patient doll she brought with her. I'm sure we can close up cuts if necessary."

"I didn't think I'd have many patients but it blossomed. Besides the men, there were some minor accidents and digestion problems from over eating at your engagement."

"We observed Dr. Eva in a several instances and I'm sure we are capable of handling it." Yiorgo told him.

"No doubt about it. You were born to be doctors. Where's Dimitri?"

"He is ordering lunch from next door." Eva said they would be eating at the cafe with Marika.

"What ever happened to Mitso?"

"A hand full of mean looking monks came for him. He was plenty sick and embarrassed when they dragged him out. What kind of punishment will he receive for breaking monastic rules? Starvation? Prayers on his knees day and night?"

"Poor Mitso. Don't think we'll be seeing him any time soon. I wonder what happened to his underwear?"

They went to the family table and when Dimitri saw Papou he flew into his arms. "I didn't know you'd be home so soon, Papou. Why didn't you tell me about the new house and that you are leaving us?"

"Dimitraki, you should know better than to think I can be without you. We'll see each other every day. Now that you'll be going back school I'll have to review your work. I'll visit the upper village often. It was my very first home and I love it."

"But you won't be there when I wake up!"

"Papou spends more time with you than anybody else, including Paraskevoula." Strati was taunting him. "Stop complaining."

Yiorgo explained to Dimitri that Papou needed alone time with his wife.

Paraskevoula asked Marika if she could continue working at the boutique. "I want to be productive. Since Georgios will be working next door at the clinic, I'd rather not be alone. I should ask your permission, my Georgios."

"Are you joking? You don't need my yes or no. You are a grown woman who can make up her own mind, my love."

Marika told her she would welcome the company. "You are an excellent seamstress. I was surprised at how well you did considering the years you spent away from the needle."

"Let's get some food in our bellies," Saranti showed up with ouzo, coffee and soft drinks.

Dimitri climbed onto Papou's lap and was about to doze off. "First you have to eat son."

"I guess I will be going back to Thessaloniki sooner than I thought."

"Why is that Eva? I could use your help. I need some free time to spend with my wife. Besides, I think the boys will benefit from your surgical skills."

"Shall I stay a little longer? I kind of enjoy these folks. I'll sleep at the clinic for now."

"I heard what you did to the men. Did they finally submit?"

"They weren't happy about it but most of them showed up. I'm expecting a few more in the next couple of days. They were scared to death." She laughed heartily.

"Dimitraki is in another world. Get the mule cart boys and let's go to my place. I brought you a few things from Hora. Saranti, why don't you take Marika up and help her pull out some of our belongings." Papou wanted to give them time together. "Eva come along with us."

CHAPTER 45

The veranda at Papou's home was huge and hovered over the sea. It was covered in cushioned loungers, umbrellas and large plants. They tucked Dimitri in a corner and each one found a spot to lie down. The ocean waves made them drowsy and they fell into a deep sleep. The moment Strati and Yiorgo opened their eyes they dove into the sea to cool off. Eva jumped in after them without changing. She swam deep into the water amazing the boys. When she came up, she resembled a sea dragon. The boys tried to dunk her but she was too strong for them and she took both of them down with one easy push of their heads.

Paraskevoula and Papou went to the kitchen to make coffee and serve sweets they brought from Hora. "These are the first things I'm serving in our new home, my Georgios." She handed him a cup of Greek coffee and a spoon to dig into the sweets.

"How did I get so lucky," he kissed her. "Let me help you put these out. Let's call the children. They've been in the hot sun far too long."

"Papou did you see Eva? She is so strong we couldn't even dunk her." Strati and Yiorgo were enjoying her company. "Swimming with Eva is a lot of fun. She isn't afraid of anything. Not even the sea monsters we told her about."

"Where are the towels?" Her wet clothes were stuck to her humongous body. She couldn't wrap herself in the small towels and decided to dry off just as she was.

"Why is Dimitri still asleep?" Yiorgo wanted to get him up.

"Let him sleep." Saranti came up to the veranda. "Here are some of your things and Marika is on her way with more." Papou handed him a cup of coffee and he sipped off the foam. "This is as good as mine."

Papou noticed Saranti's eyes light up when Marika came. His family was together and he couldn't be more content. He wondered if it was time to reveal his secret but decided he needed more time. Everyone was happy and he didn't want to pose any stress on Saranti.

Marika went to Dimitri and kissed his forehead. "He usually doesn't sleep this late. It must be the ocean breezes." He didn't budge.

Everyone spoke at once as they were downing the sweets. The boys had two and three helpings. Eva ate a whole bowl of fig jam. "It is a good thing we bought plenty." Papou told them.

"We love this Papou. Can we have more tomorrow?" Strati wanted to make darn sure there were extra helpings.

"There is enough for the next few days then we'll order more. Don't forget, school starts soon and all this playing around will have to be curbed. Studies come first." Papou put out tablets, pencils and book bags. "Eva, what do you think? Is there time for the boys to study medicine with us?"

"I'll expect them every day after school. Right fellows? If we have willing patients, the boys can observe. Georgios, they truly impressed me. They can handle anything without getting queasy."

"Saranti? You usually have work for them but I think this is far more important for their future. I don't want us to make assumptions if you are not on board."

"Papou, I was from the start. They should prepare for medical school in England."

Dimitri finally woke up. "Where am I?" He looked confused but was admiring the surroundings. "Eva, you're here too. What happened to your clothes?"

"I went for a swim. Didn't have a suit with me."

"You look funny. You will have to dry off before you go anywhere. My mom doesn't know how to enjoy herself. She would never go in the water for fear the villagers will say ugly things. Who cares? Papou says women have rights."

Marika picked him up and gave him a hug. "You slept a long time, Dimitraki. Come and have your favorite submarine." She handed him a glass of water with a spoon full of mastiha in it. He loved the way the white pastie sweet stuck to the roof of his mouth.

Saranti promised to show the boys where mastiha is harvested. He described the large bushes that are pierced allowing the sap to drip out and harden like diamonds. "Chios is the only place in the world where mastiha is produced. Besides gum and sweets, many other things are made from this substance. White sheets are wrapped under the base of the bush and the workers break off the pieces allowing them to fall and dry on the cloths. Next time I go to Hora, maybe I can bring you boys with me to visit the villages called Mastihohoria."

"Papou, your place is beautiful. No wonder you don't want to be in the upper village."

"Wanna swim." Yiorgo asked.

"Not now. I want to look around this house. Is there room for me if I want to stay?"

He started running around the house with the submarine in hand.

Marika was upset. "You would leave me alone?"

"Never. I wouldn't stay unless we were both invited."

"Papou, are these ours? I want the striped book bag."

"I was wondering when someone would ask. They are for you boys. Of course, you can have it, Dimitraki."

"Sorry, Papou. We didn't want to be ill mannered," Strati said seriously. "We thought you should tell us first. These are really nice. I suppose these tablets can be used to take medical notes."

"What can we learn in the village school? If we study medicine with you and Eva, that should be sufficient. We'll be prepared for England in no time." Yiorgo did not want to continue learning things that he deemed unimportant.

Papou explained to the boys it is imperative to have a well-rounded education. He told them they could not enter medical school without passing all subjects. He expects them to have perfect scores. "Think about how crucial it is to exercise your mind, fill it with knowledge. Medicine is your ultimate goal. As you study, your mind becomes a sponge and your grades are scores that the finest schools will review. You want to be the best medical professional in the field you chose to follow. That can be accomplished with dedication."

Everyone listened to Papou. Dimitraki decided to follow his example. He thought the boys were brighter and would probably do a better job but he wasn't going to let that deter him. Being a sea captain was a good career, also. "I intend to study even the subjects that don't interest me." He wanted Papou to be proud of him.

CHAPTER 46

"**D**octor, help. Hurry it's Koula. Doctor, please. There's blood everywhere." Angeliki was screaming.

"Eva, let's go. Everyone stays here."

"No, no, I need to help her."

Eva shook her and sat her in a chair.

The boys watched Papou and Eva hurry down the path and wanted desperately to go with them. They waited a few minutes and dove into the water. No one realized they were swimming to Koula's house.

"There was so much blood, she lost consciousness. I think the baby is gone," she sobbed. All three women cried.

Saranti tried to calm them saying she had the best doctors. "That doesn't help anyone." He wanted to embrace Marika and comfort her.

"Let Papou do his job. I have faith in him," Dimitraki said and held his mother's hand. "I think he's got more help. The boys are nowhere near this place. They probably followed them to Koula's."

"They wouldn't do that without permission." Saranti was boiling. "What do they know about pregnancies and women's issues."

"That's how they learn by observing and being there to help if necessary." Dimitri spoke seriously.

"They might be in the way." Saranti paced the floor. "Maybe I should go after them but I'm afraid of what I might do. I'm very angry."

Several hours passed and Papou finally came home with Strati and Yiorgo. They were pale as ghosts. They had never seen that much blood and thought Koula had died. Fortunately, Papou and Eva brought her around. The boys did what they could but were terrified when they saw Papou and Eva trying to save her life. They didn't have much to say and knew trouble was brewing by the way Saranti looked at them.

"Eva is spending the night at Koula's who is too weak to be transported to the clinic. I think it's a good idea to bring her sons here. She needs to rest and take her medication." Papou realized Saranti was angry. "Strati, Yiorgo, your assistance was invaluable and I am glad you didn't run away when you saw what was happening. If this didn't scare you away from the medical field, I doubt anything will. They were stoic, Saranti."

The boys stared at him in shock. Papou and Eva barked orders at them but they realized it was necessary to save Koula's life. They could barely talk. They felt every bit of their energy was drained from their body.

"Maybe Saranti can bring the children here while we rest." He put his arms around their shoulders and led them to comfortable seats. "Remember, when Koula's boys get here, we don't want to alarm them. The only thing they need to know is that she needs her rest. We won't say the baby is gone until tomorrow."

Dimitri went into the kitchen and brought sweets for everyone. "I hope this will bring color back into your faces. You look awful."

Saranti decided not to reprimand the boys when he saw the fear in their eyes. They wanted to help and didn't realize the magnitude of the problem. After all, Papou said they did well. "Relax. I'll bring Koula's sons here. I'm proud of the way you handled yourselves."

The boys were visibly shaken. They sat on the loungers and looked at the sea. Papou knew they were traumatized. They were far too young to have such experiences. Still, they handled themselves better than some doctors would have. Poor Koula did not heed his warnings and ended up losing her child. There wouldn't be another pregnancy for her. She took it terribly hard. The boys witnessed everything.

The women were huddled and crying. They wanted to see Koula but Papou was emphatic. "Absolutely no contact for at least two or three days. She doesn't need emotional disturbances. Besides she is under sedation. Eva and I will take turns staying with her. You can take care of her boys."

CHAPTER 47

VISITING STRATI AND YIORGO IN OXFORD

Saranti and Papou boarded the flight to London from the Athens Airport. Strati and Yiorgo had been going to school in England for four years with only two brief visits to Kardamyla. They were sorely missed and their father decided it was time to pay them a surprise visit. Saranti wanted to be with his sons for the holidays.

It was difficult for him to leave Marika but ten days was not a long time to be away. Nothing had changed between them except their love was deeper. Their relationship continued when they went to Hora once a month. The years were rapidly escaping and he wanted to be with her on a permanent basis but there was no chance for a divorce from his wife. He felt the villagers suspected they were having an affair but they didn't discuss it openly. They admired

Marika for showing love and commitment when she adopted Katina and nursed her to health.

Something was bothering Saranti and he wasn't sure how to approach it. He saw Papou lighting a candle one night and remembered the candelabra he received years ago. Perhaps, it was coincidental that both had the same one. Was it a Jewish symbol, he wondered?

"Papou, funny thing. I have the same candelabra as you. Where did you get yours?" For some reason he was shaking as if this conversation would change him forever. He put his hand on Papou's shoulder and looked into his eyes.

Papou felt the color drain from his face. He realized the moment of truth had arrived. He hoped Saranti would forgive him. "It is a menorah, my son, a symbol of Judaism. I sent one to you many years ago."

"But you didn't know me then!" He wasn't sure why, but he started crying. "Papou, my Papou." He held him and rocked back and forth. He was choking. "Please Papou tell me what I've needed to hear for a long, long time. Do I belong to you?"

Papou lost his composure and a deep pain filled his heart. Tears rained from his eyes. "I didn't want to hurt you this way. My love for you has no boundaries. I am your grandfather, your only living relative." The words caught in his throat and came out in short bursts.

"How could you possibly hurt me?" He pounded on his chest. "You are here inside my heart."

"Saranti, my Saranti, my beautiful Sarah's son."
He held his face and kissed him again and again.
"When I came to Chios, I knew I would stay near you
whether I told you the truth or not. My life began
again the moment I set eyes on you. I was coming to
Kardamyla when I saw you drop Marika in Vounaki
Square and recognized you. There was no denying
it, you were the image of Sarah. You know the rest.
We bonded immediately."

"You were the one taking care of me all these
years. Marika said it must be someone who loved me.
Oh, my wonderful, generous Papou. I am proud to
be your grandson. Everyone says I am your double."
He couldn't stop sobbing. "My sons take after you."
Both their shirts were soaked with tears.

Although Saranti knew about Papou's family in
Thessaloniki, it was different now. They were his
people. He wanted details about his mother and
how his father died. There was a thirst inside of him
to know his roots and his grandfather answered his
questions with clarity. "My God, the Nazi's annihi-
lated our whole family."

Papou explained that the monk's grandchildren
were saved by a priest and he joined the monastery
in Chios to hide and protect their identity. "He kept
me informed about your life. Finally, I decided to
see for myself. You were my only reason for living."

"He came to the cafe periodically and asked me
unusual questions. I thought it strange but he seemed
genuinely interested. I was truthful. After all, he was
a monk and I confided in him."

Questions flowed from him. Things that were bottled up for years came to the surface. It was as if he always understood he wasn't who he appeared to be and didn't know why. "I didn't belong to anyone until now. The people who raised me saw a stranger. They were good parents but could not accept the fact I had no resemblance to them."

"We thought this was the best way to save your life, son. We had no choice. The woman who took you had no idea you weren't her child. She was happy and content since she had already miscarried three times, the fourth counting the one in the hospital was still-born. No sooner where you removed from Sarah's arms and the dead child placed there, the Germans came for her."

Neither realized they had landed. As the plane rolled to a stop, a new set of emotions brought them to tears again. "I needed you Papou. Although it took a long time for you to reveal yourself, you were always by my side. You sustained me even before we met."

They exited the plane, proceeded to pick up their luggage, claimed a car with a driver and headed towards the school.

"The boys have to be told."

"I don't want to disrupt their studies. Should we wait until they finish school?"

"Give them some credit. They'll handle it with dignity and grace."

CHAPTER 48

The school officials knew Saranti and Dr. Cohen were arriving and brought the boys to their office under the pretense of discussing their classes. Usually these questions were executed separately but they were invited to participate together then left them waiting alone in the room.

Strati wouldn't stop talking to Yiorgo. "Do you think they want us to attend classes in another school?"

"Why Strati? You and I are their best students. That wouldn't make any sense. Don't be nervous. They'll be back soon enough."

"By soon enough do you mean now," Papou said. He had walked in with Saranti and was admiring the boys.

"Papou! Father!" They both shouted and embraced them. "We have much to tell you."

The boys had grown and although they were always respectful, there was a difference in their demeanor. They weren't children any longer. They were men.

"We missed you but decided to stay and study during the holidays and come during Easter break." Yiorgo spoke. "I think Strati was contemplating coming for the New Year but I talked him out of it."

"Why do I listen to you, Yiorgo?"

"You miss Christina. Am I right my sentimental brother?"

"Papou, how is she? Does she talk about me?"

Papou and Saranti were laughing. "We brought you pictures and gifts from Christinaki. I think, when you come home you should make a commitment. Don't let the time pass, my son. Someone else may grab her."

"I doubt it, father. She's been in love with Strati since she was a tot. There is no one else for either one of them."

"This was a long exhausting trip but the drive to the school was peaceful. We wanted to take you to the city for dinner." Papou was anxious. "The car is waiting. Do you have other plans?"

"Our plans are null and void." Strati said. "This time is for you."

The boys spoke with a distinct English accent. Their father and great grandfather were impressed with their vocabulary and stature. They had an air of sophistication and dressed the part. Papou made sure they attended the finest medical school and were groomed to be the best in their field. Oxford had done wonders for them.

The driver was waiting and the car doors were open. "Where shall I take you gentlemen?"

"There is a marvelous restaurant not far from here. Yiorgo and I treat ourselves occasionally. It is run by Greeks and the food excels in comparison to other eating establishments. If you have no objections, the Greek Islander it is."

"Follow this road through the meadows. When you see a blue and white building in the middle of a landscape surrounded by trees, we've arrived. There is nothing else around there but it is extremely popular and is frequented by everyone who is in the know. Mr. Petros is the proprietor."

Papou and Saranti were happy the boys had some form of recreation. Although from what they observed the countryside was quiet. Fortunately, there weren't many distractions to keep them from their studies.

"Strati, Yiorgo, how nice to see you again. This must be your father and grandfather. We couldn't miss that resemblance. Welcome to the Islander." Mr. Petro was charming and larger than life. He was warm, friendly and knew every customer intimately especially the ladies. He liked them plump and soft. Their satisfaction was his joy.

"Papou is a Jew, Mr. Petro, Dr. Georgios Cohen. We know you have many Jewish customers." Petro was confused with Yiorgo's statement. If Papou was Jewish, what about their father?

"Come, I will seat you in a perfect spot where the girls can admire you handsome gentlemen."

"It is well known that the Jews have a sophisticated palette. That's why they come from far to relish the delicious food." Strati told him.

"Oh. We Jews have sophisticated palettes?" Saranti spoke up as they were seated in the garden area. "Does that include my sons?" He couldn't wait to tell them.

Papou was startled. He was at a loss for words and was hoping to ease into telling the boys. "Let's have that discussion over dinner."

"Father, Strati and I always said you and Papou could be twins except for the age difference."

"So we are related. How exciting! We have been a family for many years and now it's official. Why didn't you tell us sooner?"

Before Papou could answer, Mr. Petro brought two bottles of wine, "One is on the house and the other is...well, you know." He slipped a note to Yiorgo.

"They are the Lemos family. Ship owners from Egnousa. They have their eyes on Yiorgo for their niece. They'll probably offer him a handsome dowry for his hand," he teased. "What does the note say. "Meet me tonight! The women are crazy about him."

Saranti and Papou looked at each other in disbelief.

"I apologize. I didn't mean to be disrespectful. Yiorgo has always been quite a lady's man. But don't let that worry you. His first priority is school."

"Well, I guess the talk regarding our true relationship is unnecessary. And here I believed this would be a difficult transition for you boys. Shall we order dinner, Saranti?"

"Mr. Petro knows what we want. Everything in the fish family. We'll begin with grilled octopus. Do you approve, Papou?" Yiorgo asked. They raised their glasses slightly to the Lemos family.

"Are you going to speak with them, Yiorgo?"

"Don't worry, Strati. There is not enough money in the world that would take me away from my family and friends. Our mission is to return to Kardamyla, work with Papou and eventually take over the practice when he retires."

Yiorgo looked straight at Papou. "Strati and I are grateful for the life you have provided. Father you were always good to us but financially, let's face it, the cafe would not have the income to support us in a school of this caliber."

"We want to take care of both of you when the time comes for us to return home. Marika, Paraskevoula, Dimitri and Katina are also in our hearts. We realize, love comes without warning and support anything you do with Marika."

Another round of tears flowed between Papou and Saranti which shocked the boys. They had never seen either one cry.

"We didn't want to upset you," Strati said quietly.

"Cads is what we are. We should have used a little finesse."

This remark made them laugh. "I guess, Saranti, that you and I should be less serious and more spontaneous. We are certainly learning our lessons from these fellows. Finesse? Oh my. Great word."

"There are several elegant cabins behind the restaurant. Instead of staying on campus or returning to a London hotel, I suggest we book two of them for the night. We'll phone the dean to inform him of our plans. Perhaps one of us can go back to the school and pick up a few things. Strati, how about you?" He winked.

He asked Mr. Petros to prepare a couple of rooms. "Would you care for the one you usually stay in, Yiorgo?"

His face flushed. "The weather was awful and I decided to ride it out before returning to school. It is still pleasant now but I smell the chill of winter in the air."

Before Strati left, he decided to cover for his mischievous brother. "Both of us stayed due to dangerous conditions on the road. It wasn't a waste of time. We had our books and studied together." This was probably the first lie he ever told his family. What could he say? His brother was a player.

None of this sat well with Saranti. He was disappointed in Strati for the story and with Yiorgo for his behavior. There is no telling what could occur if they weren't careful. He would talk with Papou to decide if they should intervene in their personal affairs.

They heard instruments being tuned and saw Mr. Petro running towards them. "I saved a spot next to the fireplace. The show is phenomenal. I imported the singers and musicians from the finest nightclubs in Greece. Come with me!" He was gregarious and it rubbed off on them. They sat facing the band. The clarinet player recognized Dr. Cohen and came to the table. "I played at your engagement in Kardamyla." They shook hands. "Marinela is here and will be singing shortly. *Yiasou leventi,*" he slapped Yiorgo on the back.

This was another indication that Yiorgo frequented the Islander. Saranti was disappointed but didn't know how to approach the subject. He thought about Marika. Perhaps, he didn't have the right to preach. Yiorgo and Strati were dynamic students. This did not affect their studies. Still, as a father, he had the right to give advice. He wasn't going to say anything without Papou's approval.

Obviously, Saranti had never witnessed a belly dancer. His mouth and eyes were wide open when he saw Karima come to the floor and move like a snake from table to table. People were putting money in her voluptuous bosom. When she swayed her body in front of him, he was too shocked to move. Papou placed a few pounds in her cleavage. "Saranti, this must be a first for you." He didn't answer but he looked at Yiorgo who got up and left the table.

The lights went out and the bouzouki player was strumming. A woman's raspy voice was heard singing the latest Greek hit. Suddenly a light flashed onto her face. She wore a fisherman's hat and a cigarette hung from her lips. Everyone clapped and the dancing began.

Yiorgo came back. "It is getting late. I think we should retire." He was afraid they would notice that he knew the entire band. The belly dancer was in to him and they had a fling whenever she was in town. "You must be tired from your long journey."

He had the keys to the cabins and led the way to the back of the building. "I hope you enjoyed the music."

"How often to you come here, son. I get the feeling everyone knows you." Papou pinched Saranti's arm.

"Once in a while. Here's your cabin. It is spiffy and comfortable. We'll have breakfast tomorrow either here or on the terrace."

They walked into a large space with a refined English flair and two beds. "This is perfect. Thanks for the suggestion, Yiorgo. It turned out to be a wonderful evening. Right, Saranti?"

"Thanks Papou. I'm happy you enjoyed yourself. Marinela is very popular. I surely hope you were into that type of music." He sat with them and talked about his school work which pleased them and calmed Saranti's nerves. Strati showed up and they spent time catching up.

"Let's go to our room, Yiorgo. Tomorrow is another day. They must be exhausted from their trip. Knock on our door in the morning. We don't want to disturb you in case you sleep late."

When the boys left, Saranti asked Papou what he should do about Yiorgo. He was afraid his son was on the wrong path and needed guidance.

"Nothing. If our boys weren't top notch in school, then we would speak to them." He explained their personalities were different yet they were very close and protective of each other. "I don't think they'll be a problem, my son. Let's enjoy the duration of our stay."

CHAPTER 49

Strati had gone to the terrace to give Yiorgo privacy. Karima was waiting in the room. Except for a few colorful scarves that hung on her body, she was nude and ready for action. She was a fleshy, exciting lover and came up with new things each time they were together. Mr. Petro had told Yiorgo, having sex with skinny women is tantamount to being with a wooden chair. A woman with plenty of meat emits heat, hugs the body and gives you bounce when you're making love. You work less and are satisfied more.

She moved slowly towards him growling through her bright red lips. It was frightening but he was turned on and began removing his clothing. She laid her hand on his face and pushed him back onto the bed. "Don't move." She peeled off his underwear slowly, climbed onto the bed and knelt with her backside facing his head. He was shocked that she was cleanly shaven and began playing with her protruding clitoris. He wanted to enter her but she was in control. She massaged his thighs with warm oil that had a sting to it, lifted his knees and laid her hands on his testicles moving them around gently. Suddenly, she inserted her fingers deep into his orifice.

"Stop, stop," he screamed and slapped her backside and thighs. "Harder. Harder," she yelled back as he fought and hit her. She filled her mouth with his penis and sucked him dry.

"Everything is burning."

"Don't worry. You'll be fine." She jumped off the bed, went into the bathroom, returned with cold wet towels and plastered them between his legs. She flipped him over, laid a wash cloth in his buttocks. "Get on your knees and open up. I'll take care of it." When she shoved the wet cloth into his behind with her finger it was painful but calmed the burning sensation.

He was infuriated at the invasion and embarrassed to be put in such an awkward position. He was swearing and gasping. When she turned him on his back, he was ready for another round. She mounted him and growled. He was angry with himself and tried desperately to cause her pain. He bit and scratched her. "More Yiorgo, more, bite harder." She loved it and laughed at his attempt to cause her discomfort. Their orgasms made him shake violently.

When they were finally spent, she fell onto his body and put her face on his chest. Her eyes were closed, her long black curls covered her suntanned face. He pushed the hair up and looked at her youthful, innocent expression. How could a wild woman look so sweet, he thought. Still, he was angry that he allowed himself to be vulnerable to her. Where the hell did she learn those things? Next time he would make her pay dearly.

"Get up. It's time for your show." She moaned and began kissing him moving slowly downward. He threw her off the bed onto her behind. "I'll be back in a couple weeks with new tricks that will make you cry and beg for mercy," she screeched.

"Men don't beg for mercy. Now, go and send in Strati." He laid back and fell asleep from exhaustion.

She wanted to leave him a momentum and tied a red bow on his penis before leaving.

Strati walked in to a disastrous mess. Clothes, sheets, towels were strewn all over the room. He wondered what the hell they had done when he saw the ribbon and started laughing. He threw a cover over his brother but left the bow intact. Fortunately, one of the beds was still made up. He changed and slipped under the covers, mumbling to himself.

CHAPTER 50

Yiorgo's arms and legs were spread out and he didn't move a muscle all night long. "Time to rise, brother." Strati shook him but there was no response. "Father and Papou should be here shortly. I'm taking a shower. If you're not up when I come out, I'll pour a bucket of water on your head."

Strati was getting dressed when he heard knocking. "Oh Lord." He ran around picking up everything and shoving the piles under the beds. "Minute. I'm coming." He forgot to grab Karima's colorful scarf which is the first thing Papou saw when he came in the room.

"Yiorgo is still asleep. We were studying till late." He poured a glass of water in his face and when he jumped up, he exposed himself.

"We'll meet you on the terrace." Papou hoped he got Saranti out in time.

Yiorgo was heading for the shower when he discovered his penis was tied. "The bitch." His rear end was hurting and he tried to wash away the pain. "Strati, can you take a look at my butt? It's bothering me."

"Hell no. Call Papou to examine you. He's the doctor."

"There's something wrong in there and I'm not asking Papou to check me out. What have you been studying all these years? Just a quick peek."

"Nope. I'm going out." He left Yiorgo who was trying to see his rear in the mirror.

"Damn." he put on a smart tan sweater, English tweed jacket and color coordinated pants.

A dusting of snow was on the ground and Mr. Petro brought portable fire places near the tables. French, Greek and English pastries were being served along with an array of cheeses. Neither Saranti nor Papou wanted tea so Yiorgo asked Mr. Petro for Greek coffee.

"Why do you keep moving around, son." His father looked at him strangely.

"My hip has been bothering me and these chairs are not comfortable."

Strati shook his head and smiled impishly. "You should have Papou check you out."

Saranti had a worried expression on his face. "What happened, Yiorgo?"

"Twisted it."

Papou knew the signs and whispered in his ear. "Try petroleum jelly next time."

Yiorgos face turned red.

"What did you tell him? I'm concerned." Saranti asked.

"Take aspirin for the pain." Papou had seen Karima's scarf and got a glimpse of the bow on his penis when Yiorgo jumped out of bed. He knew something crazy had happened. Fortunately, Saranti didn't notice a thing.

They were eating warm scones and honey, when the band appeared on the terrace. They had played through the night and just finished their last show. Karima flowed in like a Gypsy queen and stared at Yiorgo with a sly smile on her pretty face. "Let's go to my room son. I want to take a look at your hip. Stay here Saranti. We don't want to lose the table."

"Karima is a wild cat. How did she get you into a compromising position?" They entered the room and Papou went straight for his medical bag. "Drop your pants and bend over so I can determine if it is serious, although I doubt it."

"How did you know about Karima?"

"I'm not blind. Good thing your father didn't catch on. How long have you been seeing each other?" He pulled out his instruments.

"A couple of years now. Actually, she was my first. Papou, this is really humiliating. Do you have to do this? Can't you give me a salve?"

"Stop acting like a kid. You were man enough to take whatever you took. Let's do this quickly to assess the extent of your problem."

"Oh, no! It's painful. I'm gonna make her pay."

"It isn't too bad. A couple of scratches. Her nails must be long. Stay as you are and I'll apply numbing medication. It will hurt at first but in a few minutes you won't feel anything. I'll add petroleum jelly and that should do it. By the end of the day you'll heal."

"Ouch. Ah. This is the worst thing that's ever happened to me." He squirmed and moved around.

"Stop that and let me finish. Okay. You can get up now. Are you sufficiently embarrassed? Watch yourself next time!"

"You're nuts? Never again." He pulled up his pants. "Sorry, I didn't mean to talk that way."

"I get it, son. Don't let that worry you. Let's leave. I want to get to London to see a play or go to the museums." He put his arm around Yiorgo.

"I love you Papou. Thanks for not admonishing me."

CHAPTER 51

Saranti was a wreck and Strati kept laughing at him. "You should have taken me with you, Papou. How funny would that be?"

"Do you think a twisted hip is funny, Strati? It could be serious. Well, Papou?"

"Nothing to cause worry. He is fine and dandy. Let's get to London. We'll decide if we should stay in the city or return to this beautiful setting."

The car was huge and comfortable. The back seats faced each other and the boys laid their long legs straight in front of them between Papou and Sarant who were glad to have their children back. They massage the boy's calves lovingly while they answered questions about everyone back home.

"Did you ever think Eva would live in Kardamyla. She even has a guy friend. Do you remember Shorty? Well they are involved and she is very happy. They swim together and play backgammon."

"Shorty and Eva? I'll be!" Strati thought it humorous. "Tell me, is Christinaki the loveliest girl in Karamyla, Papou."

"She hasn't changed one bit since she was a youngster. Her eyes still shine and her lip quivers when she speaks of you. You have to spend more time at home on your next trip. The poor girl is suffering without you."

"Would it be a bad thing to get married and bring her to London with me?"

"I thought I was the crazy one. You will never be able to concentrate on your studies."

"I tend to think, Yiorgo is right on this, son. It was extremely difficult for me to leave Marika behind but one has to do what's best."

"Father, your situation is impossible. I'm talking about making it legal. With her next to me, there is nothing I couldn't accomplish."

"Papou, what do you think?"

"Strati, you are extremely level headed. Do you think she'll be happy here?"

"I would see to it."

"If it doesn't interfere with your studies, then do as you may."

"He misses her Papou. But if you want my opinion, our idea was to double up on our courses and finish school sooner. That means, we will be in study mode almost every night. We actually do that now except for one weekend a month. We can do our residency in Greece. Strati you would have to cut back to spend time with Christinaki. It would take longer to finish school."

Saranti was proud of Yiorgo for speaking up. "You are men now. These decisions should be left up to you." He knew exactly what Papou would say and he took the reins.

They asked about Dimitraki and were told he was about to leave. First he would take to the seas starting at the bottom and then school. He would be returning to the island every few months for short spurts. "It will be hard on Katina. She is used to having him around. They've grown close." Papou told them.

"I surely hope our little brother will be home when we visit. It won't be the same without him."

They inquired about the Jewish end of their family but Papou felt it best not to discuss certain things at this time. He didn't want to depress them.

"They are grown men," Saranti told him. "I am sure they can handle it."

"Father, Yiorgo and I have something to say. We are jealous of the two of you. We all look alike except for one thing. Your crystal blue eyes are the talk of everyone who meets you. Although our eyes are light, they aren't blue. You should have been more careful when you had us."

"I think that's what attracted our women." Saranti told them. "The eyes were a big part of it for Marika."

"Father, thank you for confiding in us." Yiorgo was happy to be treated as an equal.

Papou thought the conversation was fun and light-hearted. "What is the first thing we're going to do in London? Suggestions?"

"We'll go to Selfridges Department store. It is the only place in England that has a Coca Cola Soda Bar. I have been dying to try it. Perhaps we can pick up a couple of things for our women. I bet Christinaki would wear French perfume."

"I don't know if Marika would. She is old school. Maybe a shawl or scarf."

"Father, don't you think that's boring? Get her something with a colorful flair."

"Yea," Strati spoke up. "Perhaps an interesting piece of jewelry or…"

"Or a beautiful corset with satin ties."

"Yiorgo, if you weren't a grown man I would give you a thrashing." Saranti told him playfully.

"Let's buy things for the boutique." Papou was thinking about under garments.

"Lunch at the Ritz Carlton Hotel or the Mayfair. Then we can check on a play or musical," Yiorgo was enthusiastic.

"We can go to Oxford Street to see Father Christmas and the huge train sets and toys. I'm sure we'll have a great time. Perhaps we can stop at the Synagogue. We've been there with our Jewish classmates. Wait till we tell them what we have in common." Strati wanted Papou to be happy.

They had a fabulous time exploring, shopping, attending the symphony, having lunch at the fabulous Ritz. They were impressed beyond belief. It seemed that everyone was a fashion plate in London. Papou had finally given up and wanted to head back to the Greek Islander. They loaded up the car and gave him the entire seat where he fell asleep. Saranti sat between the boys with his arms around them.

"Father, did you notice how many ladies gave you the look." Yiorgo told him.

He did but denied it. "Stop that nonsense."

"We're not blind father. You are truly handsome. We had a couple of gals follow us down the street once they saw you. One of them talked to you. What was it she said?" Strati asked.

"That's enough."

"Come on, Father. We're not stupid. We know the ways of the world now. Don't we Strati? You can tell us."

"Okay. The one with the bouffant hair that came into the store, gave me her phone number."

"Wow. Are you gonna call?"

"Never happen, Yiorgo. I have the woman I want. Even though most men are promiscuous, I'm not one of them. I couldn't live with myself if I did anything to compromise my relationship with the woman I love more than life. Don't get me wrong. I'm not a saint. I enjoy a flirtation once in a while but no more than that. You know every person wants to feel attractive and wanted. It is good for their ego."

Strati and Yiorgo were amazed. His father had never opened up to them before. He was always serious. They felt much closer to him now and loved that he trusted them with his private feelings.

They talked about their family in Thessaloniki and the holocaust. It was devastating for the boys to know they would never know Saranti's parents. "You will know them through Papou. He is an extraordinary man who loves deeply. It is painful for him to talk about his friends and relatives who were exterminated by the Nazi's. Don't press him. Let him tell you in his own gentle way. He wants to protect you."

They were getting close to the Islander. Papou was stirring and opened his eyes. He saw the huge trees from the car window. "Didn't realize how long I'd slept. Saranti did I take your spot?"

"No way. I was happy to sit with our boys. Are you hungry? We'll be there in a few."

"Someone should bring in our purchases and we'll head for the restaurant. I have a taste for keftedes and *saganaki*."

"How about Lamb shanks with artichokes? My stomach is growling. "

"Anything you want, Saranti. You boys?"

"Moussaka for me and Pastitsio for Strati."

When they sat at their table, Papou ordered all the mezedakia on the menu. Two waiters brought food to the table with warm crusty bread. They were dipping, eating, feeding each other and laughing.

"I'm not sure we'll be able to eat the main meal after these *mezedes*."

"The boys have huge appetites, son. If I'm not mistaken, Marika said you had the appetite of forty men."

Mr. Petro came to the table with wine. "I see how much you're enjoying our food. If you're going to have desert, order it now. We make the best loukoumades or homemade Greek yogurt and honey."

"We have enough food here for an army." Yiorgo said while rubbing his stomach. "No dessert for me."

They overate and could barely make it back to their room. Saranti asked the boys to stay for a while. No one wanted the evening to end. The boys discussed their school work and their feelings regarding doctoring. Strati said he would be the one to deliver his babies.

Yiorgo thought he would suffer more than Christina when she went into labor. "Can you handle seeing her in pain?"

"It won't be an easy task but she will need me."

They spoke for hours about their dreams, their love of family and friends back home. "How lucky we are to have you and Papou. You taught us to respect ourselves. And believe me, we do. Our studies are the most important thing in our lives, next to you."

"Are you trying to make us cry, brother?" Yiorgo punched his arm.

This was a fabulous day and they were content being together. The boys did not want to leave the room. Being with their father and Papou made them feel warm inside. They crawled into their father's bed and slept soundly knowing how lucky they were.

Saranti covered them and laid next to Papou. "We are fortunate my handsome son," Papou told him and kissed his forehead.

The next few days held more of the same. They went to London, shopped, saw plays and ate at interesting places. Every night they were at the Islander having long conversations about Papou's family and their future. They enjoyed telling stories about their life in the village. Mr. Petro usually joined them during dinner. One of the funniest stories was about the monk's exhibition during Papou's engagement party. Mr. Petro laughed hysterically and fell out of his seat when he heard it. "This is a keeper. I will tell this to everyone I know."

During the last two days they decided to stay put with the boys. The only thing they did was visit the professors and headmaster at the school.

The dean felt the boys were tremendously dedicated but he thought they needed some down time. He indicated that they were able to sustain thus far but he believed they should take it easy. They studied night after night. Although it was rare, they were devastated if they made a minute error in their exams. He also hoped they would stay in England for their residency and not go to Greece.

Papou and Saranti could not be more proud. They would return to Greece filled with wonderful stories. They hated leaving the boys. This was probably the best time they ever had with them.

"Gentleman, I was hoping to entice you to stay for the New Year celebration. The same band will play." Mr. Petros was sad they were leaving. "Besides, I'm going to miss our late night conversations."

"Mr. Petros, please see to it that my grandsons are taken care of." Papou put money in his hand.

"Absolutely not, Doctor." He handed back the money. "I will personally make sure their needs are met."

"Save a room for them on the Eve. I want them to have a good time." He winked at Yiorgo and whispered in his ear. Be careful of the viper."

"Yiorgo and I will miss you and father more than you know. May we come to the airport?"

"I think it best that you let us go it alone. I'm not sure I can handle it, son. One thing for sure, we'll surprise you again. Maybe we'll bring our women next time. We left holiday gifts in your room."

"You'll also find presents in your luggage. We decided to match the gifts with your eye color." Strati was sniffling.

Both Saranti and Papou were about to cry as the car was moving away. They waved at the boys who were standing in the midst of a snow fall. Strati leaned towards Yiorgo who stood with his hands in his pockets. They grew sadder and sadder as they watched the car disappear.

Mr. Petro called out to them. "It's cold. Come in for a cup of hot tea.

CHAPTER 52

HOME IN THE VILLAGE

"Dimitraki why do you spend money bringing me clothes that you tear to shreds. Good thing I keep an extra dress to change into." The red bustier he had given her was in pieces on the floor with the dress he had ripped from her body.

They were both nude and Dimitri was lying between her legs with his head on her soft belly. He squished her stomach and tickled her.

"Stop that or I'll yell and they will find us laying here naked!"

Her voice softened. "Don't you wish we were kids again?" She was petting his hair and running her fingers through the curls pulling and laughing every time he tickled her.

"We're always kids when we're together. Do you remember the cave where you showed me your private part without blinking an eye?"

"Why not let you see it. It belonged to you anyway."

"We didn't bank on the old monk coming in to take a leak. He heard us giggling and didn't even take the time to hide himself. It was still in his hand when he ran out using language not fit for our ears."

They laughed hysterically. "I had forgotten that."

"Did you see his birdie?"

"I did not." She pulled his hair. "Shame on you."

"Ouch. I just wanted to know, silly girl?"

"It took us quite a while to sneak out. We waited in there for at least an hour scared to death we would be seen. I can still hear mama threatening to whip us for disappearing. I miss her, Dimitri. Do you think she ever wondered about us?"

"If she didn't then, maybe she sees us from up there now."

They laid quietly for a while painfully aware they must go their separate ways.

"At some point we have to leave our sanctuary," she sighed. "Have you seen Penelope yet?"

"You always come first. When will I see my precious god-daughters? I missed them."

"I'll bring them up this evening unless you come down to see Strati and Yiorgo at the clinic. We can meet there. Dimitra and Marika have grown since you last saw them. They heard your helicopter this morning and were elated. They can't wait to see you. And, please, please do not spoil them with a lot of gifts," she told him knowing it was futile.

"I want my girls to have everything. Their dowry is intact. Each has a home and bank account in the

States. They will attend the finest schools in the America."

"Dimitraki, you have given me more than enough money. There will be plenty for them when they are adults and realize the value of having such treasure. I don't touch the money unless it's necessary for their education. I have a private English tutor. We study together. You will be proud of all three of us."

"I've always been proud of you. I am a wealthy man, my darling. I want you to be comfortable and not worry if the fish are biting. Now, let me help you get dressed, then go tell the twins Uncle Dimitri is coming to see them."

He enjoyed putting on her clothes. "You are far more beautiful naked." He twisted her long hair around his hand and pushed it into a net in the back of her neck. "There. No one will suspect. You are perfect."

They kissed as if it was their last.

"Don't be long." She took off running.

CHAPTER 53

Dimitri scaled the large marble steps two at a time. He heard the staff calling to each other, "Mr. Dimitri is home." They were always glad to see him. It curbed his wife's abusive behavior when he was around.

"I didn't bring gifts with me this time. The packages will arrive in a few days. I've ordered leathers from Italy." He always brought them exceptional things.

"Please prepare the upper bedrooms for my guests from Ohio. Anre and Simeon are coming, too. We'll have entertainment for our parties and Anre can show off the latest fashions from Paris."

He saw a fragile looking young black girl with a frightened expression hiding behind a column. "Who is this pretty girl. Come here sweetheart." She didn't move.

"Rena was hired by Mrs. Penelope to help in her bedroom," one of the housemaids spoke up. "Apparently, she hasn't been doing a very good job because Mrs. Penelope strikes her."

"Keep quiet," another housekeeper whispered, "or we'll be next." The staff gave each other suspicious glances.

"What the hell are you talking about, Maria? Penelope strikes the help?"

He went over to Rena and took her hand. "Come into my office." The poor girl started crying. "Please sir. I have nowhere to go. I came from Africa and Mrs. Penelope bought me for her pleasure." Although she communicated in Greek, her accent was strange and Dimitri thought she didn't quite understand what she was saying.

"Her pleasure? I don't understand, child. How old are you?"

"I'm not sure. Can I be here for your pleasure? She is cruel to me?" Rena was small and thin. She looked very young, no older than eight. Her black eyes were large and sat over a long nose that lead to lips that seemed to pout.

"What you are saying? Perhaps it is a language barrier. Stay here and I'll talk to Penelope."

"No...no....don't tell her I said anything. She will kick me. I will go back to her room before she knows I'm gone."

Dimitri wasn't quite sure what to believe. He was positive his wife wouldn't harm anyone. What was this child inferring? Penelope wasn't the friendliest person but she certainly wouldn't be abusive.

"Someone give this child food. She is far too skinny. Stay here Rena. I'll see you shortly."

He opened the double doors to their bedroom suite. Priceless art of naked women in ornate frames covered every inch of the walls. A huge bed with red satin sheets took up one entire end. The ceiling over the bed was mirrored. He disliked his wife's taste and hated the gaudy room.

"Penelope, aren't you going to welcome your husband? I understand you haven't seen the light of day for months."

Her eyes were glazed over. "Well, well. You found your way back finally and I'm supposed to be happy." She slurred her words.

"Tipsy are you? I know why you drink, Penelope. You're trying to numb the pain from the last miscarriage. It is terrible for a woman to be unable to carry a baby. I'm sorry I wasn't here to help you through it." He sat on the bed next to her. "I have great news. Soon you will experience the joy of being a mother. Surely, your disposition will change when you hold a tiny one in your arms."

A female voice came from another room. "Think you've discovered what will make her whole, huh!"

"Shut up Margarite," Penelope yelled.

"I've been here for months while you were traveling the globe. She needed me and I came to her." Margarite hissed at him. She was not uncomfortable with her state of undress and paraded around the room with no respect for his presence. It was a purposeful exhibition of territorial control.

"May I have some privacy with my wife?"

"Only if Penelope says go." She was a petite blond with the same hard demeanor as Penelope.

Dimitri got up slowly and towered over her. He wasn't going to allow any of this. "Margarite, get out. We'll send your things," was all he said and she left the room trembling. "I don't want to lay eyes on her again."

Penelope stretched her long, beautiful limbs and pretended to cry. "Come to my bed Dimitri. I've missed you." It was difficult to conceal her disgust for him. She wanted to scratch his eyes out for getting rid of her girlfriend.

"I'm going to see my friends and when I come home you can tell me about your latest acquisition."

"Rena is a bitch. Nothing she ever does is right. I want her out of here." She spoke harshly.

"What was it that she did for you? You have plenty of help in this house."

"I took Rena because I felt sorry for her but she turned out to be treacherous."

"That little girl treacherous? Were you cruel to her, Penelope?"

"She is a thief and needed to be taught a lesson." She pushed herself up on her elbows and spit out the words vehemently. Her face was distorted.

It made him sick to look at her. "I didn't think you were such a woman. She is a poor frightened child. I'm taking her with me to the clinic. We'll discuss this when I come home."

Penelope realized her mistake and tried to retract her words. "I only yelled at her Dimitri. I would never strike a child."

"I didn't believe you could be that unfeeling. I'm bringing a young lady here who is pregnant and can't keep the baby. Do you think you can be a mother or shall I find another family for the infant?"

"Oh, you've made me gloriously happy," she lied. *How dare he make this decision without consulting me. I'll have to find a way to get rid of her, she thought.*

Dimitri wasn't sure he believed her. He didn't spend enough time with her to develop an understanding of the private world she lived in. There was something that kept him from bonding with Penelope. "Prepare yourself for company in the next couple of days."

He took a long hot shower, put on comfortable khaki island-wear and soft sandals. His Fiat was waiting for him when he walked out. He had Rena with him. "You are going to see a doctor friend for an examination. Don't be alarmed. He won't hurt you. No one will ever 'cause you pain again if I can help it."

CHAPTER 54

For the first time since she was abducted and sold to strangers, Rena felt a sense of relief. *Maybe he will take care of me and not sell me if I give him pleasure,* she thought. "Let me be good to you, sir." She laid on his lap and put her mouth between his legs.

"Stop," he shouted and lifted her face. "What are you doing?"

Her tiny face showed fright. "Pleasure for you."

He was horrified at this gesture and wondered how much of this the poor child had endured. "You shall never, ever do these things and you will never be abused again. We will find a good family to take care of you and give you love."

Rena had dreams of soft warm arms rocking her and a woman cooing sweet melodies. A familiar smell invaded her sleep. It was the only time she felt safe. She wanted to stay there forever. "Will they hold me and sing pretty songs?"

"I'll see to it." His eyes welled up and he would have cried but didn't want to make her uncomfortable.

He pulled up to the clinic and heard Christina's voice. "Dimitraki, Dimitraki," she was shouting. "When did you get in." She threw her arms around him.

"You are glowing."

She touched her belly and smiled.

"No? Georgios is still a tike and you are working on number three already. Where are the children?"

"Their Uncle Yiorgo has taken them for a stroll. He is more attractive to women when he's with the kids. My Strati is finishing up with a patient. He'll be thrilled to see you."

Dimitri lifted Rena out of the car and held her on his shoulder. "Would you give this child a bath and stay while Strati examines her? I have an awful feeling she's been hurt."

"Give the sweet thing to me and don't worry."

Tears rolled down Rena's cheeks as she tried to hold on to Dimitri. "Don't cry little one. I'll be waiting here for you."

"Dimitri, my brother." Strati came out of the clinic with his arms up high. He hadn't changed a bit except for a few gray hairs at his temples. He was fit and quietly handsome. His good looks didn't jump at you rather they grew as you entered his sphere. "Wait till Yiorgo sees you. We always talk about you and the fun days when we gathered in the old house."

"My plan is to have a reunion there to reminisce and catch some laughs. Think of the stories we can tell the children."

"I named son number two after Papou Georgios. My Saranti is serious and grounded but Georgios is a spitfire. You know I delivered both boys. We're hoping for a girl this time."

"Your wife hasn't changed since she was a youngster sucking her thumb and staring at you. Papou always said you two would marry."

"I am happy as any man can be. She is a wonderful partner."

"No doubt. Adoration in a man has an irresistible charm."

"I couldn't live one day without her."

"Strati, did you notice anything from across the way. Their eyes are on us. Nothing much has changed except the women are now a part of the cafe crowd, thanks to Papou." Dimitri waved at them.

"Come over for an ouzo!" They called out.

"Not today but soon."

"So, tell me about her."

"I think she's been abused. Please be gentle and kind to her."

"I am with all my patients especially the young ones. I'll spend extra time reassuring her."

"Uncle Dimitri…Uncle Dimitri. We couldn't wait any longer to see you."

The twins ran up to him with Katina following.

He lifted one in each arm and twirled them around. "You have grown into the most beautiful women I've ever seen. Let me take a closer look. Those eyes, that hair, your figures…I may have to hire body guards."

"You always tell us we're beautiful." They enjoyed his compliments.

The twins were the image of Dimitri. They had black curly hair, hazel eyes and clefts in their chin. Katina and Dimitri knew they were his offspring but never admitted it even to each other.

"I hope you won't be leaving soon." Dimitra kissed him.

"We'll be very upset," Marika said and pouted.

They whispered in his ears. "What did you bring us? Did you remember what we requested?"

"What do you think? Everything you wanted and more will be here in a few days."

"Don't you dare ask for anything. I still have my hearing!" Katina scolded.

Strati came out of the clinic and spoke to Dimitri privately. "This is serious. The girl has been sexually battered and is suffering multiple cuts, burns and infections on various parts of her body. We will probably lance and drain her sores and stitch the cuts. I'll have to keep her here at the least overnight. Who the hell would do these things to a child? They should be horse whipped. Christina is devastated."

"She is frightened. I'll have to stay with her." Dimitri tried to keep his composure. He couldn't fathom that his wife would torture Rena. This must have happened prior to her coming to his home, he deducted. After all, she was only there for a couple of weeks. He couldn't understand why she didn't realize the child had been injured. Perhaps it was because she was grieving for the miscarriage and didn't pay attention. The help told him she had been drinking daily. Margarite stayed with her to relieve the loneliness. But why did she need Rena?

He went into the exam room where Christina was sitting. Rena reached for him. He bent over the bed to kiss her cheek. "Listen to me sweetheart. The doctor will make you feel better but you must stay here for a short while. I promise not to leave you." Her lips trembled and she squeezed his hand.

"Christina and Dimitri were with her until Strati put her to sleep."

CHAPTER 55

"Tell us...tell us Uncle Dimitri. Mom resembled a skinned kitten when Marika took her in."

Katina stopped them cold. "Leave your uncle alone. How many times do you want to hear these stories?"

They were sitting on the deck in front of the clinic. Dimitri loved telling his favorite tales about Katina. He vividly remembered the day his mother brought her home. Her mother had died at childbirth and they were positive she would not make it. "If she lives," Marika said, "you'll have a sister."

"Katina was tiny and fit in the palm of my mother's hand. She was translucent and made squeaky kitten sounds. Mom wrapped every part of her body in wool strips leaving only her mouth, eyes and pee-pee free. We fed her with an eye dropper. Her tongue was a pink worm. No one believed she would survive but Marika would not listen. She kept her close to her breast and near the fireplace for days. If she needed to go out, I was the chosen one. She tied her to my chest and threatened my life if I so much as thought to put her down for a second."

The girls adored their uncle and couldn't get enough of his master storytelling skills especially the ones about their mother. This gave them license to tease her.

The twins were close and almost of one mind. There were very few differences between them. Dimitra tended to do well in math while Marika preferred writing. They worshiped their mother and Uncle Dimitri but didn't particularly care for the man they believed was their father. He was unfair to them and their mother promoting harsh punishment for what he perceived was disrespect to him. Their mother didn't know, he occasionally used a strap on their behinds. They didn't confide these things knowing she would go after him ferociously and he would beat her senseless. It didn't happen often but when it did, Katina would be out of commission until her bruises healed. They yearned to leave their environment and move in with Dimitri. They dreamed of going to America and planned to discuss it with their uncle as soon as they were alone with him. If he knew they were unhappy, he would move heaven and earth to change their circumstances.

"Dimitri, you son of a gun." Yiorgo came running towards him dragging Strati's son Saranti. He was as good looking as his brother but had a naughty flair. His sandy hair hung in his eyes which promised something exciting was about to happen. He was a magnet for the girls. There was a cute young woman with him carrying Georgios. She was outraged that anyone would entrust the children to him. "Georgios was running in the mud and needed a change of clothes. Saranti was oblivious. He believes he's an adult. Where is their mother? I want to give her a piece of my mind."

Yiorgo winked at Dimitri and embraced him. "Soulitsa is right. I am incapable of watching these children. Thank you my gracious friend. What would I have done if you hadn't come along precisely when I needed help?" He absolutely knew how to work the women,

"Well," she calmed down, "next time you want to take them for a stroll, let me know. I'll make myself available to assist. Georgios is a terror. He punches everyone in the nose. Look at Yiorgo. His face is bruised. See you," she waved goodbye.

Saranti rolled his large, sultry eyes. He knew the scenario by now. His uncle was fishing for wife material and this was the test. "Hi, Uncle Dimitri. I suspect you know what's going on," he said seriously. For a youngster, Saranti was very gentlemanly, much like his grandfather. He was an impeccable dresser and looked as if he stepped off the pages of a magazine. "Nice to see you ladies."

"You too, sir." The girls giggled. They referred to him as Mr. Proper when he wasn't around.

"Yiorgo, would you please help your brother on a special case for me."

"I would do anything for you Dimitri. What did you think of Soula?"

"A bit too young, don't you think. Although you boys haven't aged one iota, still handsome and muscular. Do you lift weights or does it come naturally?

"Probably because we swim twice a day."

"You and Strati are both the image of your dad. What's with the hair? Are you trying to be modern in this village? Your brother is much more serious and has it cropped. I even had mine cut before coming here."

"You know I'm unconventional. I do things for effect. It draws attention from the ladies." He put on his serious face and went into the clinic.

"My princesses, we'll continue our stories when we meet at the old house. I need to request a special favor. There is a young African girl having treatments inside. When she opens her eyes, I want her to be surrounded by toys. I'm thinking of calling Athens to request they send black dolls for her."

"Uncle, don't you remember the last time Simeon visited the island he brought us beautiful black dolls." Dimitra said sweetly. "Come on Marika. Let's go to the house and bring her fun stuff to play with."

Katina went along to be sure the master of the house didn't give them problems. She took the boys with her threatening Georgios to keep him from punching the girls. "If you as much as make a fist, I will stretch your ears from here to the sky. Do you understand?"

Dimitri sat on the porch with his long legs resting on the railing as he watched them rush towards their house by the sea. The love in his heart was overwhelming. His girls were not only beautiful; they were also kind. He wanted to protect them from the trials of life and to provide them with everything they desired.

When he thought of Rena, a deep pain filled his soul. Where was God when the child was abused? Why didn't he intervene? Whoever hurt her needed to pay. He would do everything humanly possible to erase her misery. He wanted her to laugh, play and feel the warmth of a family.

Strati and Yiorgo came out. "We're finished. Expect her to be awake in approximately an hour."

"Pain?"

"We'll keep her comfortable as possible. Compresses and soft cushions to lie on should help. She'll be in and out of sleep for a while. Christina is still with her."

CHAPTER 56

The girls and Saranti came rushing up with bags of toys. Behind them, Katina holding the black dolls and Georgios kicking her shins every chance he got. "Get your mom, Saranti and hurry before your brother destroys my legs."

Georgios had the face of an angel and the stubbornness of a mule. It was impossible to contain his fury whenever he perceived he was being controlled. Even at that age, he craved independence.

Dimitri picked Georgios up by the seat of his pants and dangled him. He twisted around and punched the air trying to dislodge himself from Dimitri's grip. "Okay girls…payback."

They hit him with the stuffed animals. "Beg for mercy you monster."

He yelled and kicked. His long blond hair hung in his face. He was frustrated at the assault and was planning revenge at the first opportunity.

"Tonight you will sleep in a tree. You don't belong with humans the animal that you are," his mother threatened from the clinic door. "Give him to me and I'll string him up by the legs." Dimitri threw him to her.

Saranti shook his head thinking how stupid they were. He was the only one who knew how to handle him. "I'm going home to pick up toys for Rena. Come with me Georgios. I need help." Off he went with Georgios stomping at his heels.

They entered Rena's room and began placing the toys strategically putting the dolls at her feet.

"Uncle Dimitri what will happen to her?" Marika questioned sadly.

"I will be her guardian until we find a kind family to adopt her."

Rena began stirring and moaning. Her eyes fluttered then opened wide. She looked around the room and lifted her hands to Dimitri. He petted her hair gently. When she realized there were toys everywhere, she was afraid they would be taken away. The dolls caught her eye and she tried to reach them. Dimitra brought one to her and a squeal escaped her mouth. She uttered a few strange syllables, embraced the doll and fell asleep.

"I'm staying through the night. You girls should go home with your mother."

"No Dimitri. The girls and I would never leave you here alone."

"Katina, you don't have to be here."

"Oh but I do!"

"Dad will be furious but it doesn't matter. Besides we want to be with you, Uncle." Dimitra stood firm.

"We are not going anywhere, Uncle Dimitri. We will take care of Rena and try to make her happy." Marika was unwavering.

"I'm proud of my girls." They were three angels spreading joy where ever they went. He worried that someone would take advantage of the twins. It was time to bring them with him but he didn't know how to do it without causing a scandal in the village. *I will not allow them to be hurt, he thought. Perhaps I should take them to America. When they finish their education, we'll find suitable partners. Then Katina can decide what to do with her life.*

Strati came in and examined Rena. "Everything seems to be in order. The best medicine for this child is love and toys. I'll leave her to you. Ring me, my brother, if she has discomfort. Although the way I see it, she will recover quickly.

CHAPTER 57

Dimitri carried Rena on his shoulders holding onto her legs. She had the two black dolls in her arms calling them unusual names. He thought it might be African words that she remembered. Within no time her wounds had healed. She was staying in a large bedroom on the third floor of the mansion with the twins. The only time she came out was with Dimitri. She refused to leave the room fearing Penelope would take her.

They arrived at the old house where everyone gathered for the reunion. Dimitri laid Rena on the cot and she seemed to be content. Georgios saw her for the first time. He tried to bite her all the while claiming she was a piece of chocolate. "I love chocolate," he said over and over. Those were the only words he ever uttered.

"Who doesn't, Georgios, but Rena is a chocolate girl. You can't bite her," his brother told him. Nevertheless, he stayed close and bit her ever so gently when no-one was looking. She tolerated him knowing he was too young to know better. Then, he climbed up on the cot next to her and they both fell asleep holding the dolls.

Katina put lanterns in the windows and on the tables duplicating what they did when they were young. She brewed Greek coffee and served home-made koulourakia made with Marika's recipe. "Okay, who is going to read our fortunes in the coffee cups?"

"Give us a chance to drink it first, Katinaki." Christina said. "As for me, I don't need it. I am the luckiest woman alive." She kissed Strati on the cheek.

"Uncle Dimitri," the girls begged. "You promised to tell us more stories about mom."

"Katina was the fattest kid in the village. After the first few days with us, her appetite increased to that of a horse. She didn't stop eating or screaming for more food. She had us wrapped around her finger."

"I wasn't fat, just plump."

"Ha! You use to climb on me to sleep when I took my afternoon nap. I could hardly breathe. You laid on my back, sucked on my ear lobe and pulled my hair. Your snots dripped on my neck. The worst of it was when I felt warm liquid running down my back. I went crazy and threatened to throw you in the well."

"Me and my brother were here. We never heard anything that earth shattering. Katina deafened us with her piercing shrieks when Dimitri went after her." Strati laughed loudly. "She hid under Marika's dress."

"Oh no, not that story. I was baby, for heaven's sake." Katina was embarrassed and crossed her arms around her chest.

I think she uttered her first words that day.
Mother was trying to calm her down and kept saying, "Dimitri, she's a baby."

She lifted up my mother's dress and yelled, "Mitri
she baby."

"Enough, already. Don't you have other things to
talk about?" Katina yelled at them.

"Wait, wait." Yiorgo spoke up. "How about when
we were teaching you soccer and Katina ran onto
the field and pulled down your pants exposing your
behind."

"I was humiliated and went after her. By the time
I caught her, I ran out of steam. When I picked her
up, she grabbed my face and planted me with kisses.
Now, how could I punish her after that display of
affection. I didn't return to the game. We played by
the seaside instead."

"Uncle Dimitri, you loved each other sooo much,"
Dimitra said. "I don't understand why you didn't
get married."

"After all, she wasn't a blood relative. You could
have." Marika followed her sister's line of thinking."

It was obvious to everyone that they were in love
and that the twins were Dimitri's. They chose to
ignore the subject to see how it would play out. Strati
and Yiorgo were positive he would take them away
at some point.

Dimitri stared at Katina whose eyes were tearing.
"I was just too darn late. Let's read the coffee cups."

*While they swished the coffee cups and turned
them over to dry, Strati and Yiorgo remembered Papou*

Georgios when he and their father visited them at medical school 'in England. When they discovered he was their real grandfather, it wasn't much of a difference in their relationship. They always thought of him that way. He was a pivotal part of their lives.

Dimitri, on the other hand, was devastated. He wanted to be Jewish, too. He loved Papou Georgios with all his heart and knowing he didn't belong hurt him beyond measure. He ran away to his secret cave and stayed there for hours smoking one cigarette after another.

Everyone searched for him. The boys would be returning to school and wanted to find him prior to their departure. They came back to the house to see if he had returned. Katina was the only one who knew about the cave. Dimitri didn't ever want her to go there without him. This time she wasn't going to wait. She couldn't stand to hear Marika crying and slipped out to find him. The rocks were jagged but she managed to get through and into the deep part of the cave. "Mitri me baby," she called out wanting to make him laugh.

"Didn't I warn you not to come in here unless I brought you, snot nose?"

"Mama is crying and the whole family is out looking for you. Please come home." She took his hand to lead him out.

"Is Papou Georgios worried too?"

"He is frantic."

They were standing outside of the house when he walked down the pathway holding Katina's hand.

They all shouted at once. Papou stopped them with one gesture. "I will handle this. Dimitri, I should give you a thrashing for scaring us to death. Sit down and tell me exactly what is wrong. Although, I believe I already know."

He hung his head. "I want to be a Jew and your real grandson," His voice was barely audible.

"Of course. I knew it. Do you see these big lugs? They are my blood relatives. As far as everyone else here is concerned, I chose them to be my family. You are as much my grandson as the boys and I love you from deep down inside of me. Now, tell me Dimitri, who among these people are your blood relatives? Only your mother. Do you love the rest of us any less? We are a happy well-adjusted family. If you become a Jew, I will not care for you any more than I do now."

Dimitri was relieved until Papou said. "If I ever catch you smoking, I will make you eat a fist full of cigarettes." He handed him a mint.

"The look on your face was priceless," Yiorgo said. "We always considered you our little brother and tried to protect you, no matter what you did. But this time you got caught and there was no denying you were smoking. Everyone could smell it."

"You and Strati were always perfect. Never got in trouble."

"That's 'cause our dad always treated us as adults, even at a very tender age. We were doomed if we did something that didn't meet his approval. There was no hiding anything in the village. All the men went to the cafe and would have blown the whistle if they saw us misbehaving."

"Strati didn't you ever do wrong. There must be something we don't know about."

"Dimitri, leave him alone." Christina was obviously privy to an indiscretion.

"Can we speak of it in front of the children?" Katina thought she knew but wouldn't bring it up in for fear of embarrassing her girlfriend.

"Never you mind, girls. Yiorgo and I will admit to a small incident. This only happened once. Yiorgo picked up a pack of cigs that were left at the cafe. We thought the old man was going to Hora with Marika and for some reason he doubled back due to suspicious glances between us."

"We went to the makeshift shower in the back of the cafe and lit up those awful things. We were locked in and buckets of water were poured on our heads. Dad left us there all night. Papou came looking for us in the morning and found us scrunched up on the wet ground. I don't think he knew what we had done when he let us out. He shouted and carried on that he had been searching for us."

"You mean to tell me you two couldn't climb out of the shower or at least break the door." Dimitri shook his head in disbelief.

"That's it? What happened when Saranti came back? Were you punished?" Katina asked Strati.

"The agony we went through worrying about it was enough. He never brought up the incident.

However, he never failed to speak about the nasty smell and bad habit of smoking."

"And here I thought you were perfect," young Saranti spoke up. "You mean to say that one incident with the cigarettes was bad. I'll have to do plenty to catch up. My grandfather sure had a tight grip on you." He went back to the cot with the kids.

"You're not going to tell us what you and Christinaki did before the engagement." Dimitri tried to extract secrets from Strati who swore to Christina he didn't spill the beans to anyone. They both turned red.

"I didn't say a thing, my sweet. Those were private moments between the two of us. No idea how he found out. Did you follow us?"

"Uhuh. Now we know! Fishing can bring information you did not intend to reveal."

"Uncle Dimitri listened to the racket. I think your company is here." Dimitra ran out to observe. "It's Simeon, Anre and your other friends going up to the mansion. Marika, let's go."

Katina warned them to go home. Her husband would be furious.

"We are all going to my place." Dimitri was adamant. "I need my girls to spend the night with Rena. Dinner will be served on the balcony next to the pool. You can meet my guests and take a swim before we eat. It will be a fun evening."

"The wee ones are still asleep. We'll stay and wait for them to wake up."

"If Rena is frightened or cries, come get me."

CHAPTER 58

No sooner did Dimitri arrive at the house, Katina came for him. "Dimitri hurry. Rena and Georgios are both in distress. Neither Christina nor I can calm them down."

He flew to the old place finding the two sobbing kids with their arms around each other. When Rena saw Dimitri, she immediately stopped crying and tried to reach for him while holding Georgios and the dolls at the same time. He lifted both of them saying soothing words and brought them to the big house.

His guests were already in their suites so he went directly to Rena's room where the twins and Saranti were waiting. Surprisingly, they had Angelina with them. When he put the kids down, Rena went to Angelina and offered her the doll she was carrying. It was as if she understood Angelina had a problem and wanted to be kind to her. All the while, she and Georgios were holding hands. Angelina held the doll and rocked it. She seemed to fit right in with the children.

Dimitri fell in love with Rena. Her tenderness towards Angelina and Georgios was moving. He didn't want to give her up. The problem was, he couldn't leave her with Penelope when he was away on business. The child was frightened to death of her. Then what would become of Angelina's baby? He didn't see Penelope in the roll of a mother. There wouldn't be a problem if Katina and the girls were living with him but that was wishful thinking.

He sat on the floor and played with the children. Hearing their laughter made him happy. They plummeted him with balls and he fell backwards pretending to be hurt. Rena threw her arms around him each time. Even Angelina seemed to be having a good time.

Someone was knocking on the door and the girls opened it. Frankie and Sandy walked into all that chaos and laughed when they saw Dimitri rolling around on the floor. Angelina squeezed her arms around Frankie's neck then went back to sitting with the kids. They were amazed at how well she had adjusted to the environment.

"Find Simeon and Anre in the room next to yours. They know their way around here and can take you to the pool. There are swim suits in the cabana. My friends are probably swimming already. You'll get along well with them. The kids and I will see you later." He got hit in the head with a ball, grabbed his head and fell back pretending to be knocked out. Rena and Georgios both poked him till he opened his eyes. "Boo!" They screamed and giggled.

Marika and Dimitra were whispering about Frankie. They had never seen a more perfect man except for their uncle. He was flawless. "Let's go swimming now Uncle Dimitri."

"Take the kids with you. Make sure you don't leave them alone. Put them in the small pool and watch them. I need to make business calls from my office. I won't be long."

Rena refused to go unless Dimitri went. "It is okay sweetheart. I can make my calls later." What is going to happen to her, he was thinking. She wouldn't go anywhere without him. He wrapped the youngsters in his arms and the others followed.

The girls were overly excited. They couldn't wait to see Frankie.

"I think he is Sandy's boyfriend," Marika said not realizing Angelina was his sister.

"We can look, can't we? No one in this entire village is that handsome." Dimitra was breathless with anticipation.

CHAPTER 59

Dimitri scanned the pool. "Where's Katina?'
"In the kitchen making your favorite
stuffed shrimp with Feta cheese." Christina
answered. She was floating on her back with Strati
holding her up and caressing her belly.

Frankie got out to attend to Angelina giving the
girls a delightful look at his physique. "Come on
ladybug. Get in the water. I promise you'll enjoy it."

Saranti took Rena and Georgios to the baby pool.
Rena had never been in water before but became
enthusiastic when Georgios splashed her. She slapped
the water and screeched.

Sandy and Yiorgo were dancing on the terrace to
Simeon's piano playing. They were deep in conversation. She was surprised to learn his father was a Jew
and he was pleased that she was a doctor. "I'll take
you to see the clinic tomorrow. It isn't modern as in
America but it is adequate for the village. We update
it every year. Maybe you can give us suggestions on
the latest medical equipment."

"I may need to use your facilities. Dimitri said
you would work with me."

"We're at your disposal." He had never seen a more gorgeous woman and was smitten to say the least. *He wondered about Frankie who was rough around the edges but quite a looker. From the conversation he had with her, he understood the man she chose to spend her life with had to be Jewish. She was much too sophisticated to stay in the village, he was thinking, but stranger things have happened in life. He wanted her more than any woman he had ever met.*

Dimitri was shocked to see the twins come out of the cabana wearing scanty swim suits. He walked over to them and told them to change into something appropriate. "If your mother catches you, I hate to say what will happen." They returned to the dressing room but were extremely disappointed that Frankie would not get a chance to get a closer glimpse of their figures.

Katina walked in followed by the kitchen help. They were carrying trays of seafood that they placed on the table. She extracted two pieces of shrimp from a platter and fed Dimitri. "Well, what do you think, huh?" Dimitri put his lips to her ear and whispered, "They taste like you." She punched him in the chest. "I will say what I always do when you cook. I've never eaten anything more delicious and I've been around the world."

He took her arm and sat her at the table. "Katina, why are you dressed like an old scrub woman? Wear something pretty once in a while."

"Yiani will shoot me. Forget it. I don't want to cause friction in the family, Dimitri. The girls would suffer."

He left her to retrieve the children from the pool and wrapped them in towels. "Put on robes and come to eat," he told his guests. He carried the little ones to the table.

Penelope slithered into the room dressed in gold satin pants and jacket. Her cleavage was deep and her breasts barely covered. Within seconds the room grew still. Rena quickly climbed onto Dimitris lap and held onto him.

Penelope walked directly to Angelina and cupped her chin. "Well, hello pretty girl." She faked sweetness.

Angelina did not take to her and backed away. When Rena saw this she quickly jumped off Dimitri's lap and took Angelina's hand to bring her closer to them. Georgios felt the tension and knew he had to protect the girls. When Penelope walked towards them, he ran to her and began kicking her shins with brute force. He had an awful feeling about her and recognized fear in Rena. It was an unpleasant scene but he was difficult to stop.

Christina couldn't contain her son from the attack. His father pulled him away. "Georgios, you will get a beating if you don't curb your behavior." he scolded even though he understood his son's anger.

Penelope, played the role of the victim and was rubbing her legs. "I'll be fine." She walked to the other side of the table and sat next to Sandy. Her blood was boiling in more ways than one. Although she wanted to punish the kids, she wanted to be with Sandy more. For the first time since her girlfriend was thrown out of the house, she felt encouraged. Sandy would be a new opportunity for her and she would do anything to make it happen.

"I'll have to check your shins," Sandy told her.

"So, you are the doctor. I'll need a full exam when you are available."

"Is tomorrow too soon Penelope? I will be at the clinic and Dimitri asked me to take a look at you. The miscarriages must have been emotionally difficult."

"Yes, of course." Penelope was on fire. "Open my bedroom door when you are going down. I'll be ready for you." She tried to size her up with a sexy look of longing but Sandy was already in deep conversation with Yiorgo and didn't get the message.

Everyone ate heartily and were ready for Simeon's brand of entertainment. They coaxed him to play and when he got up, Rena noticed him for the first time. She was mesmerized by his warm brown color and happy eyes. He saw her staring and motioned for her to come. She took Georgios and Angelina with her. He lifted her onto the piano bench. "Look at those long fingers. You have the makings of a piano player." She gave him a big smile. He laid her fingers one at a time on the keys and helped her play a few notes. She adored the piano and Simeon.

Georgios climbed onto the bench next to her and gazed with pride at her accomplishment. He loved her and didn't want to lose her attention to anyone else. Since she was happy, he would go along with whatever she wanted if he could stay close.

Angelina laid her face on the piano and made soft humming sounds. This did not escape Strati's attention. He wanted ask Frankie if she had ever done this before. This was a sign of a hearing problem, he thought.

Dimitri was pleased at Rena's reaction to Simeon. He thought it may be a promising union.

Both Anre and Simeon were kindhearted and would make an ideal family for Rena. She could possibly live with them in the States and when they were entertaining on board the Olympia in the summer, she could stay on the island. It was ideal. He would size up their relationship in the next couple of weeks before approaching them. No doubt Rena would be comfortable with two loving people. Actually, he thought they were a perfect match.

The children spent the night at the house. Beds were set up in Rena's room. Simeon, Anre and Dimitri kissed Rena goodnight and she couldn't have been happier. Angelina stayed in the room too, leaving Frankie the freedom to be with Sandy. He needed her to help him cope with the nightmares. Everyone else went home including Katina.

CHAPTER 60

Yiorgo came by early to pick up Sandy. She was going to size up the clinic and give Penelope a physical. She heard him honking but had slept in and wasn't prepared.

He went in and waited near the stairs looking up with anticipation. Her shoes were in her hand as she came flying down the steps. Yiorgo stood at the bottom watching her. He wanted to kiss her but was waiting for a sign that she was interested.

"I'm running late…slept in. I have to tell Penelope we're leaving. Do you think it's a good idea for you to assist with the exam?"

Yiorgo heard the melody of her voice but wasn't sure what she said. He was in a trance watching her bounce down in her yellow cotton dress. Her hair was a massive burgundy storm. Her grey eyes were fixed on him.

"Yiorgo, did you hear me?"

"I wasn't listening. I'm sorry."

"Never mind." She bent to put on her shoes and her breasts spilled over the top of her dress rocking in slow motion.

Yiorgo was mesmerized. He saw himself burying his face in her cleavage.

"Are you okay? Your face is flushed." She felt his forehead. "I think you may have a fever. Let's take your temp when we get to the clinic."

He trembled when she touched him but was incapable of uttering any kind of response.

"I'll let Penelope know we're going." She knocked on the door. "I'm leaving with Yiorgo. Come when you're ready."

Sandy was laughing as she tried to pull herself together. "I'm usually more organized." She played with her hair trying unsuccessfully to tie a multicolored scarf around her head.

"Let me do it." Yiorgo took the scarf from her hands, lifted her hair and wrapped the fabric slowly around her head. As he leaned toward her and tied a bow on the side of her face, he felt her warm breath on his neck. This was the defining moment. He was so turned on, there wasn't chance in hell he was going to give up on her, Frankie or no Frankie. "You are perfect." He kissed her cheek lightly then led her to the car. His legs were weak. Never before had he been engulfed by such powerful emotions. He now knew the true meaning of lovesick.

Sandy was not unfamiliar with this kind of attention. However, she realized this was more than lust. Yiorgo was serious about her. She really enjoyed his subtle advances but wasn't blown away. After all, Frankie was the hottest man she had ever met. Even though Yiorgo was handsome, she didn't believe he could measure up in the sex department. Yet, there was a masculine, protective aura about him that she found enticing.

Without much talk, they arrived at the clinic and Yiorgo led her in. Here, he was in command. He prepared the instruments on the tray for the exam. He also indicated that she should be aware of Penelope's odd behavior. His feeling was that she was a strange, volatile woman. There were stories about her outbursts from the help in the mansion. They thought she had a touch of insanity.

Sandy concluded, he was genuine and discovered she was attracted to him. "Yiorgo, do you want to participate? Your opinion would be valuable. I don't understand why Penelope didn't come to you to begin with. Don't you find that unusual?"

"Everything this woman does is off. I think it best that you perform the exam alone. I'll be in the next room if you need me.

CHAPTER 61

Penelope was furious. "Who does she think she is expecting me to go to the clinic on my own." she was shouting. She put on her sexy black lingerie and a red Chanel shift that hugged her body. Two thin leather strips hung from her neck. She would take her time hoping Sandy would wonder if she was coming. Usually, the women she found attractive did not let her down. She had a sixth sense and made sure they were into her brand of B & D.

Although Sandy was an enigma and her sexual preferences were still doubtful, Penelope felt this opportunity should not be missed. Besides, she was positive, she could make her fly to Mt. Olympus. No denying it. Sandy's male lovers couldn't come close in that department. Only a woman knows what brings ultimate satisfaction to another woman. She also wanted to discover if burgundy was her true color and longed to torture her into heights of passion. All the better if she heard her whimper and cry out for mercy.

"Hello…hello…" Penelope put on her happy voice as she opened the clinic door.

"Come in Penelope." Sandy was professional. "I'm ready for you. Please remove your clothing behind the curtain and slip into this gown. Don't be anxious. I will be thorough but gentle."

"I'm not uncomfortable. I'm sure you're an excellent doctor." She stripped down but kept her bikini underwear and leather straps hidden in her hand.

Sandy did the preliminary exam then put Penelope's feet into the stirrups and parted her knees.

"Please stop. First I have to confess something." Penelope sounded breathless.

Sandy was surprised but stopped what she was about to do and walked to the head of the exam table.

"I hate Dimitri. When he touches me it makes me ill."

"I don't think you should be discussing this with me, Penelope. That is something very private. Besides I have the utmost respect for him."

"Look at me, Sandy. Come closer and listen. I did not miscarry. Actually, I aborted my pregnancies and would do it again."

"My God." Before she finished the sentence Penelope grabbed her head and shoved the black underwear in her mouth. She wrapped her long legs around her and tied her wrists behind her back with lightning speed. Sandy was shocked and didn't have time to react before her uniform was ripped open.

"Stop struggling. You're gonna love this." She pinned her face down on the exam table and buried her long nails into Sandy's buttocks but before she could continue, Sandy's mustered up her strength and kicked backward knocking her against the tray of instruments that crashed to the floor.

Yiorgo heard the disturbance and flew through the door. It took him a few seconds to realize what was happening. He was mortified. "Get the hell out of here," he shouted and backhanded Penelope across the face.

Penelope was stunned and fell to her knees. "You prick. She begged for it." she screamed. "I'll deny it if you say anything to Dimitri." She crawled behind the curtain, put her dress on and ran out rubbing her swollen face.

Yiorgo cut the straps from Sandy's hands and pulled the panties from her mouth. He held her and rocked her back and forth. "My poor beautiful baby. I should have remained with you." She was crying. Yiorgo wrapped a sheet around her and noticed the blood running down her backside. "Lie down and let me take care of you."

"She aborted her own children. What are we going to tell Dimitri?"

"The truth. He will be hurt but this is the best way to handle it. This will sting a bit." He gently pressed medicine on the wounds while admiring her body. "You are the loveliest woman I have ever laid eyes on. Do I have a chance?" He looked at her with puppy dog eyes.

"Except for being with you, this has been the worst day of my life, Yiorgo. I'll have to get dressed and decide how to tell Dimitri."

"We'll do it together. You haven't answered my question."

"Yes, but not now. I'll have to speak to Frankie."

She took off the sheet and walked in her naked splendor to the closet. "You are a goddess." he whispered hoarsely.

The phone was ringing and when he answered it was Dimitri. "Yiorgo, may I speak with Sandy? I'd like to know what is wrong with Penelope. Did she find the problem?"

"We'll be right up to talk to you, brother." He hung up, walked over to Sandy and kissed her. His heart was in his throat.

His kiss was warm and tender, not something she was used to. "Not yet, Yiorgo. It wouldn't be right." It shouldn't go further. She was thinking of Frankie.

"Don't make me wait too long. I don't know if I can take it." He watched her putting on her clothes and the mounting pressure in his loins was painful. He almost burst in his pants. "Just touch me. That's all I'll ask for now." he closed his eyes and whispered. "One stroke will suffice, Sandy, please."

She walked across the room slowly and reached between his legs. He almost cried when she caressed him. Then she walked out. "Let's talk to Dimitri. It is imperative we see him before she puts a spin on what transpired."

"Dimitri will believe me. He knows I always tell him the truth. Wait for me in the car while I change." His pants were wet, something that had never happened to him before.

CHAPTER 62

Sandy and Yiorgo were in Dimitri's office explaining Penelope's behavior. His face turned ashen when he realized she aborted their babies. He didn't respond verbally to their words but his expressions ebbed and peaked with each tormented emotion.

"Thank you. I will handle this appropriately." He walked across the hall to their bedroom.

Penelope froze when she saw him. "Dimitri, it was awful. You have to understand what they did to me…"

"Don't utter one more lie. If you do, I'll have Marvin snap you into tiny pieces and feed you to the fish. Leave now. Take nothing with you. You have plenty of money. We are divorced as of this moment. Sign this paper and go. Penelope, you will not talk about our private matters. If I hear anything, you won't get a second chance to speak. I will have your tongue ripped out."

Penelope was terrified and left quickly without a plan. Finances were not an issue but she didn't know where to go on such short notice. Surely one of her female lovers would temporarily assist. She would say it was best to be on her own. Nothing else. The thought of losing her tongue kept her from getting even with the bastard, she thought. Perhaps, she would contact Margarite once she went to the airport.

Dimitri called a meeting of the help requesting they strip the bedroom. "Either give everything away or burn it. I don't want one thread that belonged to her in this room." He was surprised at how happy they were that she was gone. Apparently, he wasn't aware that she tormented the staff. They never told him for fear of retaliation.

He walked into his office and embraced Sandy. "She's out of here. Because of you, the children are safe. I'm sorry for what you endured. I'll make it up to you."

"It isn't your fault, Dimitri. You are one of the finest gentlemen I know. This incident wasn't anticipated, and you owe me nothing."

"I heard rumors about her volatile behavior but did not know about her sexual orientation. Penelope did not reveal herself to our family. We rarely spent time with her and when we did, she was on her best behavior." Yiorgo said seriously. "When I saw this, I was shocked. There is no way I would have guessed."

"I never really bonded with her. I thought she kept me at arm's length because she felt I didn't love her. Oh Lord!! She killed our babies. What kind of woman does that?" He put his face in his hands. "I want to see Katina, Yiorgo. I need her."

"I'll phone her and tell her to come up to the old house."

"One good thing has come out of this, Rena will no longer be afraid. The kids can have run of the place. I think I should go up and tell them." He walked out as his phone was ringing.

"I'll answer it." Sandy reached for the phone. It was the United States calling for Frankie. "Angelo, is that you? Myrna isn't feeling well? This is Sandy. Put her on."

"How is my Angelina? Let me talk to her and Frankie?"

"They are not available now Myrna. I'll have them phone you later. Angelina is fine. She is having a ball with the children. There is nothing worry about. Now, tell me about your health."

Myrna was rambling on about her condition when Sandy started laughing. "I won't be home for a while but I can assure you, this isn't an illness. I believe you're pregnant, Myrna."

Myrna screamed and handed the phone to Angelo. "Are you sure? It goes to show you Myrna, I still got led in my pipes. I'm the man! Where is Frankie?"

"He isn't here but I'll tell him the good news. Take care of your wife Angelo. She should see a doctor in Steubenville."

"I forgot to tell you. Timmy got married to a gorgeous Greek dame. They didn't invite anyone because Mrs. Georgia was afraid Frankie would stop the wedding. They are on their way back home."

"Frankie will be disappointed that he didn't witness the nuptials. I'll have him phone you asap."

Yiorgo was watching and listening to Sandy. Hearing her laughter made him feel wonderful.

"Good news? A baby?"

"Frankie's mom. Amazing isn't it?"

He phoned Katina. "Dimitri needs you."

CHAPTER 63

Katina dropped what she was doing and flew out of the house without explaining anything to her husband. Tripping on her ugly dress, she almost cried thinking that Dimitri had told her she resembled an old scrub woman. *Never mind what I'm wearing. It doesn't stay on my body very long, anyway. He prefers me naked, she thought.* Yiani was cursing as she left but she ignored him. Dimitri needed her and nothing else mattered.

Yiani tolerated Katina and the bastard kids that he pretended were his own. He wanted to do away with the lot of them but kept up the illusion of the family man for sake of his reputation in the village. From the day he married Katina, he realized she would never be his. There was no love between them. Sex was nonexistent. In fourteen years, she submitted hand full of times. If the twins weren't the spitting image of Dimitri, he may have believed they were his offspring.

"Don't touch me." she begged. "You smell like fish." "I'm a fisherman. That's what I do for a living." The tragedy was that Yiani couldn't control his

temper. When she rejected his advances, he would beat her. "Some day you will pay. You will suffer beyond belief." He planned to do away with Katina or the girls and make it seem accidental.

Yiani's mother was continuously in a state of denial. She always believed they would see the light and try to preserve their marriage for the sake of the children. She understood he was a mean, unattractive man. He was small without an ounce of flesh on his body. His face was covered with scares and deep lines burnt in by the sun. Worse yet, he was a drunk. Oftentimes when she tried to protect Katina and the children, he would strike her too "Shame on you, Yiani. If your father were alive he would give you a taste of your own medicine." His ugliness wouldn't matter if he was kinder. "Your drinking has done you in, Yiani."

Katina and Dimitri arrived at the old house simultaneously. They fell in each other's arms and onto the cot. "Dimitraki, my love, what is wrong?" She caressed his hair and kissed his face.

"I need you and the children, now. Leave him and come with me. I threw Penelope out. If you are worried about your reputation, we will go to America."

"When? Who will tell our girls?"

"Both of us. We shouldn't hide the truth any longer, Katina. I think down deep they know."

"Why is Penelope gone?"

Dimitri told her the story in short but powerful phrases. She gasped when he told her Penelope aborted the pregnancies. Katina held him and cried. "May God forgive her."

"May God forgive me, Katinaki. I am a man of the world who did not know his own wife. If I had understood her, this would have never happened. I was busy nursing my wounds from losing you and gave no attention to that monster. The fact that she preferred women never entered my mind. Her freedom would have been granted willingly had I known. The abuse she enjoyed dishing out to the help and aborting her own children was too much for me to bare. Poor Rena was frightened to death of her."

"Don't blame yourself. You are a wonderful person, Dimitraki and always did what you believed was right. God will judge her."

"I won't live without you any longer. There is nothing on earth that I can't have but what I need is you and my girls. I want to bathe you in luxury."

"Stop, Dimitraki." She covered his lips with her hand. "All I ever desired was to nurture you, my darling. Nothing else matters. The girls adore you. It won't be a problem for them! But we must be careful how we approach Yiani."

When Katina and Dimitri were young, they met in the secret cave to design their future. They talked about traveling the globe when he became a sea captain, how many children they would have, their home near the shore. Their lives changed dramatically when Marika and Saranti got killed in an earthquake at the lagoon. Dimitri was on the sea commanding a freighter. He didn't find out about the deaths, until months later. It was too late to save Katina from the savage she was forced to marry.

Papou was unable to protect her. Although he was still alive, he had a massive stroke when he learned Saranti and Marika were gone. Paraskevoula was devastated. No amount of love could bring him back to his former glory. Eventually, he passed and she couldn't live without him. There was no one left for Dimitri, except for Strati and Yiorgo.

Dimitri finally returned to the village and discovered Katina in the old house. She went there every day and prayed for his return. The house was in perfect order as if Marika were still alive. They shed tears and made love. She knew immediately that she was pregnant. When she returned home, she submitted to Yiani's advances. It made her sick inside.

Dimitri needed to take care of Katina financially. When he returned to his post, the incident with Konstantinides occurred and his life took a dramatic turn. By taking a bullet for the shipping tycoon, he sealed his future. He inherited the ships and married the daughter.

Papou had been a masterful teacher throughout the years and Dimitri was confident in his abilities. He turned his fortune into an empire.

CHAPTER 64

Katina and Dimitri returned to the mansion and discovered complete chaos. The children were running through Penelope's room throwing her things out of the windows. They were screaming delightfully. Even Angelina was enjoying herself. Frankie was keeping an eye on them. He was thinking that his sister had never experienced anything like this before. Had she not been over-protected, her life may have been more enjoyable.

"Frankie, have you seen the girls."

"They are in your office, Dimitri."

He told the kids to carry on and went into his office with Katina. "Are you waiting for me?"

They both threw their arms around him. "We want to discuss a serious matter with you," Dimitra said. "Since mom is here, we'll include her in the conversation."

"Mom, please forgive us." Marika looked at her mother pleadingly. "We're not trying to upset you. The misery we endure with that horrible man at home is too much for us. We want to leave with our Uncle and go to America."

Dimitri told them to stop talking and start preparing for a different life. They will move into the mansion until he is ready to depart for the states and their mother would be with them.

"I've always loved your mother and you girls are the image of me. There is no denying it any more. You are my daughters."

"What did I tell you, Marika? He really is our father!"

"May we call you father? Uncle Dimitri never really sat well with us. We always fantasized you were our dad."

"Let's wait till it is official. Meanwhile, you can call me dad privately."

"Can we go to Steubenville?" Dimitra asked. Of course, they both had ulterior motives. They wanted to get to know Frankie better.

Katina was thrilled. She imagined it would be more difficult to discuss their paternity. "Finally, we can be together."

Young Saranti had been eavesdropping and ran off to report the news to Strati and Yiorgo. They threatened him to keep quiet until Dimitri announced it.

Frankie walked into the office. "There isn't much left in Penelope's room. The kids and the help have torn it apart. People are coming around picking up her things."

"Great. You and my girls can take the children for a swim before dinner."

"Did you hear about my mother? She is pregnant! We want you to be the godfather."

"Myrna will get two for one. Katina and I will christen the baby, if it's okay with you. Matter of fact, we'll all be coming to Steubenville."

Dimitra and Marika left with Frankie. He put his arms around both of them and spoke softly. "We are practically family. No one messes with you or they'll answer to me. Got it?" The girls were totally thrilled.

"Is Sandy in the building or is she still out with Yiorgo?" Frankie suspected Yiorgo was into her but it wasn't an issue with him. He had no intention of interfering with her personal life. Yiorgo seemed to be a standup guy. If she wanted him, more power to her. He preferred a softer more feminine woman. For sure she was gorgeous but too strong for his taste. The friendship and probably sex would always be his for the taking, even if she got married.

"We saw Yiorgo leave earlier. I think Sandy is taking a swim." Marika told him.

"Do you want to go to the pool?" Dimitra was hoping.

"I have to keep an eye on the children. They have gone nuts since Penelope left. Let's take them with us."

Frankie was less concerned with Sandy and more worried about Angelina. He wasn't sure what would become of the baby since Dimitri split with his wife.

Sandy was floating in the pool. She got out to help Frankie with Angelina and the other children. Her swimsuit was a metallic shade trimmed in burgundy. It accented the color of her gray eyes and red hair. She looked like a movie star.

"No wonder Yiorgo is crazed. The poor guy has lost his mind." Frankie wanted her to know he was aware of the situation.

"Does it bother you, Frankie?"

"He is a man and not the first."

"I asked you a question."

"Stay here with him. He would do anything to make you happy. Eventually, you'll fall in love. You and I will always be an item. When you come home to visit, I assume we can do our thing."

"Why can't we…

"No, Sandy. You are a sophisticated lady who shouldn't settle. I'm not a Jew. I'll never measure up to your standards. Your family will look down on me. Yiorgo is a doctor. You'll make a perfect couple."

She was hurt but also relieved. What he said was true. But how would she survive in the village. She would have to go home a couple times a year. Besides, Yiorgo didn't ask for marriage even though the signs were there. For sure he wanted more than sex. But, she felt she should make him suffer for a while before submitting. It would make things a lot more exciting.

Food was being served on the terrace. Simcon and Anre had arrived and were helping the children out of the pool. Simeon picked up Rena. Georgios had a fit and bit him on the leg. Simeon had to lift him too. The twins waited to see where Frankie would be sitting.

Yiorgo was suddenly at the doorway with his medical bag. "I need to check your wounds, Sandy.

If I don't change the bandages, you may become infected."

"Take her to our room on the third floor, Yiorgo. Make sure you check her out thoroughly. Don't miss anything. I don't want her to have a medical problem later on. She is fragile." Frankie was egging him on but he didn't get it.

Yiorgo followed her up the stairs. Her swimsuit slipped into her behind and she was pulling on it. He almost toppled down the steps. When he went into the room, he asked her to remove the suit and lie face down on the bed. She whimpered just enough to make him crazy.

He removed some of the bandages and began kissing her behind. "Yiorgo, please kiss me here. I think you missed a spot." She got on her knees and exposed herself completely. She placed her hand between her legs and showed him a place where she claimed it was hurting. He bent over to kiss her there. He had never seen anything more perfect. Perspiration dripped from his face and he felt faint.

"Stop, stop," she cried out. "What if Frankie is on his way up?" She didn't bother to cover up.

Yiorgo got up, backed out of the room slowly while looking between her creamy thighs. Then he ran down the stairs forgetting his medical bag in the room.

Frankie kept an eye on the door. He saw Yiorgo and called his name. Poor Yiorgo was shaken and he didn't respond, until Frankie went up to him. "Is she okay? I hope you didn't miss anything."

"No, no, I didn't but I left my case in the room."

"Go on up and get it. Bring Sandy down for lunch."

Yiorgo was afraid he would have one of those episodes where he came in his pants. He was in pain and was about to burst.

"I'll return shortly."

Frankie went up to check on Sandy. "What the hell did you do him?"

"I made him suffer!"

"Get dressed and come to eat. He'll be back as soon as he takes care of his hard on."

Saranti went to bring his parents. When Strati and Christina showed up, Dimitri questioned them about Yiorgo. He said he had an announcement to make and wanted both of his brothers support. They claimed Yiorgo was at the clinic feeling a bit under the weather.

Frankie suggested Sandy should check him out and bring him back with her. "When I saw him earlier, he seemed to have a fever. Make sure you take his temperature."

CHAPTER 65

S he rushed to the clinic and found him lying on
an exam table. He could barely talk. All he did
was moan and shake. "Yiorgo, you're on fire.
Let me take your temp." His teeth were chattering
and she couldn't get the thermometer in his mouth
so she took it another way. It was sky high. She gave
him an injection and phoned the house. "Bring me
a barrel of ice. No children please. I'm not sure if
what he has is contagious."

Dimitri did not inform anyone of Yiorgo's condition. He claimed he was needed and would return
soon. His kitchen staff filled containers with ice
and put them in the car. He was alarmed when he
got to the clinic. Sandy was on the bed with Yiorgo
holding him.

"Let's pack him Dimitri. His fever isn't going
down." While they iced him, she kept saying, "You'd
better come out of this. We're gonna get married."
He was still shaking but he heard what she said and
tried to smile. "I love you Yiorgo. Do you hear me?"

His eyes were closed and he couldn't respond.
"Please open your eyes!" She was frightened that

he was going to die. She always kept her cool and couldn't understand why she acted like a fool instead of a doctor. She was borderline hysterical.

Dimitri stood around pacing the floor. This he didn't anticipate. He was sure Yiorgo would be fine and Sandy was over reacting. "Stay calm or you'll scare him to death."

Yiorgo heard that, too. He tried saying he was better but his teeth chattered. He wanted the ice off of his body and Sandy on it.

She continuously took his temperature and it was coming down. *She just wants to see my behind, he thought.*

Finally, his temp was normal and she began removing the ice. He opened his eyes and said "Cold." She jumped on the table and held him. "Angelina's baby… ours," he said before he fell asleep in her arms.

Dimitri left them alone and went back home. He explained what had happened and they were shocked. Strati said he should have been there to help his brother. Christina started to cry. "No…no…no. Don't cry." He kissed her tenderly. "You'll disturb the baby, sweetheart.

"Trust me. He is in capable hands. Let's leave those two alone. Tomorrow I will confide the latest news."

"Dimitri, what makes you think we aren't privy to what's going on? You….Katina….the girls. We always knew it would happen." Strati told him.

"The twins are mirrors of you." Anre said. "I knew it years ago when I started coming to Kardamyla."

Dimitri put his arms around his daughters. "Take care of the children. Your mother and I have a lot of planning. I also want to have a talk with Simeon and Anre in my office."

Simeon and Anre agreed to take Rena to the states and bring her to the village every summer. Simeon wanted her to take piano lessons. He also would to hire a tutor before enrolling her in school full time. They agreed that she was bright and would pick up on her studies quickly. The only thing that worried Dimitri is that she would be separated from Georgios. They were glued at the hip and he knew both of them would be hurt. "Perhaps we can get them together during the holidays.".

They were on board and totally happy they would have the opportunity to love and raise a child. Dimitri said he could adopt her and send her to the states for an education. That way, it wouldn't cause problems for Anre and Simeon. *He thought it wouldn't be a bad idea if they got a home in Steubenville. He would discuss that with them later.*

"Shall we take her back on the ship?"

"If you think that is the best way. I'll let you make the decision."

"Let's talk to her, Simeon. We'll explain our lifestyle and gently introduce her to being our girl."

When they left, Dimitri turned his focus to Katina. "Should we go ahead and do this right away or do you need time. Waiting won't make things any easier with Yiani."

Katina insisted on telling her husband she was leaving him. Dimitri didn't agree. "He may attack you Katinaki. Then I would have to kill him. Why don't you stay here with our girls and let me handle it?"

"It wouldn't be the honorable thing to do, Dimitri. I am worried he would take it out on my mother-in-law. She was on our side in every horrible situation and paid for it dearly."

"Why didn't you tell me how damn bad it was? I would have taken you away from here a long time ago. Bring the old lady with you if the girls want her."

They kissed freely and without regret. This was the first time they weren't afraid of exposing their feelings.

"There was a constant pain in my heart living without you."

"I missed you every moment of every day. I would have given away my fortune to be with you. It's over. Nothing will keep us apart again." He held her face next to his heart.

CHAPTER 66

Yiorgo opened his eyes and found Sandy with her arms and legs around his body. Her face was on his chest. It was dark outside and she was fast asleep on the exam table with him. He was nude but she had her dress on. They were lying under a sheet.

"You naughty girl." his muscular arms squeezed her closer to him. "You are a tease. You showed me everything then kicked me out. No wonder I got sick."

She smiled. "I should take your temperature again."

"You enjoyed that, didn't you?"

"Your butt is fine."

He kissed her and ran his tongue in her mouth. There was a promise in the way he approached her, a strength that she felt would lead to extraordinary pleasure.

"Now that we're alone, you're not going anywhere. I want to see you as you were in your room. You know what I mean, when you were playing with me. Show me where you want to be kissed. Do it exactly the same way," he demanded. He rolled off the table, turned her on her stomach and pulled off her dress. "On your knees lady." His voice was husky and scary.

"Are you angry, Yiorgo?"

"Shush. Let's see how far you can go with that game. Frankie isn't here to walk in on us. While you are exposing yourself, let me here you whimper."

She pulled down her panties and opened up as he told her, but started to cry. "I know I was playing with you...

"Shush. Where did you want me to kiss you? Here or here." He bit her in two different places. "Oh yes. How nice of you to allow me access." He flipped her over and dragged her to the end of the exam table. He put her feet in stirrups and pushed her knees open. "This is perfect."

"Yiorgo, please let mc go," she sounded frightened.

"After I finish the exam. After all, if we are going to be married, I need to make sure you insides are in order." He slowly began sucking her inner thighs from the knees up moving his mouth from one thigh to the other. When he reached her private place he stopped and put his lips on her belly. He wanted to taste her but thought it best to make her wait. He left marks everywhere.

She was trembling and pushing her hips up expecting him to enter her. Her hands massaged her breasts and she squeezed her nipples with her fingers. "What do you think you're doing lady? He slapped her hands away. Keep them above your head."

He opened her up and put his fingers inside moving them around and pushing deeper. "Beg me for it. Tell me how much you want me inside of you."

He heard her crying softly. "Please. Please." Her hips were high off the table.

The position she was in made him crazy. Even though he wanted her to suffer as he did, he wasn't sure he could wait. There wasn't an inch on his body that wasn't turned on. He stepped up on a stool and pushed her knees back and slowly entered her making a strong rocking motion. Neither of them held back. Their orgasms were long and strong. "Oh Yiorgo, I didn't expect you would be so damn good." She could barely get the words out of her mouth.

He fell forward onto her breasts. "I didn't get a chance to fondle your breasts. Don't get up," he said gruffly. He washed himself then brought a container of water and poured it between her legs. He took a brush and lathered her there with long strokes. She was laughing and gasping. He brought the mirror overhead to let her watch him remove the hair with a raiser.

She raised herself up on her elbows. "Stop it. You are not going to shave me down there."

"No...no...don't."

"It's mine and I want it cleanly shaven. I'll leave hair on the top. Why don't you cry and see if that works, lady?"

"I won't allow you to treat me this way. I have my rights." she tried to close her legs and get up.

"Shush, you have no rights. Behave, or I will show you no mercy. Your punishment will be severe. Open up."

She did as he said and was swearing under her breath.

He dried her and pulled her clitoris with his teeth then slowly moved up to her breasts encircling each one with his hands. He sucked each nipple like a hungry baby wanting milk. Her fist pounded his back and her other hand rubbed between her legs. "Yes...yes....yes...Yiorgo!" He went down, pushed her hand away, put his mouth there, sucked and licked the wetness.

"No more Yiorgo. I'm done. Stop. Stop." He took her feet out of the stirrups, wrapped her legs on his hips, lifted her and inserted himself deep inside.

"No. I can't do it." Her arms were around his neck and her head on his shoulder. She was limp.

"Worn out lady?" He moved her hips back and forth until he she began to respond. He felt there was another climax in her. "One more. Let me feel it." He was deep inside of her and couldn't hold back any longer. "Come on lady." He sat in a chair and bounced her up and down. "For a small woman you can take in a large one." They came together. Her head fell backward and she screamed out his name.

His lips were on her mouth as he maneuvered her into the shower. She was in no condition to do anything. He washed her body slowly. She could barely speak. Suddenly, she was alert. "I have to go. Frankie needs me and I'm late." He wanted to slap her. Instead he threw her out of the shower. "Don't come back!"

"You don't understand, Yiorgo. He needs an injection. Come with me. I'll tell you along the way. He knows about us and wanted this for me." she was still wet when she put her clothes on.

Yiorgo calmed down and got dressed quickly. "What kind of an injection?"

"You may get upset if I tell you. He is suffering and needs help to sleep. His nightmares are destroying him. I have to stay there to keep an eye on Angelina in case she wakes up at night and looks for us."

"I'll buy that. Let's go." He kissed her and ran his tongue under her lips. "You are boiling hot, lady. I'm wondering how long I can keep you satisfied."

"Forever, Yiorgo."

When they arrived, they found Frankie on the terrace. He was perspiring and calling for God's forgiveness.

Sandy knelt at his feet. "I'm sorry I'm late. Yiorgo was ill and I had to stay a while."

"Get it, now. I need it."

"Let's go upstairs, Frankie. You can sleep in your bed."

"Can't...too hot. Hurry."

"I'm going up for the medicine and to check on Angelina. Yiorgo, please stay with him. Can you wipe him off with a wet towel? Get it in the kitchen."

"You'll be okay my friend. Well take care of you." He pressed a cool sponge on his face.

"Thanks buddy. Sandy is gorgeous, isn't she? You two will be happy together." He was shaking. "Oh God help me. Please."

Sandy arrived quickly and turned him to one side. She pulled his pants down and stuck the needle in his hip. "It's okay Frankie. You'll be fine," she spoke gently as she watched him fall asleep.

"This can't go on, Sandy. There has to be another solution. Do you know what is making him suffer this way?"

"Maybe, but not sure. Can you help me take him to his bed?"

Yiorgo lifted him easily and climbed three flights. He didn't want to leave Sandy.

"Shall we sit on the terrace for a while since Angelina is fast asleep. I have a serious issue to discuss."

They held hands and smiled at each other. "You are the most enchanting woman I have ever met. If you truly want to marry me, do you think you could live in this village?"

"You're here aren't you? We can go home once in a while....I mean back to the States. What do you think?"

"I need to meet the family."

"Was this the important issue?"

"Strati and I have gone over this again and again. We don't think Angelina is retarded."

"What are you saying?"

"There are indications that she has a hearing problem. We don't believe she is completely deaf.

She has blossomed since she's been with the other children. Matter of fact, she understands a lot more than most of you think. We can take her to a specialist in Hora for an evaluation."

"This never occurred to me. Were we all oblivious to this? If she is deaf, then there is a possibility she can be taught other ways of communication."

"Perhaps surgery or an aide can restore some hearing. I can't say until she's examined."

"Let's get her to the doctor asap."

"What will Frankie say?"

"He'll probably want to be there. He adores her and wouldn't let her go without him."

"I think I'll talk to Dimitri about Frankie. He may know the problem and then we can address it. Drugs are not going to solve it. He's addicted and has to be weaned off."

"I tried Yiorgo, but am not capable. I can't stand seeing him in pain."

"Do you love him Sandy?"

"Of course, but not the way I love you. I want us to get married. Do you think Strati and Christina will approve?"

"I didn't expect to hear that from you. Would it matter?"

"Yes. They will be my family, too."

"They've observed your kindness to the children and care for you already. Our life together with Angelina's baby shows commitment. When we first met, I thought of nothing but bedding you. I realized

I was in love with you the day I tied the scarf around your hair."

"I knew it when you were ill. I was out of my mind."

"We're going to England on our honeymoon to a magical place in the country." He was thinking of Mr. Petro and the Greek Islander. They kept in touch but he was up in the years and was constantly asking the boys to visit. "Bring the children," he always told them.

"Yiorgo. There are things you need to know about me before we take the final step."

"Unnecessary. All I need to know is that you love me, Sandy."

"This discussion is important. You may not agree but I have to put it out there. Firstly, this is a special request. I'll go along with whatever you decide. How do you feel about getting married at a temple in Pittsburgh? My family would be thrilled. We can also have a celebration here for our friends and relatives."

"I'm thinking how happy Papou would be. I have no objections."

"Another even more important issue. I'm terribly frightened of bearing children. I don't want to get pregnant."

"I don't understand. What scares you about having a baby?" He hadn't really thought about it before today. What would she do if she was already pregnant? They weren't careful during lovemaking.

"I am a very small woman with narrow hips. I've seen women with the same body structure who have suffered tremendously and ended up with a cesarean or worse. Their body was ripped apart or others died. They had stretch marks everywhere and were destroyed when they were cut up. Their healing was long and arduous." She didn't tell him she was taking pills to keep it from happening. Many husbands were not supportive. They were angry and blamed their wives for not submitting to them."

He pulled her close to him and petted her hair. "My baby. I couldn't stand it if anything hurt you that way. You are an obstetrician and should know these things. Perhaps we can consult the experts and make a decision at that time. One way or another, it won't stop us from going forward with our wedding. Angelina's baby will be ours! Adopting would be another option if we want more kids. Look at Katina. Marika adopted her and they adored each other."

It was already daylight and there was movement in the kitchen. "We've been talking most of the night. Let's get coffee. A decision doesn't have to be made now. The only thing we know for sure is that we're in love and nothing will keep us apart, my lovely lady."

They were kissing when Dimitri showed up on the terrace. "Morning. Where's Frankie? I left him out here a few hours ago. He wasn't in good shape."

"I gave him an injection to calm him. Yiorgo carried him up. He approves of us Dimitri."

"Do you know why he is suffering, brother? There is a possibility I can help."

"I do know but can't reveal it without his permission. I'll ask him to tell you. It won't be easy for him."

"We're starving. Let's have a hearty meal this morning." Dimitri brought coffee from the kitchen and asked the help to make American breakfast. They talked about their plans for the future. Dimitri was worried that Katina wanted to wait before telling Yiani she was leaving him. She thought it best to bring it up after Angelina had the baby and they were ready to leave for Ohio. The girls would not return to that miserable house. Dimitri was worried that Yiani would harm Katina and wanted her to stay away from him.

"He is a crazy man but how far would he go, Dimitri. Why don't you bring Katina here to wait it out. What could he do to her under your roof. If Marvin comes, she'll be well protected."

They told him about their wedding plans and he was delighted they chose to marry in a synagogue. He was hoping to be with them. He said Papou would be watching over them. His biggest joy was when he learned Angelina may not be retarded. He didn't want to delay her exam in Hora. "Set it up immediately. We'll take her by helicopter. The children should go with her to make her comfortable. They can all be tested."

"Great idea, Dimitri." Sandy embraced him. "We'll talk to Strati today and have him phone the doctor."

"I'll do it. They wouldn't dare delay one damn minute if I call. Should we bring him here?"

"No. His equipment is in the hospital. It's best that we go there."

The help was setting up the table and bringing in pancakes, eggs, bacon etc."

"What the hell kind of breakfast is this? Who eats this way early in the morning?"

Sandy laughed at him. "You have a lot to learn about American eating habits.

CHAPTER 67

GOODBYE

The day was extremely difficult, especially for the children. Rena was packed and ready to travel with Simeon and Anre. She couldn't understand why Georgios was not going with them. She was under the impression they would always be together.

Dimitri tried to explain she would see Georgios during the holidays and every summer. He would make sure of it.

Per Dimitri's suggestion, they decided Steubenville would be the best place to take up residence in one of the homes that belonged to him. That way when Angelina went back, Rena's friendship with her would continue to flourish.

The twins could not wait to go to America and explained to Rena they would be together soon. But Rena's heart was broken. She held Georgios hand tightly while they walked to the seaside with her new family. As they were about to board the yacht, Rena pulled Georgios aside and whispered sweet words to him. They held each other and she told him Mr. Dimitri always kept his promises.

Georgios teared and refused to leave until the last vestige of the yacht had faded. Saranti tried to console him. "Let's go home. Mom misses you." He ignored his brother. Instead, he marched up to the mansion and went to the room the children shared. He embraced the black doll Rena had left him, fell onto the bed and cried.

The girls sat with Saranti at the back end of the room while Angelina stayed on the bed with Georgios. She started speaking to him in Greek explaining that this was only temporary.

Everyone was startled. They knew that she had learned to communicate but didn't realize how well. They watched her skillfully prepare Georgios for life without Rena until she returned to Kardamyla. She told him they should mount a calendar on the door to count the days. He listened to her and even began talking. He had never spoken much before. His devastation turned to hope.

"Remember, Uncle Dimitri said you can phone her every week. You'll have to speak with her." They made plans to decorate the bedroom with flowers when she came back.

Frankie showed up and was surprised when he heard his sister speak. "Hey ladybug, you're going to have to teach me Greek." She put her arms around his neck and she began massaging her belly.

"You'll be all right." Frankie trembled when he realized his little sister was having labor pains. "Don't be frightened."

"I'm not. Sandy explained everything."

Frankie was amazed at Angelina's language skills. It was only few months since the surgery and her speech was perfect. Even though she was fitted with hearing aids, they were changed often. It seemed as though they were unnecessary after the first few weeks.

Angelina was a powerhouse. Dimitri hired a tutor who said she was exceptionally bright. She picked up Greek quickly. It flowed easily from her since she spent most of her time speaking with the children. Frankie and Sandy used American to communicate but she preferred the Greek language. She had never been happier.

Angelina recognized that Frankie was nervous for her. She didn't want him to worry and believed Sandy could explain about the delivery and what would happen to the baby. "Sandy will discuss everything with you, Frankie."

She was thankful that Sandy and Yiorgo planned to be her baby's parents. She would be the aunt when she visited Kardamyla in the summer. Besides, her mother would suffer if she knew the circumstances of her pregnancy. Angelina was fifteen and wise beyond her years. She knew what to do.

CHAPTER 68

"Yiani knows, Dimitri. I think he always knew I would never be his. As for our daughters, the resemblance to you is uncanny. Anyone who has laid eyes on them probably recognized they were yours. The least I can do is tell him we are leaving with you."

"I have an awful feeling, Katinaki. I need to protect you. He is a violent man and could hurt you or the girls. Please let me do the talking. I will give him and his mother enough money for a lifetime."

"It isn't the money, my love. It is his pride. His mother will have to live with us or he will brutalize her claiming she was a part of the scheme. Let me do this my way. Maybe I can save him the humiliation. I will let him tell the villagers it was his idea to send us to America."

"I wish you would allow me to handle this. If you are adamant, I will come with you and wait in the garden. I don't like this Katinaki."

The girls were knocking on his office door. "Dad hurry. Frankie took Angelina to the clinic. She's having the baby."

"Let get going Katinaki. We'll discuss this later. Enter the clinic through the back. We don't want the villagers to catch on. We'll stay in a separate room to wait it out."

CHAPTER 69

Frankie sat in the back room of the clinic. He covered his face with both hands and sobbed thinking about what Angelina was going through. The blame is entirely mine, he thought. If only I had taken care of her the way a brother should, this wouldn't have happened.

As the group walked in, Sandy came through the clinic door. "Angelina is asking for her brother. The delivery was easy."

He jumped from his chair and ran into the room. "Uncle Frankie. Meet your niece, Francesca." Angelina handed him the tiny baby that was wrapped in a multicolored blanket. She had a mass of black hair and her tiny tongue slipped in and out of her pink lips.

"Francesca?" Frankie was in a fog.

"She looks like you and should have your name." Angelina said softly.

Sandy laughed. "Don't be afraid of her. She's strong like her mother. I'll bring in the others." They were all enamored with Francesca. While everyone was fawning over the baby, Dimitri spoke. "Shall we bring her to the mansion, Sandy?"

"That's the best place for the time being. Angelina can spend time with her before she departs for Steubenville. What do you think Yiorgo?"

He was standing in the corner of the room in a daze. This child will be my princess he thought. "The decision is yours and Angelina's."

"Angelina was brave and fearless. It was one of the easiest deliveries I've ever seen. Although she's tired, I'm sure she has the strength to go up to the mansion. Let's wait a while then pack her, the baby and Frankie in the car. I think she should have a private room. I'll stay with her."

"You shouldn't count me out, Sandy. Francesca will need both of us." He whispered to Sandy.

Sandy was surprised at Yiorgo's tenderness. "Of course, my love. Her daddy should be there. Remember that Angelina needs rest. You can hold the baby when she sleeps."

"We must get her an evil eye immediately," Katina said seriously. "Francesca is exquisite and must be protected." The girls agreed they would get it in the morning and make sure they attach it to her clothing.

"That's been done. I bought one encased in gold. But, let's not get ahead of ourselves. Remember she has family who may not agree."

"It is fine, Dimitri. We want to protect her!" Sandy was happy and would go along with what they wanted. "After all it is a Greek custom."

Frankie finally put the baby in Angelina's arms. Tears were falling from his cheeks as he kissed his sister. "I'm so proud of you."

She smiled and touched his cheek. "Stop blaming yourself. This was a miracle, Frankie."

"Let her rest for a while before we leave. You can sit with her, Frankie. Perhaps all of you should go home. We'll bring her when she wakes up. None of the villagers will see us when we exit from the back."

Young Saranti was visibly shaken. Although he was always a gentleman, this time he had an edge of anger to him. His folks had gone to Hora a few hours ago and did not know about the baby. They left him in charge of Georgios who was at the mansion thinking about Rena. "Why did they have to leave today? This was the most exciting time we've ever had. I have a new cousin." He spoke with passion.

"Don't be upset Saranti. Soon your mother will be giving birth and we'll all be here to welcome another baby." Dimitri hugged him. "Let's find Georgios and comfort him. He's hurting from the loss of his Rena."

Saranti softened up. "Can we phone the hotel in Hora to let them know the good news?"

"Of course, son. It will be a while before they arrive. They took the long route."

"Thank you Uncle Dimitri. I'll start walking with the girls."

Even though Saranti was excited about the new baby, he felt sadness in his heart. He realized everything was changing in his world. Rena was gone. Angelina would be leaving shortly and the twins did nothing but talk about going to Steubenville with their mother and father. He saw the twins every single day for their entire lives. There was discomfort in the pit of his stomach. They had no regard for his feelings and probably wouldn't even miss him, he thought. Tears rolled down his cheeks. That hadn't happened to him in years.

"Saranti is something wrong?" Marika spoke tenderly. "Did somebody upset you?"

"We've never seen you like this. You are always composed. What happened" Dimitra asked.

"What do you care about my feelings," he spoke harshly. "All you want to do is be with Frankie and go to Steubenville. We've been like family all our lives, taking care of each other. I'm supposed to go on without you." He ran up the hill towards the mansion.

The girls were shocked. He was right. They ignored him since Frankie came to town. "Saranti…. Saranti…" they both called out to him. "We didn't mean to hurt you. Please forgive us."

"You were always strong and gentlemanly." Dimitra said but he didn't hear her. He had already reached the mansion and was climbing upstairs to the children's room looking for Georgios.

"Marika what are we going to do? We can't leave him here. I doubt his folks will let him come to America. Steubenville is out of the question. It would be wrong. He'll be lost without us." Dimitra thought it best to stay in Kardamyla for the time being. As they grew older, perhaps Saranti could join them at a University in the States.

The girls found him sitting with Georgios who was holding Rena's black doll. He looked embarrassed and started to apologize for his behavior. "I shouldn't have acted immaturely. You have a right to your own lives without me interfering."

"Stop, Saranti. You were absolutely right." Dimitra spoke first. "We are not leaving you ever."

Marika put her arm around his shoulders. "We couldn't exist without you. Today we'll speak to our father and explain we are not ready for changes. If we go to Steubenville it will be for a couple of weeks to attend the christening of Myrna and Angelo's baby. I assume your folks won't mind if you come with us."

Saranti's attitude changed in an instant when he realized the girls really loved him. He was overjoyed and embraced both of them when Georgios started screaming. "Me too. Me too." They were all laughing. "Sure thing, Georgios," Saranti assured him and pulled him close.

CHAPTER 70

MYRNA AND ANGELO

Angelo and Myrna were hosting a private party in the diner. Only the people closest to them were invited. A feast was being prepared to celebrate a miracle.

Mrs. Georgia and Thea Irini brought trays of homemade Greek cookies. Easy was in the kitchen with Angelo helping put the final touches on the food. Annie decorated the tables with candles and Jimmy dropped bottles of ouzo on each one.

Mr. George came with his sons Mike and Timmy. Although he rarely left the house except for work, the boys coaxed him into coming with them. He was proud of his sons and wanted to show off. Mike surprised them by coming to town to congratulate Timmy on his marriage. The bride was unable to join him in the states without the proper papers but was expected in a few weeks. Timmy missed her. She was a pretty girl, shy and innocent. Despite that, he found her alluring. Frankie won't believe it, he thought. I'm a married man now. No more sparring over the dames.

Mike took a tour of the tables and shook hands with the guys crushing their fingers. They groaned. "I'm thinkin' you're my wrestling buddies." He was massive and though he was somewhat of a star in town, lot of guys were afraid of him. He gave them a wild wrestler look that scared them.

"We saw you on TV with Sky High Lee. Man what a show. The way you jumped up, throwed your legs around his neck and brung him to his knees." Johnboy was a bruiser and was nuts about wrestling. He envisioned himself making the moves and couldn't sit still during the match. Mike was his hero.

"The whole town went to Easy's place to watch you on his TV. Them Greeks from Weirton, Follansbee and Wintersville who work with us in the mill came too. We was cheering you. Heard your ma went berserk when she saw you on the tube. She was scared you was gonna get hurt." The big Serb filled him in.

When Mrs. Georgia came, they clammed up. "You crazy peoples." She pointed to each of them. "You want Mihali get killed, eh?"

"I can show you fellas how to take a dive without hurting yourself. Do I have any volunteers?"

Teddy was the smallest guy in the place. "I don't wanna injure you, Mike." His wife hit him in the head and laughed. "If he blows on you, you're finished."

"Come sit with you Pops," Mrs. Georgia dragged him away. The pint size woman had a tight grip on him.

Myrna was greeting everyone at the door with warm hugs. The only glitch, a few ladies of the night showed up without invitations and pushed their way to the head table. "Excuse me. We are closed tonight for a private party."

Candy spoke up. "So damn sorry. Thought you were open for business. We wanna place an order. Where's Angelo?" They looked amused. "Tell him it would have to come strictly from him," she purred. The three of them looked like clowns. Their cheeks and lips were painted in bright red, their eyes lined in black. They were dressed in revealing clothes. People stared at them and the women made funny comments. "Circus must be in town."

Myrna turned on her heels quickly and went to the kitchen. She whispered to Easy who nearly blew up. He came out swinging, grabbed Candy and dragged her out kicking and yelling. The other two ran before he could catch them. They screamed and cursed. "You weren't abusing us the other night when you came to see us strip." They lied wanting to embarrass him. Easy went out again and chased them down the street. A couple of police officers stopped him. "Easy, calm down." He mumbled under his breath and returned to the diner. "Come in for meatballs."

"If it wasn't for my pregnancy, I would have beat them senseless."

Angelo witnessed the scene through the kitchen window. "The nerve of those dames. Why didn't you tell me Myrna? I would have taken care of them." He knew better than to get involved. Candy had been sending him messages that she wanted him back. Fat chance, he thought. No way was he leaving Myrna and his family ever again.

"I didn't want you to ruin your handsome face. They would of scratched your eyes out."

"This is one for the books." Mike and Timmy were laughing. Timmy knew the girls and was explaining to his brother who they were. His father heard him and was infuriated.

"Don't be angry, Pops. Angelo ain't seein' them broads any more. He's devoted to his wife, especially now that his baby is in the oven."

Thea Irini was flabbergasted and wasn't sure how to react. She sat between Mike and Timmy who fawned over her. "It's okay Thea. Your husband was a hero tonight.

"He always protect family." Her voice trembled.

The customers were whispering. A few of the men recognized the strippers but ignored them for fear their wives would realize it. "How the hell did they get in here?" Dominick spoke quietly.

"No tellin' buddy. One of them was Angelo's girlfriend." Myrna's brother Carmine thought he'd better stay away from the club for a while. He didn't want his wife to catch him with his pants down. She threatened to cut off his nuts if she even suspected he went there. "Them bitches are dangerous."

Meanwhile, Jimmy was going from table to table pouring ouzo in special glasses and adding water to make the clear liquor smokey. He explained that to keep from getting inebriated, the ouzo should be sipped between eating small portions of food. Unfortunately for him, he had a drink at every table and was drunk before he got back to Annie. He pulled her on his lap and asked her to sing Besame-Mucho for him. "Come on my sweetheart." He tried to pick up the tune but his voice was terrible.

"Jimmy, I love you. Every inch of you is fabulous except for your voice. Let me sing it for you. He picked her up and danced around the tables with her as she sang their favorite song.

Angelo came out of the kitchen and did a soft second to Annie. "All right everybody. Let's dance." He and Myrna had perfect rhythm.

Easy and Irini were a funny pair. He was large and couldn't maneuver her in the tight spaces. "I take you to keetchen," he said and tangoed into the back. She enjoyed his antics and batted her eyes at him.

Mrs. Georgia was hoping her husband would invite her to dance but Mike took her for a spin instead. "Where did you learn to tango, mom?"

"On ship." Oh, how she remembered. "The Olympia."

Annie finished the song in Spanish and picked it up in Greek. Jimmy was ecstatic and lifted her onto a table. "This is your stage." They were having a ball. When she sang the last cord, he kissed her. He adored her and whatever she did was magic to him.

Mrs. Georgia thought her daughter was crazy but she was Jimmy's problem now and he should deal with it. Mr. George, on the other hand, liked every-thing Annie did. Both the boys thought Jimmy was the best man for Annie. They never saw her enjoy herself till she met him.

Myrna and Angelo stood at the head of their table. "Before we serve the main course, we need to express our gratitude for your support of our Angelina." She began crying. "You tell them the good news Angelo."

"We got a call from Frankie who told us that Angelina is not retarded. She had a hearing impediment that progressed because it wasn't discovered by her doctor. She had surgery and most of the hearing will be restored as she heals. They are teaching her communication skills. Apparently, she is doing quite well." Angelo had his arm around Myrna's shoulders. "If my darling wife wasn't pregnant, we would be leaving for Greece to be with our children. God bless Mr. Dimitri for his help with our baby."

Everyone was delighted and they came up to the couple one at a time to embraced them. Irini said their prayers were answered. Easy was crying and blowing his nose.

Timmy whispered to Mike and Pops that Easy's nose sounded like a trumpet.

Mr. George enjoyed attention from his sons. His wife did nothing but give him dirty looks to make sure he didn't lose his temper. He was afraid of her and chose to keep quiet when she was close by.

"Myrna, I no have better news in my life." Mrs. Georgia said. She knew Angelina was pregnant and had no intention of revealing the secret. She doubted they would bring the baby to Steubenville. "When they comin' home?"

"As soon as she finishes her treatments. I'm hoping before my baby comes. I couldn't be happier. God has finally smiled on us."

"We're here for the meatballs Easy promised us." Angel and Gus were as round as they were tall. They spent their days going from restaurants to bars and had very few confrontations with criminals except for occasionally busting gambling establishments. Itching to solve Chester's murder, they zeroed in on Timmy to see what they could pick up. "Heard you got married."

"Yep. Sure did." Timmy didn't trust these cops. He worried they were on a fishing expedition.

"How's your buddy Frankie?"

There it is, he thought. "Don't know."

"Why did he leave Steubenville?"

"Ask his folks." He left the table and motioned Mike to follow.

Easy brought food. "Angelo makem good meat-balls." He sat down.

The police officers were suspicious that Frankie was involved in Chester's murder. They wondered why he suddenly left the country with his sister. "What happened to Frankie? When is he comin' back?"

"Why you ask 'em? You no hear bout Angelina? Mr. Dimitri take to big doctor check for problem. They find she no retarded. She no can hear good. They do operation in ears." He wanted to punch their lights out but left the table instead so he wouldn't give anything away.

"Jesus Christ." Angel told his partner Gus. "We must be barking up the wrong tree. Besides, I heard tell, Frankie was out of town the night of the murder porkin' some babe."

"Who the hell told you that? Was it Easy?"

"Who else? He knows everybody's shit. The whole town goes in his place and coughs up their business. Easy could be covering for Frankie." Angel thought he was on to something. "It's a gut feeling."

"Knock it off. I think you're jealous of Frankie and you want to pin the murder on him. There ain't no evidence. All your gut is good for is farting." He laughed at his own joke.

"I'll keep my ears open, asshole, in case I find indication to the contrary."

"Whoever did it was brutal. That ain't Frankie. He's a lover not a killer." Gus downed a glass of ouzo. "Oh man. This stuff is potent." In no time he was feeling dizzy. Let's get the hell out of here. We ain't gonna get anything on him."

"Oh yea? I say we find the dame he was jumpin'. When he comes back we can question him."

"Did you see the size of his buddy's brother, Mike. He'll break you in pieces. There ain't nothin' to find out. Lay off before you get yourself in a shitload of trouble. Dig? I'm goin'."

Most of the group were leaving and taking leftovers with them. Angelo's cooking and the Greek cookies were a hit. They left uplifted and satisfied.

Myrna and Angelo sat with Easy, Irini and the Paidousis family. They were tired but happy. "We'll clean this in the morning Angelo. Let's enjoy our friends."

"You relax, Myrna. Jimmy and I will clear everything." Annie kissed her on the cheek leaving a red lipstick mark. "You did enough. Angelo and Easy have been working all day."

Thea Irini and Mrs. Georgia got up to help.

"No way," Annie said. "Sit with your husbands. How often do you get a chance to be together." She took Jimmy's hand and they did their duty, joking and playing while they worked. Jimmy gave her a pinch and a kiss every chance he got. They ran around like lightening trying to outdo each other.

"I'm happy about my Angelina but do you think she'll come back speaking Greek? What are they teaching her, I wonder? Is it sign language or words?"

"You ask 'em Frankie tomorrow. Irini what you say?"

"Dunno my Easy. I miss angeloudi. Mrs. Georgia she go with on ship. How she be?"

"She wonderful. We have nice time on ship. No problem. Sleep with me. Have fun. Eat good. Everybody they sick, bad ocean but Angelina no."

"Maybe we should phone at midnight. They are eight hours ahead." Angelo told them. "Let's stay awake. Tomorrow is Sunday and we're closed."

"Okay honey. Hope I can. I'm awful tired."

"You go to bed, baby. I'll make the call and tell you the latest when you wake up. Besides you already know the important stuff. Our little girl is getting better by the day. I'm going to be the best father when our children return home."

Myrna laid her head on Angelo's shoulder and dozed off.

Mrs. Georgia insisted they leave to give Myrna a chance to rest. "I see you and Myrna tomorrow my house for to eat supper." She and Thea Irini were planning a surprise baby shower.

"We'll be there but I hope you can keep Mr. George in check. He's got it in for me."

"No vory. He be okay. We go now. Annie.... Annie?"

"We finished in the kitchen." Her face was flushed. She and Jimmy were smooching,

"You no can wait? Maybe we go church tomorrow and talk to father you get married."

They were both giggling. "We only kissed a bit. That's all."

"Leave them be," Mike hollered. "They're only young once."

They left arguing about what was proper for an engaged couple. The consensus was that anything goes. Since Easy had keys to the diner, he was the last one out. He switched off the lights and locked up.

Angelo was petting Myrna's hair. "Come on my dumpling. Let's get you up to bed. Everybody is gone."

CHAPTER 71

Angelo was waiting for Myrna to wake up. She had been sleeping later and later since becoming pregnant. He didn't want to disturb her but the news about Angelina was good and he couldn't wait to share it. Dr. Sandy filled him in on the latest happenings. Frankie refused to speak to him. He still had anger issues.

She finally opened her eyes. "What time is it? Did I oversleep again?"

"It's okay my pet. You need your rest. I've been waiting to tell you the wonderful news about our baby."

Myrna sat up and drank the orange juice Angelo put on her bedside table. "Our baby?" She was confused and still in a dream world. "Oh you mean Angelina. Tell me, please. When is she coming home?"

"Not yet. She is still in recovery stages but is healing quickly and speaking in phrases. Sandy said we will be amazed at her progress. Angelina signs and speaks in both Greek and English. The children are helping her and she's loving it."

"Oh, Angelo. I wish we could go to her. Let's ask the doctor."

"You remember what he said last time we went for your exam. It is preferable you don't travel. You were very sick and I don't want to chance it, sweetheart. Angelina is in excellent hands."

"But how long will she be there?"

"Dr. Sandy will know when the time is right. Maybe a couple more months."

"How is our son?"

"He's doing well and taking excellent care of Angelina."

"Did you speak to him?"

"He was busy, love. Now let's take a shower and get dressed to go on our Sunday date. I'm not taking you by the river. It is too windy and I don't want you catching a chill."

"He's still not talking to you. Right? Don't worry, Angelo. He'll see how much you've changed and he'll soften up."

Angelo caressed and kissed Myrna's belly. He pulled her up, undressed her and helped her into the shower. "I don't understand it," he pulled off his pajamas, "belly and all you turn me on." He sucked her breasts and put his hand between her legs.

"You nasty old man. Get your hand out of there. I couldn't do anything even if I wanted."

He lathered a cloth and washed her. "Turn around, my pet." The minute he put his penis on her behind, he came. "Sorry. I can't help it if you drive me nuts."

"I'm as big as a house."

"Yep but you're my house and I'm crazy about every damn inch of you."

They dried off and he helped her dress. "From the looks of it, you need larger clothes. Let's go to the Green Mill for lunch then the Hub for new maternity outfits."

"I'm not sure I can walk that far. I know the doctor told me to be active but I get worn out quickly."

"Lean on me, my dumpling and off we go. Shall we stop at Holy Name for services?"

"Oh yes Angelo. I want to give thanks for our Angelina. By the way, you look tremendous in your Sunday suit."

Angelo ran his hand over his collar then tipped his hat. "All for you."

It was difficult for them to go anywhere. They were well known in town and people always stopped them on the street to chat.

"Myrna, we heard about Angelina. How wonderful for you! You feeling okay." Rosa touched her belly.

"Just great. Angelo and I are content."

Lucky woman, she thought. Her man came home and now they are having a splendid time together. Her husband was lazy and wouldn't take her across the street. "Did you see Myrna and Angelo." She waved to her friends and they came rushing over to see them. There was nothing to gossip about any more. The couple was extremely happy.

He put his arm around his wife proudly and pulled her close to him." I take excellent care of my woman. That's why she looks and feels terrific."

"Going to church? My husband is still sleeping."

"Myrna and I have a lot to be thankful for."

He held her arm as they climbed the steps. "I'm starving Angelo."

"We'll sit in the back pew, exit quickly after the service and hail a cab. It won't be long before we get your favorite lunch."

CHAPTER 72

Even though the restaurant was packed Angelo and Myrna were escorted to the first available booth. Tony and Vito were there, as well as, other known celebrities in town.

"Hey Angelo. Great meatballs! When you get a minute, can we talk."

"Today is reserved for my wife. Stop by my place tomorrow."

The conversation didn't go unnoticed. Vito asked Angel and Gus to join them. "We hear tell you are asking questions regarding Chester's murder. Leave Frankie and his folks out of this."

"We heard through the grapevine that Chester was taking Angelina to the park. Frankly, I think her brother discovered it and took the bastard out." Angel whispered.

Gus left the table and walked out. He wasn't gonna get caught in this conflict. He walked up Market Street to Thrift Drug Store and sat at the soda fountain.

Vito reached under the table, grabbed a handful of Angel's privates and squeezed. Angel fell forward and passed out. "Hurry, get an ambulance." Tony yelled. "Heart attack."

Nobody moved.

Angelo jumped from the booth. "He was okay last night at my place."

"Go back to your wife. He'll survive."

He wasn't going to question these guys. Not too long ago, he was the brunt of their fury and he knew what they were capable of doing. Good thing Myrna's back was turned and she didn't see a thing.

Angel opened his eyes and grimaced. "S. O. B."

"Get out or the next one will be worse." Vito was foaming at the mouth.

Angel limped out holding himself between the legs. He had never felt this kind of pain and realized this was the end of the road regarding Frankie. He threw up outside then went to the soda fountain where Gus was having a malt. "Ice...hurry..."

"What the hell happened to you?"

"Ice you bastard. Lots. Now!"

Gus jumped behind the counter and filled a container with ice and followed his partner to the bathroom. "Malaka, why are you holding your nuts?"

Angel pulled down his pants and put ice in his underwear. "The two dickhead mobsters went after my balls. Oh man, excruciating pain. I fainted. I'm gonna get them sons of bitches."

"You're gonna what? I'm going to the station tomorrow to hand in my resignation. You're on your own brother."

"You can't do that to me. We've been partners since the cows came in."

"The only way we're staying together is if you leave Frankie alone. Got it!"

"Okay. Okay. Okay. Go order me a root beer float!"

"Yiasou Gus." Jimmy and Annie were at the counter having a malt loaded with whipped cream. They were feeding each other. Jimmy put whipped cream on her pert little nose and her dimples then licked it off. She laughed and put some on his face. "Mmmmm. That's the only way to eat it?"

"Yiasou!" Gus really enjoyed those kids. It reminded him of his youth.

"When's the wedding?"

"Soon. When Timmy's wife Angela comes from Greece. "

Angel came to the counter. He walked as though he had a pants full, and could barely sit on the stool.

"What's wrong Angel?" Annie asked. "Did you get into a fight? If you're hurt, see a doctor right away."

Myrna and Angelo came in loaded with packages. Myrna went over to Annie. " I bought sharp maternity clothes from across the street. I'll bring them tonight to show you and your mom."

Angelo talked to Gus about Angel. "Thought he had a heart attack. Those guys don't mess around. What went down?"

"I'm sitting right here. Ask me if you wanna know. They crushed my balls."

"No shit. They tried to shoot mine off. Trust me, I was beggin'. They actually did me a favor. I came home and couldn't be happier. Why were they after you?"

"For diggin' in places where I shouldn't put my nose. I'm finished with bull. I got bigger fish to fry."

"Did you find out anything about Chester?"

"Not a damn thing. Must have been an outside job." He wasn't about to bring up Frankie's name ever again, especially after what Angelo told him.

"Come by the diner any time." Angelo went to sit with Myrna. "Milkshake, baby? What about the kids. What can I get you?"

"Thanks. We had enough." Jimmy was lighting a Chesterfield.

"Those things make my wife sick. You know… because of the baby."

Annie plucked the cigarette from Jimmy's mouth and put it out. He didn't mind. "Sorry, Myrna. Tonight at dinner, no smoking." Next to Easy, Angelo and Myrna were two of his favorite people in Steubenville. He felt at home in their presence. His mother-in-law to be, on the other hand, was difficult. He tried to go out with Timmy once in a while to play a game of cards but she followed them. There was no messing around or she would verbally tear him apart.

Old man George was the opposite. He was a lamb unless the family was embarrassed by an act not befitting a gentleman. Mr. George's temper was beyond belief if one was reckless with their reputation. It was difficult, for instance, to forgive Angelo for humiliating his family even though he was now a model husband. Every once in a while, he would lose his temper if he perceived Angelo did not respect his wife. Mrs. Georgia was the only one who could calm him down.

"Angelo, your wife looks tired. Maybe she should rest before dinner tonight. Jimmy and I are going home to help my mother or she'll have a fit."

"Let's take off together," Myrna said. "We can dish along the way."

They bid goodbye to Angel and Gus who were devouring their floats.

Annie was whispering to Myrna. "Angel looks like he has a problem you know where."

"It may be hemorrhoids, honey. He just couldn't sit on the stool. Should I approach him with a solution?"

Angelo started laughing. "Are you crazy, Myrna? What are you gonna ask him? Can I take a peek at your butt?"

"I wouldn't go that far, Angelo. I would simply inquire about his discomfort and maybe he would fill me in. Then I could tell him what to use."

"Why don't you invite him over for a spaghetti and you can discuss the matter with him." Angelo roared at the possibility.

They thought it was the funniest thing they had ever heard.

"Angelo, quit teasing Myrna," Annie said. "Besides, I don't think that's his problem. From the way he was sitting, he may have fallen and hurt himself elsewhere."

"I think his balls hurt." Jimmy said seriously.

Annie screamed and covered her face with her hands. "What's the matter with you?"

"He's right Annie. Gus told me he had an accident and hurt himself there." Angelo told them.

"I could tell from the way he was squirming," Jimmy said.

"Why did you let me go on and on about his hemorrhoids when you knew the problem all along." Myrna punched her husband playfully. "What should he do?"

"Let's not get obsessed with Angel's nuts. I'm sure he'll figure it out."

"But Angelo, he's probably in pain," Myrna whined.

"Jesus Christ, Myrna. What do you want to do, ice his privates? This whole conversation is ridiculous."

"I guess you're right Angelo. Maybe you could do it."

"You want me to bring him over," Jimmy said. He was in a state of hysterical laughter. "Who will ice him, you or Myrna?"

"We're home kids. At least I had a good laugh. See you tonight. Come on my pet. Let me take you upstairs for a rest before dinner. No more talk about Angel's parts. You hear me?"

"Well okay but as a friend, you should give him advice."

"Oh, Jesus. I ain't a doctor, Myrna." He took her upstairs to rest mumbling to himself. "

CHAPTER 73

Jimmy and Annie were rushing home to help organize the party. "I can't believe what you said about Angel. How can you talk like that? I was totally embarrassed. You could have said it another way."

"What other way? Balls are balls. Did you want me to say loukoumades?"

Annie screamed again.

"Sorry precious. I should realize you lead a sheltered life. I, on the other hand, fought the high seas with a bunch of dirty old men who said much worse things."

"Don't do it again." Her face was a deep shade of pink.

"I won't." He kissed her.

Mrs. Georgia was watching them from the living-room window and thought her daughter was in distress. She went out on the porch and put her hands on he hips. "Where you was and why you kiss on street? Neighbors see."

"Annie and I are engaged and can do pretty much what we want mom."

"Keep quiet Jimmy. You know how she gets."

"Come in do work, lazy bums. People comin' we need finish. Jimmy set chairs in basement for men play cards. Annie go kitchen help Thea." She walked in and slammed the door.

They both followed instruction but not before a long sweet kiss. "I'll be careful what I say from now on, Annie. Forgive me!

CHAPTER 74

Myrna and Angelo arrived a bit earlier for what they thought was dinner. When they saw all the women wrapping gifts and the baby furniture, they finally realized it was a shower organized by their friends. Myrna grabbed her face, "Oh no, you didn't."

Annie was laughing. "You got here before we finished. We wanted to yell surprise."

Myrna of course was moved to tears and was passing out hugs to the girls.

"Go basement play cards Angelo," Mrs. Georgia pushed him towards the stairs.

The girls put Myrna in a comfortable chair. "I'm starving she yelled out. I'm always hungry. That's why I'm here before my time." They brought her a large plate of food which she devoured. "What am I gonna do. I'm as big as a house and I can't stop eating. There is no room for Angelo in our bed."

As she was opening the presents, her back began to ache. It couldn't be labor. It was much too soon, she thought. She didn't wait for cake and ice cream.

"Call Angelo. I need to go home. Sorry but I'm feeling uncomfortable."

"We'll bring your things to the house tomorrow, Myrna." Annie helped her up and to the car because Angelo was incapable.

It was difficult for her to climb the stairway but she managed to \get into bed and immediately fall asleep. Angelo heard her moaning every once in a while, but knew she wasn't due yet. He went down to the kitchen in the morning to prepare food for the lunch crowd. While the mill workers were coming in to eat, they heard loud screaming.

"Someone is yelling upstairs, Angelo."

He ripped off his apron and ran. "Help yourselves. Everything is on the house."

When he reached Myrna, she was hollering. "I'm having the baby you buffoon." She pulled his shirt, grabbed a fist full of his hair and pulled him to his knees.

"Myrna, baby, let me go. Somebody help me," he was yelling. "I can't deliver a baby."

He ripped himself from her grip but not before receiving a slug that resulted in a bloody nose and swollen eye. He went half way down the steps and yelled, "Call an ambulance. Call Easy. Call anybody. She is having the baby." When he went back up he was shaking and trying to stay away from her but she grabbed his arm and began biting it. "No Myrna. I can't do anything if you don't let go. Help. Help."

Easy suddenly appeared at his side, pried her mouth open and stuck a towel between her teeth.

"Bite hard. I called an ambulance. Let's try to take her down. I'll hold her arms from behind and you get her legs."

Half way down, Angelo slipped and slid backwards bouncing his head on the stairs. When he hit the bottom, Myrna was sitting on him. Fortunately, she was all right.

"Grab her," Easy shouted. "Let's take her to car." He had plenty of help from the patrons but they ignored Angelo who was out cold on the floor with his legs still on the wooden steps.

As Easy headed towards Ohio Valley Hospital, the ambulance arrived. The paramedics saw Angelo and wanted to know who beat him up. They thought he had a concussion and were trying to revive him when Thea Irini showed up. She saw him on the stretcher and became hysterical. She started phoning family and friends to say that Angelo was beaten within an inch of his life an ambulance was taking him to the hospital. "They rob diner," she sobbed.

Easy was pacing the floor wondering where the hell Angelo was. They told him Myrna was in the last stages of labor and the baby would be born soon. He saw the ambulance pull up and the paramedics were bringing Angelo in on a stretcher. Not far behind were Angel and Gus trying to get the details of the beating. They heard it was a robbery.

Easy ran out to find out what happened. "Concussion we think. He was beaten pretty badly."

"What? Nobody beat him. He fell down the stairs."

Angelo was fighting the paramedics. "My wife is having a baby. Let me up now."

Gus was standing over him. "Who did this to you? Did you recognize anyone? We heard it was a group of thieves."

"Get the hell away from me you, numbskulls. I fell down the steps." He was embarrassed to say his wife attacked him.

They wanted him to submit to an ex-ray of his head but he refused. "Easy, where is she?"

By then his friends were descending on the hospital to find out if he was okay. "Oh my God! You look awful. Did they catch anybody? How much was stolen?"

"They took everything I had. I will need a small loan to continue my business. Now, move out of my way because my wife is having the baby." He went into the father's waiting room with Easy. "Word sure gets around. Who said I was beaten and robbed?"

"Thea Irini," Easy told him. "You lookin' like war on head." Blood was caked on his face.

A humungous child was brought to the window and shown to Easy. It was a natural mistake. "A boy." They said to him. Easy's mouth dropped open.

Angelo was in shock when he saw the kid. "The baby is mine," he said angrily. "Good Lord, a monster child."

"Your wife had a difficult delivery and is resting. You should visit her tomorrow? Hold the baby for a few moments, if you like but please let me wash the blood from your face." The nurse motioned for him to follow her, wiped him off and handed him the child.

"Hercules," Angelo spoke to the newborn. "He looks at least three years old." The baby took hold of his finger. "Strong, ain't he? His face is perfect just a bit big. Large kid." He was talking to himself. The expression on Angelo's face was of disbelief and admiration. "I produced a Hercules. Wow."

The nurse stood aside and was telling the staff, "You won't believe this kid. The father wants to name him Hercules. Can't think of anything more appropriate."

The child did not fit in a crib so the nurses took turns showing him through the window to everyone who came to visit. Each person had a shocked expression. Angelo enjoyed watching them.

"His name is Hercules. Myrna doesn't know yet. No wonder my poor woman needed a C section. This bad boy couldn't come out the regular way."

He begged to see his wife but they didn't want to disturb her. "Come by in the morning. She will probably stay for a few more days. The baby can go home tomorrow. Do you need help with this heavy weight?"

"I made him and I can take care of him.

CHAPTER 75

ARRIVAL IN THE STATES

S andy and Angelina were saying their goodbyes at the Pittsburgh airport. "We will see each other in Greece next summer, sweetheart. Please don't worry about Francesca."

"She'll be well taken care of," Angelina said with conviction and gave the baby to Yiorgo. "Goodbye my sweet angel."

Vito and Tony were taking the luggage to the car. Dimitri instructed them to pick up Angelina and Frankie from the airport.

Frankie was feeling abandoned worrying about who would administer his meds. "Sandy," he looked at her pleadingly. She embraced him. "You have enough for a few days after which you will come to the clinic in Pittsburgh to be cleaned out. Yiorgo and I will be waiting. You won't be alone."

Yiorgo didn't want Sandy touching Frankie that way. The thought that he was once her lover made him uncomfortable. He looked around for her parents hoping they would pick them up soon. Even more importantly, he was praying they would approve of him. He knew they were tough from the stories Sandy told him. *What the hell is wrong with me, he thought. As long as she wants me, everything will work out. Oh lord, if I lose her, I won't survive. He held the baby close to his heart.*

Frankie shook Yiorgo's hand. "Thank you my friend. You'll be the greatest husband and father. I knew you were a good man the first time I laid eyes on you." He kissed Francesca on the forehead and turned away fearing he would cry.

CHAPTER 76

They got into the car and Dimitri's men took charge. "Steubenville, here we come." Vito said. "Don't wanna scare you but heard the diner was robbed and your dad was beaten. It ain't serious."

Angelina was shaken. "I know my daddy is living at home now. Is he going to be okay? How's mom?"

The guys were surprised that Angelina was speaking to them. They didn't respond to her directly. Instead they addressed Frankie. "Your mom is in the hospital. She had the baby. Your father is back home. Hercules is with him."

Angelina started laughing. "Hercules? Is that the kid's name?"

"Wait till you see him. Everybody is talkin' about the size of the kid." Tony told Frankie. "Hercules is the perfect name for him."

Frankie asked all the important questions wondering what had transpired and when his mother would be home. Angelina's baby was born without a glitch, he thought. Why would his mother stay in the hospital?

Angelina spoke with an accent. "Look here. You can speak to me, too. Why isn't my mother bringing the baby home? Is something wrong?"

"Nothin's wrong. Needs more rest, is all. She's gettin' visitors. Your dad was there all day. Man he's been struttin' his stuff." Vito was laughing thinking about how he scared Angelo into going home.

"Drop off our things and go directly to Ohio Valley hospital. We want to see for ourselves that mom is okay."

Frankie was glad to be going home. He knew the family would be thrilled with Angelina's progress. The old man needs an ass kicking, he was thinking, at least those thieves gave him one.

"Step on it guys."

When they hit Fort Steuben Bridge, Frankie had flashbacks of bloody Chester falling into the river. "God forgive me." he mouthed quietly. He was frightened wondering if they heard him. I have to get control of myself, he thought or I may scare Angelina. Until today, the pain and fear consumed him mostly at night.

"Somethin' wrong, Frankie?" Vito looked in the rear view mirror and noticed he was perspiring.

"Tired. Wanna sleep." When they drove into Steubenville and passed High Street, Frankie had a meltdown and was shaking. "All my fault. Mine... mine...mine." He needed Sandy.

"Drop Angelina and take me to Pittsburgh. I forgot a package with Dr. Sandy."

Angelina suspected something was wrong. "Frankie, don't worry. Look…Angelo's is packed with people. Go ahead and leave. Call me when you get there."

They put her luggage in the doorway and left.

Angelina walked into the diner looking like a princess. Everyone had surrounded Angelo and were making funny faces and noises at Hercules. They didn't notice her until they heard the little black girl call her name. Rena, Anre and Simeon had arrived earlier and were building relationships with Dimitri's friends.

Rena and Angelina ran into each other's arms. They were speaking in Greek and holding each other tightly. Rena wanted to know if Georgios missed her. "He is preparing for your return this summer. We'll go together." Rena jumped up and down and kissed her.

One at a time they gravitated towards Angelina and were flabbergasted with her speech. Yiayia Georgia, Thea Irini, Easy, family and friends embraced her. Angelo was showing her the baby and kissing her. "I missed you my beautiful girl. Your mama will be thrilled." He looked around for Frankie.

"He left something in Pittsburgh and needed to return."

Angelo was hoping to bond with Frankie. He planned to apologize for his ignorance,

"Did you get a huge crib for him, daddy?" Angelina ribbed him. "You are going to need a nanny with muscles.

This reunion was filled with love and joy!

CHAPTER 77

Frankie gave himself an injection but it wasn't potent. Sandy had been cutting the dosage and he needed something stronger. He was shaking uncontrollably when they dropped him off at the high-rise where she lived.

"Sandy isn't home but we'll take you up. You don't look so good." When they let him in he fell to the floor, rolled himself into a ball and cried. "God help me, please. I can't live this way. I wanna die."

Sandy and Yiorgo came in. She ran to him when she saw how bad off he was. "Frankie, Frankie."

"Help me, Sandy. Please."

"I gotcha honey. Turn over. Get me my bag Yiorgo. Hurry." She pulled his pants down over his hip and fumbled with her medical bag till she retrieved the needle.

"Hurry, Sandy. I'm not going to make it this time."

She quickly injected him and rocked him till he fell asleep.

Yiorgo was angry. "How long, Sandy? Forever."

"Stop it Yiorgo. Tomorrow he is going to rehab and I will be there to take care of him. Now give me the baby and put him in the bedroom."

Yiorgo lifted him and tossed him in bed angering Sandy. "Take Francesca and leave the room. I'm going to undress him."

"No you are not. I'll do it. Now you leave the room."

"Jealous? Well too bad. I'm not. I've seen him naked a thousand times."

"Since you are my woman, I have nothing to be jealous of. Right?" When he took off Frankie's underwear he turned red. *How did that little woman take that huge thing in,* he was thinking.

"Stay if you want. In the olden days, the women listened to their men." Sandy proved to be a handful.

"I will be next to my friend all night. He is in bad shape. Anything can happen. You may be with us if you want." Francesca was fast asleep. She placed her on the chaise and surrounded her with pillows. "Yiorgo, my love, size doesn't matter. Besides, you are not lacking anything in that department."

"I'll be here with you in case something happens." *Next time we're alone I will screw her brains out. She'll forget Frankie ever existed.* He sat on the lounger and pulled her on his lap.

"Sandy, the phone is ringing."

She answered in the living-room. Yiorgo heard her gasp no, no, no. "Yiorgo your brother needs you. I'll stay with Francesca."

"You are white as a ghost. What's wrong?"

She stared into space. "Talk to him."

"You have to come home Yiorgo. Dimitri needs us and I'm splitting my time between him and Christinaki. She is devastated and Dimitri has barricaded himself old house with the body. It's been two days now and we can't get him out. Noone is able to reason with him."

"We'll be on the next available flight." He was crying. "We have to go back to Greece."

"You are not going anywhere unless we get married. I'm calling my parents. They will bring someone over here this morning to perform the ceremony. Then you can go. I'll contact TWA to see if there is a flight today."

"And you?"

"I'll come when Frankie is stable. We can take him to rehab after we're married in the morning."

Yiorgo was furious. "Francesca is coming with me. It will be good for Christina to keep occupied. Saranti is worried about her."

"Okay Yiorgo. I concede. You are her daddy and a fabulous one at that."

"Please don't be upset with me. I don't have the heart to leave him alone. Believe me, you are the center of my world. I won't be away from you for long. I adore you."

Yiorgo was crying quietly as he went to take a shower and prepare for the wedding. The flight would be in late afternoon. He couldn't stop thinking of Dimitri and Katina. How could he console him and the girls when his heart was in pieces?

Her folks showed up with a Rabi who went through the marriage quickly. They were sorry they had to cancel all the pageantry. "We'll be back as soon as my brother is better."

CHAPTER 78

Dimitri was waiting outside of the house when Katina went to tell her husband she was leaving him. He was uneasy and decided to go in even though she asked him to let her handle it alone. As he pushed open the door he heard a rifle go off. Katina had a shocked expression on her face. She put her hands on her chest and blood gushed through her fingers,

"Katina, Katina no, no, no." He picked her up and ran towards the clinic screaming like a wounded animal. Katina touched his face. "The girls, Dimitri." she whispered. "Love you."

Strati and Christina came out to see what was happening. "Katina, I love you. Katina, please don't leave me. Help her. Do something."

Strati tried to take her inside the clinic but he wouldn't let her go. "She's gone Dimitri." He closed her eyes. Both he and Christina were crying.

"No, Katina, please wake up." He carried her up the hill to the old house, placed her on the cot and laid next to her. "You'll be fine Katinaki. I can't live without you, Katinaki mou."

Strati followed him but could not do anything. He refused to let go of her. "She is going to wake up. Get out Strati. I won't let you take her from me." He wet a cloth and wiped the blood from her lips. "You're cold Katinaki. I'll cover you and lie by your side. My arms will keep you warm.

"Do you remember our first time Katinaki? It was so wonderful." He told her stories of the their past adventures but when she didn't respond he sobbed. Finally, he was exhausted and fell asleep.

A pale light fell on his face. It was dawn. He heard noises in the kitchen and smelled coffee. "Dimitraki, Dimitraki," her sweet voice was calling his name.

"I knew you wouldn't leave me, Katinaki mou."

"I came to make you coffee. I won't be back again but you will see me in your dreams. Papou said to stop feeling sorry for yourself and mom sends her love. When the time is ripe, you will come too. I'm in an angelic place enveloped in their arms."

"But I need you here with me."

"I can't stay, my love. Let go of my body. It is but a empty shell. Take care of our daughters and live a happy life. Let's have our last cup of coffee together. I'll be waiting for you on the other side."

He sat at the kitchen table and sipped his coffee. "Why? Why? Why? I would have given you the world."

"You already did, my darling. Now I must go but I will always be near you." Her image faded when he tried to embrace her.

Dimitri was crying when Strati walked in and held him. "She came to me this morning, my brother. Take care of the girls, she said. Papou and mom are with her. This body is an empty shell. Do what you must with it. I didn't want to lose her," he voice caught in his throat. "Papou sent me a message to stop feeling sorry for myself."

"Sounds like him. He had strength of character and he loved us all. Come on. Let me take you home. Saranti is with the girls. They need you. Yiorgo is returning tonight with Francesca."

The house was surrounded by villagers. "We broke every bone in his body and he has no place to go for healing. He'll probably be dead by tonight." They slapped his back as he went by. "We lost the sunshine in our lives."

"I'm going to see my daughters. For those who have doubts, they are my offspring."

"How could we not know? Whoever sees them sees you!"

Katina's mother-in-law was scrunched up in the doorway. She was terrified. "I didn't know where to go."

"Come in old woman." He helped her up. "You were a good yiayia to the girls. No one blames you for this tragedy."

ABOUT THE AUTHOR

Maraki was raised in small, ethnically diverse town. Her father, a seaman, migrated to Ohio. She had a stay at home mom who read poetry and sang to her every night. Thus she began writing poetry at a young age. She married, moved to Chicago and had a daughter and two grandchildren.

She wrote two poetry books, a travel column in *What's Happening*, a restaurant column for a national magazine, and stories for several newspapers and magazines. The inspiration for her first book came from her upbringing.

Maraki is now engaged in writing another novel.